For Emma

For Emma

THE DEATH OF ME

OF ME

A HELOISE CHANCEY MYSTERY

M. J. TJIA

ISIS
LARGE
PRINT

First published in Great Britain 2019
by
Legend Press

First Isis Edition
published 2020
by arrangement with
Legend Press

A catalogue record for this book is available
from the British Library.

ISBN 978–1–78541–901–0

Published by
Ulverscroft Limited
Anstey, Leicestershire

Set by Words & Graphics Ltd.
Anstey, Leicestershire
Printed and bound in Great Britain by
T. J. International Ltd., Padstow, Cornwall

This book is printed on acid-free paper

Prologue

When I close my eyes, I can see the pile of men, five or six of them — who can tell how many in such a tangle of limbs — lying beneath the buckled, torn roofing. Arms stick out, some legs, and even one head, torn from its body, covered in so much dust, plaster and blood it would be difficult for his closest relatives to claim him.

That was my first strike. Outside the police station by the river.

The second strike was even better. I miscalculated how much black powder was necessary and the bomb left a small crater in the ground outside the palace gates. Fewer casualties, though. That bombing only claimed two lives. But the terror in the eyes of the survivors, their frantic scrambling to escape the area, the welts and scratches that oozed blood, it all warmed my heart. It really did. Because really, these deadly little excursions were nothing more than rehearsals for my real goal: taking down the man who stands in my way. Who stands in the way of many, really. I'm not entirely selfish.

My finger traces the chill outline of the sphere that lies on the table before me. The dark cast iron encases so much more death. My eyes take in the wooden fuse drilled into its centre, and I smile as I imagine lighting it. I hope I see the spray of bricks, rising in the air as buoyant and light as a child's building blocks. The smoke, black and acrid, billowing into the sky, obstructing for a few moments the sight of my beautiful work. People, flung to the ground like discarded rag dolls; others crouched in supplication to my work, their arms raised in submission, their mouths open in awe. For those few moments, they will know, and I will know, that true power lies with me, not with their God.

CHAPTER
ONE

Violette and I step down from the *voiture de remise* — a much smarter conveyance than the hansom cabs in London — and take stock. Rue de Clichy is quite narrow, and tall buildings block whatever sunlight there might be. Wind blusters down the avenue, buffeting my hat, tipping my wide skirt as though it's a church bell. Further down the street, a solitary cherry tree, still missing its spring coverage, vies for room in a tiny square with parked phaetons and buggies. We stand in front of a patisserie and my eyes scan the golden pastries on offer, pausing on a pear *croustade*. Despite the midday repast Hatterleigh and I enjoyed not one hour before in the Palais Royale, I know I'd enjoy its sticky syrup on my lips.

"I think it is over there, Madame," Violette says, pointing across the road.

Violette is my handmaid while I'm in Paris with Hatterleigh, a French girl I've borrowed from a friend. Amah didn't want to join me this time, said she had things of her own to do in England. I think, though, she's sulking, because I've postponed our trip to Venice. I promised to take her when the weather is more clement, but I recognised that twist to her mouth. She doesn't believe me.

I follow Violette towards a building that takes up nearly half the block. A generous number of French doors and tiny balconies line each level, shutters open revealing blank windowpanes. We walk past a shopfront on the corner that advertises a *Grande Pharmacie Commerciale*, beneath another sign, *Dentiste*, on the floor above. Pausing outside a pair of doors painted in a rich, maroon lacquer, Violette gestures to a discreet sign above the doorway, written in gold lettering. "Debtor's Prison, Clichy," she announces.

Taking the letter from my bag, I re-read Somerscale's instructions. It definitely says to meet him here. At the Debtor's Prison. But how a man worth twenty thousand pounds a year could find himself in such a place is beyond my ken. I bang on the door's brass knocker and it's not many moments before a rather short fellow, with grey hair and a grubby vest, answers the door.

Speaking swiftly in her native tongue, Violette tells the man why we are here. He grunts and turns, waves his hand for us to follow him along the dim corridor. Two men, guards presumably, in navy blue uniforms, lounge on pine chairs and we pass them to climb a set of dusty stairs until we reach the first landing. A vast space yawns wide before us, impressive columns punctuating the long gallery every few metres. But the area is uncarpeted, the fireplaces bare. Grey light flows into the room past the tattered curtains, lighting upon a number of men, twenty men perhaps, huddled in

4

groups on the worn floorboards. One man stands by the French doors, reading aloud from a newspaper and, as we pass through, he stops for a moment and stares, as do the rest of them, craning around to see us.

"Tailors," mutters the caretaker. "Paying back what they owe."

A large pair of scissors and a flat iron lie on the floor in the middle of the nearest cluster of tailors, who bow their heads again to carry on with mending the squares of cloth in their laps. Some of them wear hats, as if they are just passing through, or are in polite company, and hanging from a nail wedged into one of the columns is a natty overcoat and top hat. A poster is pinned to the wall, but my French is rusty, I can only make out the words 'work' and 'scoundrel'.

"No women?" I ask, thinking of the harried seamstresses I have known, who failed to keep up with demand, who found themselves in another trade all together.

"They are on the top level," the caretaker says, nodding towards the ceiling as we climb another set of stairs. "They are lucky. They have more light. And when the sun is out, they have more warmth too."

Finally, on the third floor, he leads us down a narrow corridor and unlocks a door to our left. He ushers us in, locking the door behind us.

"Heloise, how wonderful to see your lovely countenance," says Sir Simon Somerscale, rising from a window seat. He approaches us, taking my hands in his cold ones. He's a thin man, maybe a good ten years older than I am. He has a pleasant face, and I know a number of beauties who are quite jealous of his fine cheekbones. "And this is . . . ?" he asks, noticing my maid.

"This is Violette. I know your message asked me to come alone, but she fulfils the role of chaperone today," I reply, pointing out a kitchen chair for her to sit on by the door. Unpinning my hat from my hair, I admire its purple felt and coloured ribbons before placing it on the table. "My French is not what it was, although I can still *parlez vous* with jewellers and dressmakers all I need. You may rest assured, she only has very limited English. She will not know of what we speak." I place my hands on my waist and gaze around the room. It's a neat space, with clean, serviceable carpets and oak furniture. The curtains are of a sturdy white linen, and the sofa upholstery, a pond green colour, is inexpensive yet unsullied. "It's not every day I'm summoned to visit someone in prison." Which is not entirely true. Many a friend have I visited at the debtors' gaol in Whitecross Street. Glancing back at Somerscale, I grin.

He bids me to take a seat at the table. "Ah, but you must understand, this is one of the better lodgings available here. Surely you passed the other unfortunates who may never find their way out of here again." He takes up a crystal decanter, and the dim light from the window glints against the edges of the cut glass. He pours us each a measure of wine, and says, "My man, Victor, brought me what luxuries he thought I might need. But how sad he was — almost in tears, I assure you — when he was not permitted to stay here with me. He does love to obey my every whim."

"This fine establishment won't allow you to keep staff?" I ask. "How will you get along?"

His lips lift into a smile, but his brows crease into a mock frown. "Madame, you have forgotten that I have seen military service. I am quite capable of looking after myself."

I laugh. "Somerscale, I'd wager these beads of mine," I grasp the pearls that circle my wrist, "that you had as many staff to do your bidding at the port of Balaclava as you would in your Arlington Street mansion."

His eyes widen for a moment as he stares into space. "Heloise, you scamp, I believe you are correct."

I sip my wine, and gaze at him over the glass's rim. "How did you find yourself in this hole, Somerscale?" I'm at a loss to know why he, an English gentleman, is to be found here, in a debtor's prison in Paris, and for what reason he requested my company. Over lunch, while Hatterleigh told me of the powerful stallion he'd purchased at Longchamp and Lady Paige's indiscretion with her Hindustanee servant, I puzzled over Somerscale's missive. What sort of debt would imprison such a wealthy man? Has he lost his fortune to cards, like many greenhorns I have known? It seems very unlikely. Has he invested poorly in some dubious rail company? There have not been any stock exchange busts lately that I know of. Or ... I take in Somerscale's even features, blond hair, lips so finely chiselled I have even caught myself wondering what they'd be like to kiss, despite feeling a total lack of attraction for the man. I slap my glass down onto the tabletop. "Somerscale, do not tell me that a fair beauty has fleeced you?"

He leans back in his chair and sighs. "You are almost correct, Heloise, almost. Let's just say I am here over an affair of the heart."

"You must be funning, sir!"

"Not at all. I made the mistake of loving a young lady who served me in Chateau d'Argent. You have eaten at this restaurant, Heloise? Best *escargot* in France. Unfortunately, my pretty butterfly has parents who feel I owe her more than she is worth."

"Trifled with her feelings, did you?"

"Not at all," he says, indignant, yet with a rueful smile. "We had a delightful time together. Absolutely worth the fifty pounds I agreed to give her."

"A hopeful *lorette*, was she? Or should I say 'disappointed'?" I couldn't blame the young woman for trying to land such a catch.

"More *grisette*, Heloise."

"Oh dear." I throw the rest of the wine back and gaze at him, my eyebrow cocked in what I hope is a cynical manner. The truth is that I find this French system of ranking the types of women who use their charms to make money quite irksome. I'm thankful — bloody relieved, in fact — to find myself in the top tier, but I'm uncomfortably aware that, like in any social order, there are those scrounging at the bottom, fighting for more, desperate for a better life.

"Her parents demand I marry her, would you believe?" he says, pouring more wine into my glass.

8

"But I ask you, Heloise, what would my wife say to that? Talk about committing a crime."

"So, how did all of this mess land you here?"

He shrugs. "Her family mean to take me to court for breach of promise. They have demanded five hundred pounds from me. I offered them a hundred, which was double my original proposal, after all."

"But this is ridiculous. You can afford to pay them a paltry five hundred pounds, Somerscale."

"Heloise, it's the principle of the thing. I will not be swindled by a family of French buffoons."

I laugh, shake my head. "Oh, Somerscale, just pay the poor girl." I scan the room. "And surely you're bored with being cooped up here?"

He nods. "I am indeed. I've been here almost four days, and I'm not sure I can spend another night on the lumpy mattress they have afforded me." His face becomes serious as he stares into the bottom of his glass. "But I believe it might be best if I stay here a little longer."

"Why?"

Somerscale leaves the table to fetch his cigarette case from the mantelpiece. "Take one," he says, offering me a Russian cigarette. I feel his eyes study me as he lights it. "Tell me, how did you get away from your Hatterleigh?"

"Told him I had a fitting for a new gown."

"Good woman," he says. "There is a reason I desired you to come alone. I have something, something rather delicate, I'd like to ask of you."

My backbone stiffens a little. Please don't let this man make advances upon me. I have never really felt any frisson of attraction for Somerscale, and I certainly would not want to begin an affair in such a place. I turn my head imperceptibly, catch a glimpse of Violette out of the corner of my eye. She's nibbling on her thumb nail, staring at the tips of her shoes.

Somerscale draws deeply on his cigarette, and lets the smoke out from his lungs in a long sigh. "And I'm almost positive that your Hatterleigh would not give his assent, if he was to find out."

"Well, luckily I do not need his approval in all that I do," I say, annoyed, discarding the opportunity to use Hatterleigh as an excuse to extricate myself from an awkward situation.

Somerscale smiles at me, lazily, and says again, "Good woman. You are what the French call *recherchée.*" Straightening in his chair, he leans on the table towards me, business-like. "I am supposed to meet a man tonight. At a certain taproom in Bocages des Anges. Do you know the area?"

"Of course I've heard of it. It's notorious. Never had the pleasure of experiencing its charms, though."

He nods slowly. "That's the problem. I'm very reluctant . . ." He broods for a moment, watching the runnel of smoke lift from the tip of his cigarette.

"What?"

Shaking his head abruptly, he says, "I'm a fool, Heloise. Now that I really think about it, I should never have involved you. I might have endangered you already." He pushes his seat back and strides across to

10

one of the French doors. He lifts the curtain away a fraction, peers down onto the street.

"What are you talking about, Somerscale?" I say, following. I go to look out the glass too, but he holds a hand out to stop me. I halt, "Well, now you have to tell me. I positively won't leave until you have told me of what plans you had in your head for me." I take one last toke — I'm not overly fond of Russian cigarettes — and toss the end into the grate of the fireplace.

Somerscale folds his arms. "I'm supposed to meet a man tonight, on very important business. In a sordid little place in the Rue de l'Âme Damnée. But obviously," he looks around the room, "I can't make it."

"And you thought I might go in your stead?" I ask, amused. "What made you think of me?"

"Lord Conroy, my cousin you know, told me last year of how he commissioned you to, shall we say, 'rescue' his niece. He spoke very highly of your discretion, which is why I thought of you in this matter, knowing you were here, too, in Paris. I need someone to meet this man for me. Tonight."

"It's that important?"

"Imperative." The word has the deep thrum of a drum's note.

I feel a tickle of excitement. A little adventure. I could do with the distraction, for there is only so much spending and carousing a woman can do before it begins to pall. "Somerscale, I'm curious. Why ask me, when you have any number of male friends — gentlemen, servants, rogues even — who could take up

11

this matter? And why can you not just arrange for him to meet you here?"

Somerscale runs his fingers through his blond locks and drops down onto the sofa. "I can't tell you much, Heloise. If you take on this task, I will divulge just as much as is necessary. I can say this though, the meeting involves a mission I have embarked upon on behalf of certain people at Westminster." His voice lowers on the last word, and he glances nervously at Violette. I look around at her too, but this time she's sucking the end of her plait, and has her eyes raised to the ceiling as she hums something to herself.

"Westminster?" Something political? Covert? My stomach constricts with the thrill of it as I take a seat next to him.

Somerscale nods. "Westminster has intercepted a letter regarding a planned crime. They're trying to identify the fellow who sent the message and the rogue he's organised to meet. They're supposed to meet up tonight."

"Do you know why?"

He lights himself another cigarette. "All I know is that they're to exchange some crucial information which I am to divert, disguised as this fellow's contact. It may well save lives."

"But how is this man to know you are the one he is to meet?"

"A special code is mentioned in the letter we intercepted, which I'll tell you of, should you take on this little assignment."

"Is he dangerous?"

12

Somerscale's eyes are anxious as they find mine. He shrugs. "I am not sure, Heloise. And for all I know, it might even be a woman. God knows, women have made very useful spies in the past. All I know is that the person holds information about a terrible conspiracy to commit . . ."

"Murder?"

"Carnage, Heloise. Carnage."

It's as if a cold draught passes across my skin at the tone of his voice. I sit back into the sofa. "Surely the French police should be told of this, then? I don't understand why you must become involved."

He taps ash onto the floor. "The plot we intend to foil is to be undertaken on English soil. Not in France. From what I gather, my contact, as we will call him, has taken refuge here in Paris, as it has become too dangerous for him in London."

"You expect the fellow to be British?"

Again, he shrugs. "I assume so. But who is to know for sure?"

"But then how are you to know him?"

He shifts in his chair so that he is facing me. "Do you mean to take on this task, Heloise? I can only tell you the details if you agree to go in my stead."

I take in a deep breath, so that my bosom strains against my stays. Somerscale stands and makes his way back to the curtained French door. He beckons for me to follow.

Twitching the curtain aside, he stands against the wall and peers outside again. "I'm being watched," he says. "A dark man, thin, bulky overcoat." He glances at me and his voice is testy when he says, "It's no use grinning at me like that, Heloise. It's true, not a figment of my imagination." He bids me stand next to him, and nods down to the street. "There! By the old woman selling shoes or whatever's on that confounded cart. See him?"

I see the man Somerscale's talking of; he's reading a newspaper, looks up briefly as a carriage passes him by.

"There's another damned fellow too, somewhere about." He rakes his hands through his hair. "Mind you, I can't be sure how many of the rascals have their eyes on me."

"You think it's connected to your business tonight, to Westminster?"

"I'm sure of it. They've been following me for days."

I plonk back down onto the sofa, while Somerscale fetches me a fresh glass of wine, which I hold in my lap. I don't want to become too befuddled. "Therefore, you need someone to meet him in your stead. Someone who will not be suspected of this little piece of espionage. Someone like me?"

"Exactly." His smile is triumphant. "If a friend or servant of mine turns up, they will know I have sent him in my place, and all will be lost. The information might be compromised. But if you go . . . Who will suspect you?"

"But, Somerscale, these men who are keeping an eye out for you, they would've seen me come in here. If the tavern is being watched, or I am followed, they will suspect you have sent me to undertake your commission."

14

"That's the beauty of my plan," he says, proudly. "You are infamous, my dear. As soon as they ask around and find out that you're none other than Heloise Chancey, *Paon de Nuit*, they will think nothing of this visit. They will assume you are here for —" his lips curve into a smile again, "shall we say — a connubial visit. I am almost sure they will not follow you, or even think of you again. They will never dream that I require you to carry out this sordid assignment."

I'm stung enough by his sentiments to briefly consider turning down his request. His words make it sound as if I gallivant about town lifting my skirts for any old humbug with lashings of money and middling looks.

But when I look back at Somerscale I see a steady challenge in his eyes, mischief even. He's watching for my reaction, blast him. Wants to see if I rise to his bait. Perhaps he even thinks he might catch a glimpse of my famous temper. But I will not let him see that I care one hoot about his careless words, or what he thinks of me. I lift my chin, laugh, and say, "Well, in that case, I will gladly take on this dirty little job of yours but, I warn you, it will cost you a very pretty pile of gold francs. Almost as much as if I actually were here on a connubial visit."

CHAPTER
TWO

Amah

Amah Li Leen pauses in her stroll through Hyde Park and gazes down upon a crocus, its furled purple petals peeping out at the tepid sunlight. It's as loath to admit spring has arrived as Amah is herself. But the daffodils are merry, dance and preen to the chilly breeze that cuts across the grassy folds of green. She pulls her coat tighter, wishing she'd wrapped her scarf about her neck.

Three stalwart picnickers unload sandwiches and bowls of strawberries and dried fruit from a basket, lay them out on a plaid blanket. Why are they seated under the waxy leaves of the magnolia tree, and not out in what sunlight can be garnered? Amah lifts her own face to the sky, waiting for the sun's warm fingertips to touch her cheeks. A frosty gust of wind whips the ribbon of her bonnet and she gives up. As she treads upon the path, the heels of her black shoes clacking to the beat of her thoughts, she wonders if she will ever see Makassar again; wonders if she'll ever feel that heat that seemed to seep into the very marrow of her body.

Making her way along Park Lane she looks up at the grand buildings, their French style reminding her of

Heloise; of her daughter's sojourn in Paris with Hatterleigh. Her lips tighten but, really, she doesn't feel all that put out. She believes Heloise's promise of taking her to Venice at another time and, at any rate, racqueting about with Heloise could be very tiring. Amah has enjoyed the restful time she has spent in London, walking and reading by day, embroidering a silk shawl by evening. And Agneau has taught her numerous new dishes to cook: a fine soup made of onion, and a choux pastry which she adores, almost as much as his quiche. Tonight she will teach him how to prepare a beef sauce for, in truth, she did not think much of his beef in red wine. She stops for a moment, gazing into the display window of the apothecary's. Perhaps she should make a quick visit to Limehouse, ask Miriam for more bean paste. She shakes her head and resumes her walk home — surely there is enough in the jar she fetched last time.

As she arrives at the corner of South Street, a man and woman brush past her.

"Cab," the man calls out, waving his leather satchel towards a line of hansom cabs across the way. He's a ferrety-looking thing. His clothing appears to be of the highest fashion, but Amah's discerning eye catches out the shine of his trousers, the flashy cheapness of his coat. His companion — her plump prettiness marred by goggling eyes and a dissatisfied pout to the mouth — demands he wipes down the cab seat with his kerchief before she will enter.

"If we could just afford our own carriage, we wouldn't have to stoop to hiring cabs all the time," she

17

says, the nasal tone of her voice rising on an accusatory note.

Amah walks past, smiling grimly behind her lace veil as the man steps into the cab to wipe down the seat. Should have told her to do it herself, Amah thinks. That's one thing she did right with Heloise, she didn't bring her up to be useless. Or whiny.

As the woman pulls herself and her wide skirts into the cab, the back of her crinoline swoops into the air, and her split drawers yawn wide over the marbly flesh of one buttock. Amah looks away, but not swiftly enough. She will never understand why the silly women of London insist on wearing those ridiculous cage contraptions.

Amah makes her way along South Street until she's looking up at Heloise's house, her gloved fingers resting on the handrail.

She wonders if Agneau is in the kitchen, conscious of a tightness in the pit of her stomach. Something like excitement. A feeling she has not experienced in many a year. Perhaps Agneau is already . . .

The front door swings open.

"Thought it were you," says Abigail, pail in hand. "Saw you through the window."

Amah trots up the steps, follows the housemaid into the hallway. She shies away from going straight to the kitchen, despite being parched. She will first sip some cold tea in her room, take off her bonnet, straighten her hair. She catches that thought. She will *not* straighten her hair. She frowns at herself as she climbs the stairs to her rooms.

18

"Any word when the mistress'll be back?" asks Abigail.

"Who knows. She is a mystery to us all."

"I just thought, you's being her lady's maid and all, that you'd have to know when to be ready."

Amah wonders if the girl is fishing for information. Is sure of it, in fact. She's sharp, is Abigail. But she'll get no fodder from her. "I am always ready, Abigail. So should you be," she says, without looking back.

In her sitting room, Amah takes off her bonnet and lays it on the walnut sideboard, ignoring the urge to check her features in the mirror. She tugs off her gloves and then tends to the fire that has faltered in her absence. She holds her fingertips above the comfortable blaze, watches pink life come into her skin again. Glancing across at the embroidery on the table, she wonders if she should while away some of the time — wouldn't do to look too eager — with taking up the needle or with reading by what daylight is still available. She decides upon the latter and goes into her bedroom to fetch her Dickens.

She gasps, stopped short in the doorway. For next to the book, upended on her bed, is her oak jewellery box. Beads, several brooches, a gold bracelet, her pearls and earrings are strewn across the eiderdown. The jewellery box's little drawers lie empty and one of its mirrored doors has been mangled from its hinges. Her eyes take in the rest of her bedroom — the chest drawers gape open, her shifts and petticoats spilling forth. Her gowns are scattered across the floor, her portmanteaus ransacked. Ribbons, hair nets, bonnets, a bottle of creme are heaped on her dresser. For a few startled seconds she wonders if Abigail is responsible. Perhaps she had an accident while dusting or was in the midst of cleaning Amah's room. But it doesn't take her long to realise much rougher hands have been at work. Rough hands bent upon mischief.

She rushes to her dressing table and, with trembling fingers, pulls the miniature drawers and frame away. She eases out the secret compartment. A long breath escapes her lips when she sees the silk purses are still there. Digging her fingers to the bottom of a red pouch with a drawstring tie, she brings out a tiny gold orb, a figure of a dragon entwined around its circumference. Her mother's earring. All Amah has left of her. She clasps it in her fist for five tight heartbeats, feeling its knobbly presence in the palm of her hand. She places it back into its pouch and returns the drawers and dressing table to how they were.

Amah gazes again on the mess of trinkets on her bed and stiffens. What of Heloise's jewels? She races out onto the landing and down the flight of stairs. In Heloise's sitting room some books have been tugged from shelves but her bedroom seems untouched. Amah opens the door to Heloise's dressing room to find the same kind of chaos as she had found upstairs. Amah tuts when she sees Heloise's newest trunk of dresses lying open, on its side. And what would she say if she saw all her favourite hair ornaments dumped on the floor like that? Good thing she isn't home, with that temper of hers. She'd shout the place down, swearing and kicking like one of those smelly sailors on Toxteth Docks.

With lips set in a firm line, Amah steps across to a large painting on the wall nearest the wardrobe. She takes hold of the left side of the gilt frame and pulls the painting wide, as though it is a cabinet door. The green safe, built into the wall behind, looks undisturbed. Just to be sure, Amah winds the secret numbers — a blend of her own birth date with Heloise's — into the combination lock and heaves the heavy, iron door open. Velvet boxes, coin albums, neat stacks of ribboned correspondence and contracts fill the dim space. Amah lifts a page in an album to spy a row of gold coins and opens the closest velvet box, revealing a rope necklace of pear-shaped diamonds. She closes the safe door again and clicks the painting back into place. Amah eyes the portrait of a young couple; their stony gazes, their umbrella buckling under the weight of gusty rain. They look to be at the bow of a barque, and not too happy about it. She's always wondered if the expression on her face was similar, that day many years before when their ship approached England.

Hands on hips, she turns to survey the mess. Her initial fright has simmered down to a hum of anger. Nothing seems to be missing, just as in her own rooms. What could the burglar have been after?

She looks back towards the safe. Heloise's jewels, of course. What did the girl expect after lording it all around town draped in diamonds and emeralds? Amah tuts again, shakes her head. Virtually asking to be robbed, foolish girl. She thinks of Heloise in Paris —

without Amah's sharp eye on her — and a faint feeling of alarm stokes the fire of her anger. Always trouble, that girl.

"Abigail!" She calls for the maid before she even reaches the corridor. "Abigail, come here please. And fetch Bundle."

Abigail lumbers up the stairs. "He's not here. He got a message to say his sister were ill."

Amah stares at the girl. "I didn't know about that."

"Happened as soon as you left, it did."

"Come in here." She gestures for Abigail to follow her into Heloise's bed chamber. "You'd better go fetch the constable for me."

The duster drops from the housemaid's hand as she gapes at the mess.

"What happened?"

"Well, clearly, we've been burgled," says Amah. "Did you not hear anything?"

The maid shakes her head, jaw hanging loose.

"Stop gawping," says Amah. "Go fetch the police." She catches the servant by her sleeve. "First, tell me, are you sure you did not hear anything?"

Another shake of the head.

"Was anyone else in the house? Any tradesmen? Visitors?" Heloise has pretty shady characters keep her company sometimes, after all.

"No, Amah, just the man about the chimneys."

Amah cocks her head to the side. "What man?"

"He come to check the chimneys. Said he'd been sought. Showed me a piece of paper saying so."

"And you just let him in?"

22

"He had a piece of paper!" says Abigail, stridently, but with a slight quiver.

"And what did he do, this man?"

"Well, he looked at all the fireplaces, didn't he? Said we had to be very careful that they did not cause a house fire. He'd just come from a nasty case in Forest Hill, he said."

"Did he? And you stayed with him the whole time?" She hesitated. "Of course."

"Well?"

"Well, actually, there was another knock at the door. And Bundle being away, I had to answer it."

"Where did you leave him?"

"We'd just come down from the servant's quarters."

"Onto my landing?"

"Yes." Colour is bright in Abigail's cheeks. "But he were a nice man, Amah. He would never do anything like . . ." Her eyes wander over the mess in Heloise's rooms. Something seems to occur to her and she takes a step towards Amah. "But it must've been him, isn't that right? It must've been him."

Amah stares at her for a moment. "Who was at the door?"

"This dratted woman wanted to know if I'd seen her dog. Run away in the park, he had. She showed me sketches she'd made of the mongrel. Long-haired thing, it were."

"Were you with her long?"

"Not long." She looks troubled now. "But she asked were there any more servants in the house. Demanded to speak to Agneau when I said there were only him."

23

Amah's eyes widen. She can't help but be diverted. She would have enjoyed seeing the indignation on Agneau's face at being summoned from his kitchen. "And how did he take that?"

"Well, he wouldn't come, would he?"

"You didn't invite her in, too, did you?" Amah's voice is sharp.

"No, of course I didn't."

"Of course."

The servant's fat bottom lip starts to push forward and Amah wonders if she is about to cry.

"It's true, Amah. It's true. And when I was finished with her, the man was walking down them stairs again. He said all was in order and left."

Amah gives Abigail a hard look.

"It's true."

"So you let in a mysterious chimney inspector, and then you were distracted by a woman searching for her dog?"

"Uh-huh." Abigail nods. Her ears are red now. "It's true. He really were here. He really were. I'm not making this up, Amah. Even when I dust in here, I never disturb madame's jewellery. Never touch it."

Abigail is usually a bit mouthy, sure of herself, and Amah's a little puzzled by her agitation until it occurs to her that Abigail thinks that Amah believes her to be the culprit.

"I don't think you did it, you foolish girl."

"I would never, Amah. Never." A flush of tears bright in her eyes.

"I know that. Go now. Go fetch the constable."

24

CHAPTER
THREE

As I make my way into the Hotel Chevalier, Violette hard upon my heels, I think again of how much the hotel reminds me of a gothic castle in some Radcliffe novel, with its turret-like structures and lichen shadows in the stonework. But inside, the entrance hall shines with marble and brass, and Hatterleigh insists the Hotel Chevalier has the very best suites in Paris. He also likes it because it's in close proximity to his cronies who live along Faubourg Saint-Honore.

As we climb the carpeted stairs to our third-floor suite, I tell Violette to take some time to herself.

"*Oui, Comtesse*," she murmurs.

Here, in Paris, I am referred to as Comtesse, or Countess, which I originally found irksome and just a little embarrassing. I have learnt, though, that Lady Hatterleigh abhors Paris's exotic underside and never accompanies Hatterleigh here, so I have become accustomed to being called Countess. In another world, at another time, perhaps it would be my rightful title, after all?

I'm slipping the gold and pearl bracelets from my wrists and placing them on the dressing table when

Hatterleigh enters our boudoir and puts his arms around me.

"What have you been up to, you minx?" he asks, nuzzling my neck.

He smells of cologne, sweat and whisky.

I grimace, moving along the cushioned stool away from him. "Where have you been? I thought you were just at the Jockey Club?" But I grin too, as he pulls me back into his arms. He presses his mouth to mine, and I could get tight just inhaling the liquor fumes upon his breath.

He takes my hands and leads me across the room to the bed where we collapse, laughing, amidst a twist of my petticoats and skirt. It takes a ridiculous amount of time for him to unhook my dress, untie all my stays, so that by the time we fall upon each other, we are quite feverish.

Later, he drops onto his back, panting. "You'll finish me off one day, Heloise."

"Well, what a nice way to go," I reply, turning over to snuggle into my pillows. Really, I want to see what time it is on the fancy ormolu clock on the bedside table. Still early. Somerscale said the meeting is scheduled to happen at midnight, when the tavern will be at its liveliest.

Hatterleigh slaps my bare bottom. "Come along, Hel. We're to meet Cyril and his lot at the Maison Dorée."

I bury my face into my pillow to stifle a groan. Cyril Breeden is Hatterleigh's dastardly brother-in-law. He's as sly as a snake, and his tongue darts in and out of his mouth as he talks. On the surface he's jocular with us, is good company, but there is a certain glint in his serpent eye that he reserves just for me when others are not looking. I've tried to explain it to Hatterleigh, but he waves it away, says I'm imagining things.

"I'm sorry, *mon gros gâteau*, but I have a prior engagement." I roll over to look at him.

"Where are you going?"

"To meet that friend of mine I told you of," I lie. "Rosina. Remember? We shared a room for the year I lived here."

Hatterleigh thinks I'm familiar with Paris and its language from a time I attended an educational salon for young ladies here, when, in fact, I never set foot on French soil until well and truly after my schoolgirl years. Well, at least he *pretends* to believe my story. Maybe he knows of my time here with Faucher, who was the French finance minister at the time; that stout whirlwind of energy who has now retired to the countryside with his third wife and their brood of young children. He taught this Liverpool scamp much: of the language, Paris fashions, its gossip. Not to mention the niceties — and sensualities — of bedroom etiquette.

Hatterleigh lies on his side to face me, and twirls a loose curl of my hair around his finger. "Where was this *pension* again?"

"Boulevard du Temple." Isn't that where I've seen rather grand buildings? I'm pretty sure Hatterleigh wouldn't be familiar with it, in any case.

I lean into him, find his lips with mine again, try to distract him from his questioning.

"Ah, *ma mie*. You are an *énigme*." He runs his tongue across the swell of my breasts. "Perhaps I will come along and meet this Rosina."

"Don't be ridiculous, Giles," I say, shoving him a little. "You will be bored silly. We're meeting at that church of the invalids or whatever it is, would you believe? She wants to show me the new stained glass windows. She's very pious, you know. Nothing like the company you keep." I grin at him, willing myself to remain nonchalant. He must be dissuaded from accompanying me. "And then we are to have supper at her mother's house in Rue la Fitte. I will take Violette along with me as escort, if that is what worries you."

"That does sound rather dull, Heloise. I don't know how you will stand it." He rests his head back onto a pillow and yawns. "Well, when you become bored with that, which you undoubtedly will, come join us at Bal Mabille."

While Hatterleigh is in his dressing room with his valet, Chiggins, I lie in bed and ponder what to do about this assignment of mine. I've heard stories of this Bocages des Anges, but the area is really so disreputable, even Hatterleigh has never been there for a lark.

As I run my fingertips across the grooves of the carved bedhead, I imagine what it might be like to wander alone in such a notorious place. At night. Picking my way through throngs of men, who will be drunk and prowling for prey and, suddenly, what feels like a pebble skittles across my innards. I've become adept at avoiding becoming game to such fellows. Of course, I have experience of the rough backstreets of London and the tough docks of Liverpool but I feel less sure of this place, less familiar with its haunts and menaces. Really, I should have someone to escort me. If I were still in London, I would take Taff, or Bundle even, along with me, but here I only have access to Hatterleigh and his lot. And to them, I would have to reveal too much.

My mind lights upon Violette. Of course. I will take her with me, after all. Sabine, her employer — who was mistress herself to a fat Duke something-or-other not that long ago, and now runs a very exclusive bawdy house in the centre of Paris — assured me that Violette was not easily shocked. And, truth be told, the girl was dressed more like a harlot than a handmaid when she first came to me. I would not be surprised if she isn't a maid at all, but actually one of Sabine's girls. I think of her pretty face and dark ringlets and wonder what she did so wrong that she was tossed from the inner circle of Sabine's doxies. Maybe she has the pox? Her pale skin is clear, nice apple-red cheeks, but of course I can't know what disease might lurk under her skirts. Or perhaps she simply doesn't have a good way with the gentlemen. Some women just don't.

Hopping out of bed, I approach the windows that look out onto the road. Remembering Somerscale's words about spies, I peer at the scattering of people down on the pavement, and cannot see anyone familiar. Although that thin man . . . Is he the chap from outside the prison? It's difficult to tell, because he has a straw hat crammed low over his forehead. I shake my head. I'm imagining things. When climbing into our carriage outside the Clichy debtors' prison, I was quite sure no one took particular interest in us and, when walking into our hotel, I took note that there weren't any buggies following us, nor suspicious looking loiterers. Seems that bastard, Somerscale, was correct. Nobody has an interest in a loose woman such as myself. Tutting my tongue against my teeth, I move to the escritoire.

"What are you frowning over?" asks Hatterleigh, entering the boudoir. He's attired in an elegant black tailcoat.

"Oh," I say, caught off-guard. "Just penning a letter to Amah to see if that trunk of new gowns has arrived in South Street."

"You're mighty friendly with that maid of yours," he murmurs, concentrating on tying the tidy, white bow tie at his throat. "I'm surprised she can even read."

I think of the row of books that are locked away in the bedside cabinet in Amah's room in Mayfair. *Frankenstein*, its cover red and velvet-soft like the wings of a moth. The Dickens with its sombre engravings, and *Sense and Sensibility*, in three parts, its covers as dogeared and rough as bark. Each a gift from my father, so Amah says.

"She's not a barbarian, Giles," I say as I scrawl a message across a leaf of paper, irrationally annoyed that he speaks of my mother in such terms. But how is he to know Amah's my mother? I glance up at him, and study his features as he takes out his pocket book and withdraws a few notes from it. I try to picture the expression on his face were I to tell him about my heritage, about the Oriental blood that courses through my veins. My lip lifts at the thought of his eyes bulging in absurd outrage. Amusing, yet a tiny corner of my soul curls in upon itself.

I blow across the damp ink, then fold the paper over as Hatterleigh bends down to kiss me on the cheek. "Are you sure, my dear, you won't join us?"

"Quite sure, Giles," I say, grasping his face between my hands to kiss him. "When Rosina and I are finished up, I will find you. Leave directions with Chiggins."

I wait a couple of minutes after he has gone before I ring for the bellboy. I give him my letter with instructions on its delivery. After eating an early supper of *côtes de veau en papillotes*, followed by the very tiniest slice of *tarte tatin*, I call for Violette.

When she enters the suite I say to her, "Violette, please fetch that lovely gown you were wearing when you first arrived here." Not many moments later, when she returns with it over her arm, I see that it is perfect for our evening in Bocages des Anges. A hideous piece of lustrous yellow satin — that showcases maximum bosom, from memory — over a puce and blue striped skirt. A dress that positively hollers 'harpy'.

"Violette, later this evening I have an assignation with someone in Rue de l'Âme Damnée," I say to her, in my stilted French.

"In Bocages des Anges," she gasps. However, she's not shocked. "*C'est passionant.*"

"Yes," I say, trying to share some of her excitement. "But I have heard this is a crude part of town. I'm afraid that it is not a good idea for two women to enter the area alone." I pick up her dress. I had the vague idea that I might squeeze into it for our outing tonight — for my sumptuous clothes would stand out in such an area — but it's quite worn, and there's a nasty stain beneath the underarms.

Luckily, right at that moment, there's a knock at the door. Chiggins walks across the drawing room to open the door. He's only a small man, his countenance almost engulfed by his huge beak of a nose. His step is still steady, but it won't be in an hour or so. As soon as his master disappears for the evening, Chiggins hits his bottle of gin or claret or whatever it is that valets indulge in during their long, boring evenings pressing trousers and polishing boots.

Swinging the door open, he sweeps in two lads who carry a trunk between them. They're attired in matching blue uniforms with gold epaulettes that, upon closer scrutiny, are frayed and grubby. They plonk the trunk onto the floor between the sofas, and the taller one hands me a letter, before they both take themselves off again.

"But, they are ushers from the Theatre Petit Lazare," Violette says, surprise in her voice. "Why do they bring you this chest?"

Ripping open the note, I watch for Chiggins to close the doors upon us, before I answer her. "I know the manager there. I asked him to send us some costumes

32

for our jaunt tonight." I scan Pascale's scribble, nodding. "Perfect."

I open the trunk, and Violette and I peer into a tumble of clothing. I lift out a pair of trousers made of a brown linen, patched in places with red and yellow squares. Shaking my head, I mutter, "What does he think I can do with these?" and drop them on the floor and gather up another pair of trousers, navy blue, with a neat grey pinstripe. I consider them. "Perhaps."

"Comtesse, why do you need these costumes?"

"Because," I say, turning to her to hold a white cambric shirt up against her chest, "I do not think it is a good idea for two women to go alone into this area." Also, if anyone did see me at Somerscale's, they might have their eye out for me, alone, or with my maid again. "I think it will make much more sense if we go as two gentlemen."

"Me?" She draws back, swiping the shirt from my hand. "I will not dress up as a man. That is *diabolique*."

I grin. "*Quel dommage*. But not to worry." I pick the shirt up from the floor. "We can go as a couple — a man and his lady — out on the town for the evening. Thankfully, I enjoy dressing up as a gentleman." I point at her yellow dress. "And you can wear that after all." God knows, I don't relish having her grimy gown against my skin. "Remember, you have to look like a woman who knows her way around Bocages des Anges. In other words, the opposite of an angel."

As she scrambles into her satins, I rummage through the rest of the costumes in the trunk. Luckily Pascale has sent me a variety of men's clothing that is on the smaller side, because when I conceived this plan, I immediately realised that Hatterleigh's clothing would be far too large for Violette and me; and, of course, it would be difficult to pry his precious clothing from Chiggins' protective fingers.

"What the hell is this?" I say, lifting out a tricorne. Underneath it, I find a shirt with black and white stripes. "Ha. It seems Pascale seeks to send me out as a buccaneer." Next, I uncover a hat with a pheasant's feather curled along its length. "Or a Spanish fellow from last century, even. It's a wonder the silly man hasn't sent me along a sword." I pause. Which actually might've been helpful in such a situation. I must remember to slip my pistol into my pocket before we leave.

Finally, I settle upon the white shirt that Violette had eschewed, and a grey overcoat. The navy trousers are still a little too big for me, so I sneak a look into Hatterleigh's dressing room. Luckily Chiggins has taken himself off somewhere, so I pinch a pair of Hatterleigh's braces, and one of his many top hats. It's too big for me, but that's fine, as it hides my hair, which I've piled high on my head. I tuck an artificial blossom, something like a nasturtium, into the satin hatband. Last, I open the drawer in which I know Hatterleigh keeps his firearms. My pretty pistol with its ivory handle lies amongst Hatterleigh's more sturdy, dark pieces. I hesitate, and choose one of his, a rather sleek piece, black and gold, and I check that it's armed.

When I return to the drawing room, I retrieve a lacquer box from the bottom of the trunk.

There's a look of disgust on Violette's face when she sees what's inside. "What is that? It looks like a furry caterpillar!"

I pick it up between my fingertips, and hold it to my upper lip. "It's a moustache." I grin as I carry the box to the mirror in my dressing room. I sprinkle some of its adhesive on the back, and then press it against my skin. It only takes a moment to hold, but I know if I sweat too much, it will peel off again. With a charcoal pencil I thicken my brows. I add a smudge between my eyebrows, and rub a little of the charcoal into my cheeks to give the appearance of stubble. Cramming the hat lower onto my forehead, I grin as I stare at the dishevelled young man in the mirror. Not bad at all.

To finish up, I wind a cravat around my throat and shove the pistol low into the coat's inner pocket. "Ready?" I ask Violette.

She's made herself up perfectly for a jaunt to Bocages des Anges. Shiny, cheap bangles clang up and down her arms, and a string of fake pearls, glistening with a silver sheen, nestle between her cleavage. I think I can actually see a peep of pink nipple rise like a sunset from the right side of her bodice. She's been very liberal with the rouge and powder, too. I let her wear my purple bonnet and velvet cloak.

While I wait on the side of the road for Violette to find us a cab, I take in the evening crowd. Apart from the usual people one might expect to find on such a busy thoroughfare — porters, a stable-boy, numerous couples ambling along, two or three pretty fancy girls — there doesn't seem to be anyone taking particular interest in me. Two men deep in conversation brush past me and a coachman knocks into my shoulder as he shoves past and, momentarily, I feel piqued. But then I grin, because I realise my disguise works. I am invisible. Just another chap out on the town.

CHAPTER
FOUR

Amah

Amah slices the beef into thin portions that she then scrapes into a large bowl. She adds some of Agneau's black sauce — which isn't quite right but has a certain piquancy that will do — and with her hands, she rubs the brown bean paste into the meat.

She's conscious of Agneau's dark eyes on her.

"The meat should have been marinating for much longer than this," she says. "But what with the burglary and the police . . ."

She pumps water into the scullery basin and washes her hands. She's wiping them on her apron when Agneau takes them in his, pats them dry with a cloth. Amah becomes still. She wants her reaction to be as matter-of-fact as Agneau's own attitude.

"The constable was not much help, in the end."

"Ah, *oui*. *Le gendarme*. What did this man have to say about it all?" Agneau leans his hip against the bench, wiping his own damp hands on the tea-towel.

She thinks back to the young man who came to take their report. Nice enough boy. Tall, red hair. But unsure of what he could do to help.

"He didn't have much to say. What could he say? Nothing was actually taken, I don't think."

"Then what was the scoundrel doing here?" Agneau's thick brows rise. He lifts his hands and shoulders. "Why make such a mess and not take anything?"

Amah has wondered the same. "They must have been looking for something specific."

The chef nods. "Yes. Yes, they were most probably after Madame Heloise's diamonds. But why not take other trifles while they are here?"

"Perhaps they ran out of time." After listening to Abigail re-tell her story again to the constable, Amah is quite certain the man purportedly checking the chimneys and the woman who lost her dog were working together. What a silly girl Abigail is to have been so easily duped. Amah shakes her head. Taking up a small tin of rice, she scoops three handfuls of the grain into the flour sieve. She picks through the husks, washing the loose starchy bits away. She then pours the rice into a saucepan with three cups of water.

Amah backs away as Agneau moves to her side. He picks up the bottle of bean paste and sniffs it.

"Interesting." He dips the tip of his small finger into the paste and dabs a little on his tongue. Smacks his tongue against the roof of his mouth, tasting it. "Very interesting."

He steps in front of the bowl of beef, his sleeve brushing Amah's. His height, his bulk, is too much for her. She turns to the stove, pushes the saucepan across the flame. She wrenches her thoughts back to the would-be robbery.

"I just hope they do not revisit us."

"But do not worry, Li Leen," says Agneau, the only one of Heloise's staff to have the effrontery — the excuse of Continental foreignness — to call Amah by her first name. He crosses to the scullery to fetch another cutting board. He pulls a cabbage head close, chopping it into fine, stiff slivers. "Bundle has secured the house. Do you not hear that banging right now?" He cups his ear theatrically. "That is a workman nailing a new bolt into the back door."

He stands next to her again. The saucepan of rice hums with the pressure of simmering water. His voice softens as he says, "And, of course, if you were to be afraid, you can always come to me."

"I'm never afraid," she snaps, perhaps more sharply than she intends.

He raises his hands in the air. "I know. I know. You are very strong. Very formidable."

She looks for anger or irritation in his face but sees none. She places a skillet onto the top of the stove and waits for it to heat up. "And you said that Bundle's sister was fine?"

The cook shrugs. "That is what he said."

"So he must have been lured away."

"That is what Bundle believes."

Which means their trespassers have watched the house. Know their movements. Probably even waited for her to go on her afternoon walk. Her back stiffens at the thought. She stirs the meat, fragrant smoke rising from where it sizzles. She watches it brown but, in her mind's eye, she's picturing the criminal couple lying in wait, perhaps strolling up and down the street or, more likely, biding their time in a coach. A burning smell reaches her nostrils, breaking her reverie, and she sees that the beef is blackening at the edges. She whips the skillet from the fire and spoons the meat onto a platter.

"Burnt," she says.

"No, no. Just a little charred."

She frowns down at the dish. It smells delicious, almost as it should. But she knows it will never be exactly right. That these things cannot be wholly recreated so far away in time and space.

Agneau picks up a piece of meat between his thumb and finger. His bottom lip shines with a little grease as he chews. "Delicious. Next time we will compare recipes for preparing frogs' legs. Yes?"

She nods. "When the rice is ready, put a little of the cabbage on top, and then the beef on top of that."

"Where did you learn to cook like this?" He tilts his head to the side, resting a hand on the kitchen table.

"From my mother." Before they moved to her stepfather's house. When times were more simple. Happier.

"How long have you been here?" he asks. "In England?"

Her smile is grim. "A long time. Long enough to remember when it was very difficult indeed to find bean sauce." Never comfortable with talking of the past, she turns the subject to him. "How long have you been working here?"

40

He pulls a face as he thinks. "Eight, no, nine, years." He pours a glass of claret, offering it to her, but she shakes her head no. "You would like the south of France, where I am from. It is warmer than here. Perhaps I will take you there one day." His eyes smile as he salutes her with the wine glass.

On her way to the third floor, Amah passes through Heloise's rooms to pour herself a small glass of Irish whiskey. Earlier, she'd helped Abigail clean up the mess and replace Heloise's things. Even neatened, though, her dressing room is a riot of colour and clutter. Hat ribbons trail the racks and baskets of feathers and silk flowers, butterflies and birds line the walls. Pages ripped from fashion journals are tacked to the wall and litter the dressing table. Shoes — bejewelled, leather, suede, lined with fur, boots, slippers, sandals — fill the boxes of a wall cabinet.

But Heloise's bedroom is neat, elegant yet impersonal. Amah takes in the smooth carpets and the plumped up, sumptuous bed and she is surprised by a dip of loneliness. She thinks back to that day long ago when she first found Heloise — her Jia Li — missing from her small room. Her girl, gone. Even before Amah had confirmed that Heloise's brush and favourite night dress were absent, Amah had known that the girl had left her for longer than a few hours. There was something about the room. Some essence of her shining girl lost to the shadows in the corners, muted by the dust motes that floated by the beam of Amah's lamp. Rage and alarm hammered in her ears as she scrabbled through Heloise's things, wondering where she could be. Who to ask for help? What to do?

Amah takes a sip of whisky. Presses her eyes shut, willing herself back into the present moment. She hears a carriage rumble by on the street below. A boy calls out, perhaps with the evening paper. She lowers her nose to her glass, breathes in the whisky's fumes. Takes another sip. Feels her shoulders ache with the loosening the alcohol brings to her body. She walks back out into the corridor, closing Heloise's door gently behind her.

In her own bed chamber, Amah changes into her nightgown and washes her face. Leaving the curtains open wide — she wakes long before sunrise, after all — she climbs into her bed, pushing the pillows up against the bedhead to lie against. She picks up her book, *The Cricket on the Hearth*, and it flips open at a page creased from the rough treatment it had received at the hands of the intruder. She smooths the fold with her fingers, and then turns to the page she is up to.

Reading of the cricket reminds her of a poem her mother used to recite to her when she was little. A Chinese poem, of cricket song and a thatched roof. Of grieving cicadas. Her mother's voice catching on the words *alone in all this empty forest*.

Again, that dip of sadness. So much of her life spent with others, but with the wraith of loneliness trailing her steps. Those years in Liverpool, however, interspersed with light — warm, glorious light — that had blazed in her heart so strongly she still feels its remnants flicker from time to time. Its heat, right now, making her think of Agneau's strong hands, kneading

42

dough, handling sides of mutton. Wondering what it would be like to feel him cupping her waist, or the flat of his hand hot on her thigh. She blinks. What are these thoughts?

She rolls onto her side and stares out at the dark sky yawning above the house across the road. Remembers a night, chillier than this, when her back was burrowed into another's warmth. His heavy arm wrapping her close. She wonders what he is doing right now. Can he see the same stars as she gazes upon? The ones that are in the shape of a stingray, or those bright stars that slither into the darkness. Is his sky black like hers, or covered with milky cloud?

She wonders if a person can ever go back. If she wished for it hard enough, if it would one day return. What would it change though? What's done is done. Amah thinks of the times Heloise has fretted about missing a ball or sulked over a failed investment, and how she tells her daughter that regret is a waste of time, a waste of energy. But mostly Amah knows that regret can sup on the soul, morsel by morsel, until it's as brittle and emaciated as a cicada shell.

CHAPTER
FIVE

From the carriage, Rue de l'Âme Damnée seems as cheerful and festive in appearance as a carnival. Bright lights, some encased in coloured glass, gleam upon the road, and the houses are as garish in colour as jockeys' tunics at the Grand National. Once we are strolling its uneven pavement, though, it's clear that the moon is kinder than the light of the sun would ever be. The merry bunting is dirty with age, and the stench of sewerage and cat piss reeks from dark, narrow alleys. The street is quite crammed with buggies, people and refuse.

I take Violette's hand and place it on my elbow, as we tread across the muddy cobblestones. I walk with that swagger so many men adopt: chest out, slight spring to the step, like a rooster with an eye out for a luscious morsel of some sort. I pat my moustache to make sure it is still in place.

"*Maisons de passe*, Comtesse," Violette says to me, nodding towards the low-set lodgings on either side of the road. Disreputable houses. "For soldiers' women. *Grivoises.*"

Grivoises. Yet another rung in that charming ranking system.

The curtains of the first house we pass are wide open, and we are able to peer right into the well-lit living room. A woman smiles down at me through the glass and pulls the bodice of her gown down to her waist, revealing a plump, pendulous breast. She winks, then pulls the bodice back into place. At the next house, there are two women, arms entwined around each other's backs. The blond girl lifts her partner's skirts to allow us a glimpse of her quim, while the taller woman plucks the girl's blouse down to uncover her tiny nipples. It's much the same at each house along the row, except for one, where a man, dark and ruddy in the face, is seated on an armchair facing the window, and all we can see of the woman is her bare arse, while her head bobs up and down in his lap.

Violette blows a raspberry and laughs, bounding ahead along the malodorous street, weaving between other carousers. She has to ask first a tobacconist and then a boy selling boiled eggs for the way to the Dernier Livre. He points towards a ramshackle, two storey building. Its sign, swinging from the eaves, is painted with five gold coins.

Anticipation prickles my skin as I tug at the red and white striped cravat that I've tied about my neck. Somerscale had given it to me; said that, according to the letter they intercepted, this was how the crook would recognise me. He'd told me to tie the cravat around my wrist, or attach it to my bonnet, not knowing that I'd be disguised as a man.

I glance around, not quite sure if I'm feeling jumpy from the excitement or apprehension. I feel like there are eyes on me; I can almost feel their scrutiny quiver against the back of my neck, and I wonder again if I'm being followed. Could Somerscale's spies truly be onto me? I'm nudged from behind as two drunks approach the tavern, and a group of revellers, both male and female, stumble past, squealing and shouting.

The Dernier Livre's doors fling open and a man bursts through, stumbles to the side of the road, where he hacks up into the gutter. Three horses, tied to a rail, shy away, the closest one bumping shoulders with Violette. She shoves both the horse, then the man, out of her way.

"Now, now, missus," says a man, in English, stepping from the tavern, "don't you worry yoursel' none. He's no more harmful than a ladybug in a blizzard." He speaks with a lazy, American drawl.

He saunters forward but trips, falling to his knees next to the other man, and stays there a few moments, howling like a hyena with laughter. He's so drunk, it takes him two goes before he can struggle to his feet again. By now a couple of stableboys and Violette are laughing at his predicament too. Once standing, he nudges the other fellow with the tip of his boot. He's a tall man, his blond hair worn long and stringy under a misshapen derby hat. "There's no saving him, madame," he says to Violette. "Do you know him, too? Michelle, or some such lady's name, he said his name was." He grins down at Violette, an admiring glint in his bloodshot eyes.

She looks at him, uncomprehending, so I say, in a hesitant manner, as if English is not my mother tongue,

"We have never met this man, sir." I shrug, and lead Violette past them in through the front doors of the Dernier Livre.

The taproom is quite small, but terribly crowded. People stand in clusters or are seated at the five or six wooden, round tables that are available. The air is redolent with stale body odour, the pong of boiling onions and damp feet and I am sorry that I cannot fan my face with my scented sandalwood fan. When we walk towards the bar at the back of the room, the soles of my feet stick to the floor with each step.

As we wait to catch the eye of the barmaid, I glance around the room and almost immediately notice two men standing in the corner. They have their faces lowered, but one of them — the thinner of the two — has a straw hat on. I feel a tingle in my fingertips. Is he the man from outside Somerscale's? The same man I'd spied from our suite? He throws his head back to gulp his beer, and his gaze meets mine fleetingly, and then takes in Violette, who is primping her curls with her fingertips. He nudges his companion and says something. They both stare at her for a few moments more.

A hand claps me on the shoulder. "Not got your rot-gut yet?" The Yank again. He leans against the bar, his sleeve soaking in a puddle of spilt drink. Violette watches him distastefully as he sways next to her. "Lemme buy you a drink. Name's Ripley."

"But where is your friend, *mon ami* Ripley?" I ask, using my fake French accent again. I avoid sharing our names with him.

He stares at me, vacant for a moment, then guffaws. "That screwy chap outside? Skedaddled, he did." He bangs the counter to attract the barmaid's attention. "Time to smother the parrot, I reckon. My new pals here will have one too," he says to her, nudging me sharply in the arm.

The barmaid's a dark, young thing, and her heavily kohled eyes are bored as she pours three glasses of absinthe. Before she can continue, the American drunkard swipes up one of the glasses and swallows the emerald green liquid in one mouthful. He punches his fist against his chest. "Phew-ee," he says, pushing his glass forward again. "Pour me another one, would ya?" He takes a handful of coins from his pocket and plonks them down on the bar, where three roll to the floor next to the barmaid's feet.

The girl stares at him for a moment then rolls her eyes, before finishing off our drinks with water and sugar.

Sipping my absinthe, now a pleasing pear green, I glance around the room again while the confounded Yank blathers on to an uncomprehending Violette. The man with the straw hat approaches the bar and orders a tankard of bitter beer, and I see his gaze steal towards my maid again, before he returns to his companion across the room. Violette's laughing in a coy manner at something Ripley says about the curl in her hair just as a new group of people enter the tavern, pulling up chairs to the already teeming tables. From what I can see, most of the Dernier Livre's patrons are exceedingly tight, as they shout at each other, merrily sloshing

48

sherry and bitters across the tabletops and floor. Mostly, the crowd is made up of ripe, ready women, and their soldiers, some still attired in red and blue uniforms. I just can't peg anyone in particular for our contact. As our noisome companion regales Violette with a long story about his horse back home, a boy, no older than six years, tugs my trousers and points to my feet. I nod and surrender my boots to his brush and polish, readying a coin for him in my fingers.

That's when I notice one man who stands out from the rest. He's seated at a table by himself, not far from where we stand. His skinny frame is engulfed by a drab coat, and what with the whiskers that cover his face and the wide-brimmed hat pulled so low onto his brow, it's difficult to make out his features. Only his hands, claw-like as they grasp his tankard, reveal that his age is advanced. I adjust my striped cravat, but can't be sure if he looks my way or not. Momentarily, another man blocks my view, opening his coat wide, so I can see his inner pockets are lined with silver spoons, tongs, chains and even a little clock. I shake my head. I don't want any of his stolen wares.

Our American friend is telling us of his home in some place called Bushwick as he takes swigs from a bottle of brandy. I do hate a man who jaws too much, and Violette looks to be heartily tired of his charms too. Luckily, his 'pal', Michel, stumbles back in through the front doors, and makes a bee-line for us, attracting the Yank's attention. Michel shoves his way between Violette and me, and leans against the bar.

An old woman, with bright beetle eyes, shoves a basket of daffodils in my face. "A pretty flower for your love?" she says to me, in French. I wave her off. Hell, I didn't realise men were so hassled. Pedlars just never seem to leave them alone. I always thought women were the more heavily harassed when out in public, although in a different manner, of course. I watch the frightful Ripley steal his arm around Violette's waist, which he hastily removes with a loud laugh when I pull her to my side. He immediately starts to prattle on again, something about Michel, who droops over a tumbler of beer at the bar between us. He stinks of vomit and horse manure.

I order another round of absinthe. An older man has joined the barmaid to serve drinks. Someone calls him Bernard, begs him for credit, but the tavern owner just shakes his head and continues to polish a pewter mug. It's clear from his swarthy skin and the sharp angle of his chin that he's the barmaid's father. Once prepared, she pushes our drinks towards me across the counter, and her eyes catch mine as she strokes her fingertip down the side of my outstretched hand. A smile lilts the sly puss's mouth. Her father glares at me, and grunts something to her.

"Michelle here — dang unfortunate name — was telling me there's a fortune to be made in some place called Otago," Ripley says loudly, trying to catch my attention. I lend only half an ear to his talk of a far-off gold rush as I scan the room again. I try to search out who might be our elusive contact, but nothing jags my attention. I give the Yank a brief smile, which encourages him further. "Bottom of the world, that is. Just waiting for our ship to be ready. You should join us. Plenty of gold for everybody, so I've been told." He goes to put his glass on the counter but misses, so it smashes at our feet.

Violette laughs, and I look to the barman to see if he's incensed, but his attention has been diverted to the other side of the room. Tables scrape across the floor and vicious squeals fill the air. We surge forward with the rest of the patrons for a closer look at what is causing the racket, just in time to see a brutish fellow, front tooth missing, haul a woman across the floor by her hair. She breaks free, her yellow hair a weedy tangle, and howls with rage. I gasp when she kicks the man square in the guts. He's so drunk that, despite his superior size, he topples back onto the filthy floor. A girl, her face red with tears, tries to pull the woman back, but loses her grip on her arm. She beseeches a rat-like man to intervene, but he just smirks as he watches the fun. The blond woman continues to kick her assailant until she falls across his broad body and, taking his chance, he grasps her by the hair again, and bangs her head against the floor, one-two-three times, until a blotch of blood blooms on her forehead. Clenching my fists, a dark veil of fury closes in upon me. The crowd and noise fade. I step forward, my hand feeling for the pistol in my pocket.

A hand grasps my arm. I scowl up at Ripley. "Let go of me!"

"Nah," he says, pushing me back. "I reckon this is the time for a real man to intervene."

51

His movements are surprisingly quick for a man who's imbibed the number of drinks I've witnessed him throwing back in the last half hour. He scoops the moaning woman up from the ground by the shoulders and presses her into the arms of the bawling girl. Bending back down, he grabs the brutish fellow by the collar and heaves him to his feet. Although of much the same height, Ripley doesn't have the bulk of his opponent, but he still manages to strike a heavy fist into the other's fat stomach, so that the bully folds over, spittle dripping from his wet mouth. Ripley then knees him in the noggin, so the big man falls onto his back again, and writhes on the floor like an afflicted cockroach.

As I inch forward to watch the fight more closely, jostled from each side, I am reminded of another tiresome thing men must put up with; both the barmaid and Violette cling to my arms, gasping and squealing as they peek through their fingers at the skirmish before us.

Most of the crowd clap and cheer for the Yank, who has a stupid grin on his face and lifts his arms in the air like a boxing champion. Except for the smirky rat-man, who doesn't look pleased at all. I notice a glint of metal and, stepping forward, I swipe up a wine flagon, and swing it as hard as I can against the side of his head. He topples forward, a nasty-looking dagger clanging to the floor next to him.

As Ripley takes in what I have done — how I have saved him from a savage stab — a look of surprise vies with the grin on his face. He looks from the dagger to me and back at the dagger again, but, before he can say anything, Bernard, the tavern owner, grasps him by the elbow and indicates for him to leave. Ripley tries to remonstrate, but Bernard ignores him, or maybe cannot understand his English, and summons two burly men to assist him in ousting the Yank. On their way out, Bernard grasps me by the arm too, and drags me towards the doorway. First, Ripley is thrown headlong into the street, his long legs taking him as far as the gutter where he falls to the road, and then I am kicked in the hind so that, after the initial momentum, I roll across the pavement and land neatly against Ripley's chest.

"Well, dang it," he says. "That didn't seem fair."

Violette helps me to my feet as the Yank tries to pull himself up with the assistance of a horse that's tied to a post next to him. The horse rears its head in fright and steps away, and Ripley falls to his knees again. This is repeated twice, before he finally manages an upright position.

"I vote we move onto that music hall there," he says, pointing to a lurid-looking place across the road.

I shake my head. "*Non, non.*" I glance back into the Dernier Livre. Light spills from the narrow windows and, twice, the front door swings open as patrons leave.

I haven't fulfilled my role for the evening. I haven't connected with Somerscale's contact. I must find a way back inside.

As I walk the short path to the tavern's entrance, I notice that the bulk in my right coat pocket, where the pistol is ensconced, somehow feels different as it bangs against my thigh. Reaching into my pocket, my fingers close about something that does not have the familiar grooves and chill of the gun. Instead, I feel sharp corners, flat planes. Something like a booklet.

I freeze, puzzled.

"Comte- . . . Monsieur?" says Violette, close behind.

I look around at Ripley, who's trying to smooth out the bumps in his ruined derby, before cramming it back onto his head.

"We must go home, Violette," I say, in French. "I do not feel so well," I lie, smiling weakly at Ripley. "Must be the knock to my head." I shake his hand in a hearty manner and whistle for a cab.

The Yank noisily beseeches us to stay. I lean from the cab's window to apologise, and tell him he can find us at a non-existent hotel on the outskirts of Paris. As the buggy pulls away, I take one last look towards the Dernier Livre. A figure in a straw hat stares out at us from the tavern's front step.

After sending Violette off to bed, I drag the booklet from the coat's pocket. It turns out to be a tattered travel guide and map of Paris. I flip through the pages twice, looking for any markings or words. On the third time through, I can just make out a very faint circle has been drawn around a paragraph at the bottom of page nine. Also, there is a slight crease in the corner of the page, where it has been turned down in the past. I'm just trying to decipher the French words on the page when I hear the suite's door handle rattle. My heart jumps as I leap to my feet. Hatterleigh. And me, still dressed as a man.

Racing into the boudoir, dimly lit from the one lamp on the bedside table, I shed my male attire as fast as a swift swoops for a grub. I cram the clothing into its box and slam the lid shut. I am just taking a seat at the dressing table, naked, when Hatterleigh enters.

"But what is this?" he says, tapping the trunk with his shoe.

"I had Pascale send over some costumes from the Theatre Petit Lazare," I say, leaning into the mirror. "I thought we could have a soiree here tomorrow night. Play a game of charades."

"Ah," he says, shrugging out of his overcoat. "That could be amusing. What are you doing there?"

I press my fingers to my upper lip, grinning, as I turn to him. "Practicing for tomorrow night. What do you think?"

He catches sight of my lustrous moustache and laughs. "Very becoming."

He moves to his dressing room, calling out for poor old Chiggins. Snatching up the travel guide again, I have another look at page nine. My French is rusty, but the word *cimetière* is not so difficult to decipher. My heartbeat quickens. It seems someone wants to meet me — or Somerscale, to be precise — at the cemetery.

CHAPTER
SIX

Amah

Amah comes in from her afternoon walk, closing the back door behind her. She pulls her bonnet ribbons loose as she listens to Agneau discuss something with his scullery boy. She is not sure what they speak of for his murmur is too low. Standing in the shadows of the narrow corridor, she watches them through the kitchen doorway, where Agneau is bent over the kitchen bench. He chops a bunch of parsley finely, then stops, offers the knife to the boy, urging him to have a try. As he turns back to the stove, Amah whisks past, glad of the hallway rug that muffles the click of her heels. Avoiding the servant stairs, whose creak would surely give her presence away to those below in the kitchen, Amah makes her way through to the front of the house. Her steps are quiet as she climbs the carpeted stairs and she can't help but startle when a voice behind says, "Amah."

Turning, she sees Bundle looking up at her.

"Yes, Bundle."

He holds up an envelope. "A young fellow delivered this earlier. Said to give it to the mistress of the house as soon as possible."

56

"Did you tell him Mrs Chancey is away from home?"

"I did. And he appeared to be nonplussed. Said his instructions were to make sure the mistress of the house received the message as soon as possible. He said the message has something to do with an assignation for today."

Amah's eyes are on the missive in Bundle's hand. Probably one of Heloise's ridiculously assiduous admirers bent upon a private assignation, or a reminder to attend some absurd folly or other. How Heloise enjoyed such foolishness.

She holds out her hand to the butler, taking the missive. "I'll take care of it, Bundle. Thank you."

"Thank you, Amah."

Amah turns the letter over in her hands as she takes the stairs to her own rooms. She really hopes it is not some embarrassing drivel from one of Heloise's admirers. Taking up a letter opener, she slits the envelope open, pulling out a single sheet of paper.

Dear Madame,

I believe I might have in my possession something that is of value to you. Please meet me at The Mitre on Great Marlborough Street, today, no later than five o'clock. I will wait for you in the private dining room to the left of the corridor. To whet your appetite, I have drafted a rough copy of what I think will be of particular interest to you.

Yours sincerely,

JC

Amah's eyes widen as they reach the bottom of the page for, sketched in graphite, is a neat replication of her mother's earring. Golden orb, coiled dragon.

She drops the note on her desk and turns to look at the dressing table in her bedroom. But how . . . ? She checked her secret drawer after the intruder rifled through her things and the earring was quite safe. Her skirts rustle as she hurries to her dressing table, again pulling free the drawers and frame to reveal the hidden aperture. She squeezes the silk pouch, feeling for the hardness of the earring between her fingers and palm before opening it to double-check. Yes. The earring is still nestled deep in its pouch. But if the earring is here . . . if the earring is here . . . The other earring must be . . . Her breathing quickens as she thinks of the possibilities; if indeed the letter is in regards to the matching earring. She's puzzled, but she feels a thrill of excitement.

Amah shoves her jewellery and drawers back into place. Glancing at her watch, she sees that it is almost four o'clock. She opens her desk and takes out a leather wallet in which she keeps spare money. She empties the notes and gold coins into her reticule. Snatching up her bonnet and the note from where they lie on her desk, she strides out into the hallway and down the servants' stairs. She's about to call for Bundle to fetch her a cab but pauses at the sound of Taff's voice. He stands in the kitchen, gulping down a cup of tea, and she notes that he's wearing a neat tweed coat and moleskins rather than his usual attire of red and black satin that Heloise insists upon.

"Taff," she says to the coachman, "what are you doing right now?"

"Just taking Miss Heloise's horses for a little trot, Amah," he says to her. "Popped in to see if Agneau here'm needed anything picking up."

"Could you drive me to . . ." She checks the slip of paper. "Great Marlborough Street? To a tavern called The Mitre."

"What you'm need there, Amah?" he asks, popping two almonds into his mouth.

She ignores the urge to tell him that it's none of his concern, conscious of Agneau's dark eyes on her. "Just some business on behalf of Mrs Chancey," she says, her voice reproving. She moves into the corridor, hoping the coachman will follow, equally eager to make the meeting in good time and to remove herself from Agneau's inquiring gaze.

They walk out to where Heloise's handsome chestnuts wait. Taff tosses a farthing to the boy holding them steady and then opens the door of the barouche for Amah.

"What you'm up to, Amah?"

She makes ready to climb into the carriage. "Nothing at all. I don't know what you're talking about, Taff." Although she feels a nonsensical urge to tell him about the earring. But what nonsense he will think it is. He might even try to talk her out of meeting the anonymous letter-writer.

"Don't sell me a dog, Amah," he says. "I've known you many a year now, and I can see when there's a bit o' colour in your'm face."

She lifts an eyebrow at him as she pulls the veil down over her face.

The roads are clogged with coaches, cabs, equestrians, pedestrians. Stray dogs and thin children dart in and out of the teeming milieu, causing more confusion. Costermongers line the gutter, brandishing baskets of coal, pottery, baked eel, puppies. By the time they pick their way around a phaeton with a broken axle, they are running late. Amah lifts her watch to look at the time. The cover of the watch is thinned with age, and Amah's thumb rubs the slight dent where Heloise had sunk her straight little baby teeth into the gold many years before when she was teething.

When Amah sees the sign for The Mitre swaying outside the tavern, she hops down from the carriage before Taff has a chance to assist her.

"Where will you wait, Taff?" she calls up to him.

"How long do you think you'll be?"

"I'm not sure." She looks uncertainly through the front door of the tavern. The interior is still dark. An ostler comes out, points Taff the way of the stables.

"Look for me in the taproom, Amah," he says, guiding the horses forward. "I'll have an ale while I wait for you'm."

Amah lifts her skirts over the mud and steps into The Mitre's tiny lobby. The thin carpets smell of dirt and ale, a peculiar reek of cabbage and something rancid reaches her nostrils. On her right, several men sip quietly from tankards in the taproom but, when she's not approached by anybody, she continues down the corridor. As she steps, the boards under the carpets dip and creak. A bit further on, to her left, a door is ajar, and she can hear a voice say, "What could be keeping her? We have been waiting an age."

She's heard that voice before. Plaintive. Whiny.

The door's hinges squeak as she pushes it open. Sure enough, seated at an oak dining table, are the two people she'd passed the day before on the street — the woman with the big eyes and the man with the ferret features.

A pulse of disappointment moves through her. She, had hoped . . .

The man notices her hesitating in the doorway and stands, bows, asks her to join them.

"Mrs Chancey?"

Amah doesn't say anything as she takes a seat opposite. Who are these people? How'd they get hold of her mother's earring?

The young woman sighs. "How can we do business with you when you wear that ridiculous net over your face?"

But with each moment, Amah is increasingly loath to reveal her identity. It becomes clear to her that these are the people who were in Heloise's house. They weren't looking for Heloise's diamonds. Could it be that they were after the other dragon earring all along?

"You said that you had something of mine?"

"I never said it was yours." The woman sits back and crosses her arms. "But I bet you'd like to get your hands on it again."

"May I see it?"

"We have it safe."

"If you are unwilling to show it to me, what am I doing here?" asks Amah. The stress of the last hour, along with her dashed hopes, leave her feeling disinclined towards polite games with these people.

"We thought . . ." the man glances at his partner.

"We thought that perhaps you would like to purchase the item back from us," the woman says.

Amah realises that she's much younger than she first imagined, no older than nineteen, twenty years of age. The man, however, looks much older — late thirties perhaps — although, Amah guesses, of a much less stern temperament than the woman.

"Well, I must insist on seeing it before I agree to any terms," says Amah.

Her heartbeat picks up a little as the woman nods to her partner. He takes a small purse from his coat's inner breast pocket. Folding back the opening, he taps the purse gently so that the earring falls onto the table with a light clatter. Warmth floods Amah's chest as she gazes upon it. It's clearly the twin to her mother's earring that she keeps hidden at home. She thinks of the palm she'd placed it in over twenty years before. How she'd taken his fingers and curled them over the earring, the one gift she could offer.

"But how did you find it?" Her voice is hoarse and she needs to repeat herself. "Where?"

"Never you mind that," says the young woman, tartly. "Now, how much is it worth to you?"

But Amah must know how these people came to have her earring. Were they working for him? Was it stolen? Or worse . . . Was it sold to this reprehensible couple for mere money?

"I will pay you what you ask, but please tell me how it came to be in your possession?"

The young woman takes to her feet and approaches a trolley that holds a profusion of bottles and glasses.

"I find it fascinating that you are so very determined to find out how we came across this trinket," she says, pouring a small glass of sherry. She offers it to Amah who shakes her head. As the young woman returns to her seat, she swings around and grasps Amah's veil, pulling it away so that Amah's hat wrenches to the side.

She goggles at Amah, half falling across the table, spilling the sherry on the carpet.

"You're a foreigner!" she gasps.

Amah straightens her hat, pushing the netting back from her forehead. "I've lived here many a year now." Her voice is flat.

"But you're a foreigner," the woman says again. "You're coloured." Her protuberant eyes widen even more. "And you're old. We thought you were young." She turns to the man. "We thought she was younger, didn't we Joshua?"

He nods. "We did, my love. We heard that the lady of the house — Mrs Heloise Chancey — was a young lady."

Amah sees her chance. "Ah. But I am here on behalf of Mrs Chancey. She's my mistress. She is abroad at the moment and has left me to take care of her affairs as I see fit."

The woman takes her seat again and contemplates Amah. Someone calls for the ostler from the road, and a servant walks past clutching a pair of newly polished boots.

"And yet, I think your interest in this earring is more personal than that. I don't believe your story of working on behalf of your mistress. Tell me, what is your name?"

Amah sits up straighter. "I will tell you my name when you tell me yours."

The young woman watches her some more and something seems to occur to her. She claps her hand over her mouth and says, turning to Joshua, "I don't know whether to laugh or heave, Joshua. Do you know what this means?"

But he doesn't seem to. He shakes his head, says, "No, my love. I have no idea."

She squeaks with frustration.

"Should we not go back to the earring?" he says. "This lady might still want to purchase it."

Amah clenches her teeth. Anger settles over her, leaving her feeling as hard and implacable as marble. She wants to utter waspish words but hasn't quite lost sight of her desire to settle the business of the earring.

The young woman leans across the table as she asks Amah, "First, tell me, do you have children?"

Amah's fury slips for a moment at the unexpected question. "That is none of your business."

"You do. I can see that you do," the woman almost pants, clapping her hands together. Her eyes stray to the tabletop as she tries to calculate something in her mind.

Joshua clears his throat. "The earring. How much is it worth to you?" he asks Amah.

Amah looks at the gold orb again. She thinks of the notes and coins in her reticule. She'll start with an amount that she thinks the earring might be worth. "£5?"

Joshua looks startled, but the young woman laughs.

"We were thinking more like £200," he says. "We were hoping that it was of particular value to you."

The young woman interrupts him and there's a mean gleam in her eye as she says, "Let's double it. I think £400 would be more suitable. Now that we know who we are dealing with."

The malicious smile on her face makes Amah clutch her hands tight in her lap.

CHAPTER
SEVEN

Rain falls heavily outside the prison, and the smell of wet soil and waste drifts through the gaps in the windows as I wait for Somerscale to say something. My fingers pick at the pink ribbon of my pretty bonnet, where it has come loose from the purple felt. Violette must've been too damned rough with it last night. I will have to gift it to her now.

Somerscale stops pacing for a moment. "You say you found this in your pocket?"

"I did. And the bastard stole my pistol, while he was at it. Regular little pick pocket, whoever he is."

"You didn't get a look at him?"

I grimace, ashamed. "Sorry."

Somerscale scrapes a kitchen chair across the floor so it's facing mine, and takes a seat. He takes my hands in his. "Heloise, think on it. Surely someone must have stood out to you?"

I spent the whole night thinking on this. Made an inventory in my mind of who could have been the villain we were trying to contact; anyone I could remember, who was in my vicinity the night before.

"There was one man who seemed a little odd," I say, thinking of the old man seated alone in such a busy taproom. "He was so heavily concealed in his coat and hat, it was difficult to see anything of him."

"Did he approach you?"

"I don't think so. But you have to understand, everyone was packed in the Dernier Livre as tight as a row of minnows in brine. And certainly, when the brawl began —"

"What brawl?"

"A brute beating his missus. This silly Yank who'd befriended us waded in and saved the day."

"A Yank?"

"Yes. Ripley, he said his name was." I'd thought of him much throughout the night. How he'd stayed close to our sides. And I can't help but recall his words and wonder: *"I reckon this is the time for a real man to intervene"*. Was he merely casting aspersions on my manhood, or had he actually seen through my disguise? "He sought us out almost immediately we arrived. But I don't think there was any period he would've had a chance to sneak something into my pocket." I think of when we stood outside the tavern, both before and after our time within. I'd certainly been repeatedly jostled by passers-by. Could the swap of pocket contents be from then? "He had a pal. A man named Michel. But he seemed far too drunk to have been our culprit, really."

"Or seeming three sheets to the wind was a good disguise," replied Somerscale.

He's right. Didn't I perform a misleading part myself?

I stand and take a place next to the windows. Peeking down onto the street, I look for Somerscale's spies. "Are you still being watched?" I ask.

He shakes his head. "I think they've given up on me. Why?"

"I did wonder if the same fellow you pointed out to me the other day was the same one I saw outside my hotel and also in the tavern. He wore a straw hat."

Somerscale's head bobs. "Could be. But there are many men who wear those sorts of hats, after all." He gestures towards my chair again and, as I take a seat, he asks, "You don't remember anyone else suspicious?"

"Well . . ." I think back to the evening before. "The only person I remember actually pressing up against me was a girl who served drinks. It was when we were watching the fight I found her and my maid grasping my arms in fright." I think of the barmaid's sleepy eyes, her knowing smirk, and it occurs to me, not for the first time, that a bar-room brawl is not something that is likely to have startled such a sly, shrewd thing. "I think I heard someone call her father — the tavern's owner — Bernard or something. The more I think of it, surely it is quite likely that they would be in on it, if their taproom was chosen as the meeting point?"

He looks down at the travel guide again. Thrusting it in front of my face, he points, "He's circled the last paragraph. Something about a monument to the dead." He taps his finger on his forehead three times, thinking. "I think I know the one he means. It's this statue of an extremely robust Greek type, some sort of angel of death, I presume. Perched on top of a very handsome mausoleum, from memory. He must want me to meet him there."

68

"That's what I thought, too. But why make a new rendezvous? Why not just give me the information last night?"

Somerscale looks troubled, shrugs. "Maybe he was spooked by something."

"True." I trace my fingertip underneath the last line. "I think there's something written under the word *catacombs*, there. See? The number *1300*."

He pokes around in his vest pocket until he brings out a monocle, through which he squints down at the faint writing.

"Maybe he means for you to meet him there at one o'clock? This afternoon?"

Somerscale glares at me. Finally, he shrugs. "Well, I can't exactly meet him, can I?" he says, slapping the travel guide against his thigh.

He must see the hopeful look on my face, because he says, "No, Heloise, your role in this assignment is finished. Meeting him in such a quiet spot would be far too dangerous. I can't allow it. Westminster wouldn't allow it."

"But you can't go!"

"No, I can't." He strides over to a desk in the corner of the room and, dipping his pen in ink, he scrawls a quick message. After sealing it closed, he brings it to me. "Heloise, as soon as you leave here, take this missive to the Grand Hotel. I've kept my rooms there. You'll find Victor, my valet. He'll know who to send it on to."

Taking the letter, I tuck it into my purse, and hurry from his rooms. It's still quite early — most Parisians would still be breakfasting — but this letter must pass through many channels before it lands in the right hands. When I reach the road, I pull the lace veil over my face to protect it from the rain. My eyes search the many carriages on the street for my hired *voiture de remise*.

That's when I see him. The man in the straw hat. I'm sure it's him this time. Same heavy moustache, thin frame. And he's staring at me. I gesture for my carriage to collect me, and he too waves over a buggy, and jumps in. After calling out my destination to the coachman, I hop up in and, as we lurch away, I can just see from the corner of the side window that he follows not far behind. I turn around again, back straight against the upholstery. Who is he? What's his game? Is he one of the Westminster set, or worse, one of the criminals they have their eye on? And why follow me? What do they know? My tongue worries at the tiny chip in my front tooth as I mull over these questions.

A light sheen of raindrops mist my clothing, and my gloves are a little damp as I peel them from my fingers. Feeling in my purse, I pull out Somerscale's letter and look at it.

I can't lead them to Victor. It might give Somerscale away; the letter might be intercepted. Then all my work so far will be wasted. Leaning forward I tap the roof of my carriage and call through the opening, "Monsieur, monsieur. Forget the Grand Hotel. Take me back to the Hotel Chevalier." I'll have one of the bellboys deliver the letter to Victor as soon as I arrive.

70

Ducking into the foyer of the hotel, I glance up at the gilt clock on the wall, and almost gasp at how late the hour has become. It had taken longer than expected for the carriage to find its way, what with the rain slowing the traffic and a collision between a dray heaped high with radishes and a smart tilbury which caused a half-hour standstill.

Striding over to the reception desk, I yank Somerscale's letter from my reticule.

"Yes, Comtesse?" asks the woman manning the desk.

I smooth the creases from the letter. "I need this . . ." I look up at the clock again. There really will be little time for Somerscale's man to organise anything. "I need this sent as soon as possible. Immediately, s'il vous plait."

Taking the grand staircase two steps at a time, I'm quite certain it will be too late. I will have to take Victor's place. I rush to my apartment and ring for Violette. Casting my hat and tippet onto the sofa, I rummage through the theatre box again, searching out my disguise from the night before. Violette helps me clasp the braces to my trousers, and tie my cravat. Pressing the moustache to my upper lip, I murmur to Violette that this time she will not need to accompany me. She can have the rest of the day off, but I will need her again that evening, so she can dress my hair before I attend the opera with Hatterleigh. I feel a slight tingling in my fingertips, and a little sick in the stomach. All I have to do is meet with this fellow, at the monument, and retrieve something from him. In the middle of the day. In public. It really should be perfectly safe. My stomach swoops again.

"What will you fill your afternoon with, Violette?" I ask, trying to transform my anxiety into bright curiosity. I watch my maid's reflection in the glass.

She's sucking on the end of her plait again, as she pins my hair onto the top of my head. "*Cela dépend*. I will go out, if that is permissible."

"Of course, Violette. Will you go far?"

The girl shakes her head. "Not too far. I will have just enough time to visit my love, Alexandre. If I walk very quickly I will be with him in less than an hour."

I turn on my seat and look up at her, grinning. "That's a long way to go for a quick cuddle."

Her brown eyes are a little blank when she looks back at me. "But I like to see him whenever I can. I do not have that many chances. He has become too big for my mother to bring to me."

"He lives with your mother?"

"But, yes. His father was already married and did not want us." She clamps the hat down on my head, so that its rim rests on my eyebrows, and her lips hook up into a sad smile. "I don't think mother wants us much either, but she does what she can. As long as I take her money to support Alexandre."

Ah. "Your son."

She nods.

"How old is he?"

"He is nearly five," she says, helping me pull on my boots. "He's very small though, for his age. He's always been frail. I don't think Mama keeps her rooms warm

72

enough, to tell you the truth." She looks troubled, but then shrugs. "But what can I do? Madame Sabine certainly doesn't allow children to stay in her house. And I am lucky Mama can look after Alexandre; many girls I work with have to send their babies into the countryside. Sometimes they never see them again."

I pick up my purse and shove some money into my trouser pockets. Handing a few coins to Violette, I tell her to catch a cab. "Don't waste your precious time walking. And buy him some cake too." She thanks me with a short curtsey and as we return to the drawing room, I catch sight of my bonnet lying on the sofa; the one she ruined last night at the Dernier Livre. "And here, you have this. And the tippet. They match each other handsomely." I pile them into her arms and see her to the door, waving off her words of gratitude.

Standing in front of the hallstand mirror, I admire my handiwork. Just like I did the evening before, I resemble a neat, diminutive chap. I regret that I don't have a pair of spectacles to add to my disguise or even a monocle of some sort. Grinning, I walk to the windows, shoving my arms into my coat sleeves.

I freeze, the coat halfway up my arms.

The man is down on the street. He's sucking on a pipe, his thumbs looped into his vest pockets. Straw hat on his head.

I dart into my room and look at the time on the clock. I only have three quarters of an hour left to make my rendezvous. I can't lose any time. Dropping the dark overcoat to the floor, I race into Hatterleigh's room. Where did he say he was going this morning?

Riding in the park, or maybe to the Jockey Club? It doesn't matter. As long as I can swipe his claret velvet coat, without him knowing, I'll be fine. Surely I won't be recognised in that.

I linger near the glass doors of the foyer until I can find the opportunity to slip out beside a family that passes through, loudly professing their desire to promenade along the avenue. I sidle along the inside of this little group of people and, out of the corner of my eye, I can see that the man has no interest in us, at all. In fact, besides casting a testy glance over the family, he resumes his doleful observation of the hotel. At the first corner, I shake free from the jolly set, and whistle for a cab.

"Cimetière du Romilly," I call, as I jump up into my seat.

It only takes fifteen minutes to rattle our way to the cemetery. Alighting from the carriage, I toss a coin to the driver. Glancing up and down the leafy laneway, I cannot see any sign of the man or any evidence I've been followed. I allow myself a satisfied grin as I turn to gaze upon the entrance to the cemetery. On either side of the majestic gates, walls of an imposing height curve in a wide arc. Sculpted into the wall's stone work are wreaths and Roman torches and something written in Latin.

Reaching into my vest pocket, I draw out Hatterleigh's gold watch I've had the foresight to bring. Already one o'clock. I'm late.

Hurrying through the open gates, I come across a heavily jowled man who's sweeping the path. I ask him where the monument to the dead is, but my French must be unclear, for he just swings his arm wide, taking in the whole cemetery. I try again, this time miming a large statue, of a man with wings. Finally, the man smiles, flashing his tea-brown teeth, and points to a path that leads east. I thank him as he waves me on.

Plane trees line the wide path, blocking the sun, and the temperature seems to drop a few degrees as I walk in their shadow. I hunch my shoulders and yank my collar up. I take a quick look behind me, but there's nobody there. On another day, this might have been a pleasant stroll, an opportunity to stop and admire the opulent gravestones, or sigh over the pretty, moss-covered crypts dedicated to lost mothers and babies. To savour the hush of stone and flora.

But not today. Today my heartbeat matches my hasty footsteps along the cobblestones. I curse as I pass a bend in the path that just reveals more path, snaking its way through what seems to be an endless array of tombstones. Finally, feeling quite breathless, I reach a crest in the road, and the plane trees fall away, revealing a long lane of catacombs, lined up next to each other, not unlike a row of quaint, miniature terraced houses. I break into a trot, and can feel sweat prickle my upper lip under the moustache as I make my way. Turning a sharp corner, I find myself in a clearing that backs onto the cemetery's outer wall. I stand still, very still, my ears straining to hear what sounds like a patter of footfall. The steps recede. Someone running away?

In front of me, a magnificent, marble statue of an angel — pale, beautiful, muscular — crouches atop a

75

large crypt, which is easily the size of a small villa in Kensington. This must be it. The angel of death. I haven't time to admire his finely wrought plumage, or his delicately chiselled lips. Walking further along the path, I glance around for any sign of someone else lurking in the shadows of the yew trees. I hear voices in the distance and, not two seconds later, an elderly couple come around the corner, stop to admire the monument. I eye their neat clothing, his cane, her basket, and decide they are not the culprits I'm to meet. I gaze up into the budding foliage of the nearest tree, pretending to admire the scenery, until they have disappeared from sight again.

I trudge towards the crypt, glum that I've missed the assignation. Standing to its left, I shield my eyes from the day's dull glare as I stare up at the angel. I would expect an angel of death to look forbidding, angry even; this angel, however, has a serene, almost sad expression upon his face. And he's young. I decide I'd trust him better if he did appear fierce. I've known too many pretty young men whose sweet simpering covered a callous heart. Angel of death indeed.

The rain starts up as I circle the crypt. At the back of the building I find a wide iron door. And it's ajar. Raindrops drum against my top hat, and a drop of water splashes against my cheek. I look around again, but there is still nobody about. Raising my hand to the door handle, I pause. With my other hand, I yank my switchblade from my pocket and then, taking a deep breath, I inch the door open.

The inside of the crypt is so devoid of light, it takes my eyes several moments to adjust and, even then, I can only make out dark, square shapes. I stand in the doorway for close to a minute, alert to a shift in the shadows or any other sign of life. When I am satisfied it's not a trap, I take one last glimpse over my shoulder, and step inside. The crypt's interior is cool, the sound of the downpour muted. I half-expected there to be an unpleasant odour within, maybe even a slight scent of decay, but the crypt smells no more offensive than a dusty library. My eyes, now accustomed to the gloom, take in the shelves that line the walls, and the long, wooden boxes that are upon them. I have to know what's in them. The ground is gritty against the soles of my shoes as I approach the closest box. Lifting the lid a few inches, I peep in. Neat, ivory bones, gracefully slender, share their bed with knuckly, knobbly pieces of bone, more yellow in colour. I'm in an ossuary. I drop the lid down again. The sandstone walls are lined with shelf after shelf of boxes. There must be the remains of hundreds of people in here. Thousands, even. The room seems to diminish in size, presses in against me.

A moan — soft, almost imagined — comes to me from the back of the crypt. Stepping forward, blade brandished, I try to stay to the left to allow for whatever light that spills through the doorway. A moan again, guttural almost. My heart whooshes so loudly in my ears, I wonder if I'll hear another. I edge my way to the furthest corner and, squatting, I poke at the dark bundle that lies along the wall under the lowest shelf. The man's eyes are bright in the darkness as he stares at me, and his breaths rasp. His mouth moves, but no words come out. I grab his coat by the shoulders and, digging my nails and fingers in, try my best to pull his heft out from under the shelf. It takes me two goes before I've moved him five inches. He's clearly spent, can't help me at all.

Bringing my hands back to myself, I notice they're damp, from something that's thicker than rainwater, that has a metallic whiff. A dark smudge smears my shirt cuff.

I can't see the colour of his eyes in the bleak light, but they're wide in a face that is almost obscured by facial hair the colour of tar. His locks are long, and I can't be sure if it is hair oil or sweat that gives them their sheen, but going by his heavy body odour, I would hazard that he hasn't seen a bath or barber in many a week. A red kerchief around his throat rises and falls with his labouring breaths, and his coat lies open, a slick blackness spreading across his white shirt and brown vest. Stabbed? Shot? In the dimness it is difficult to tell. I almost wince away as his hand lifts to my face and brushes my cheek, fingers chill, but I realise in time that he's just trying to hand me something.

As I clutch the note from his hand, he manages one strangled word. *Bombe*. His last breath gurgles deep in his throat, and he becomes still. I scrabble away from his body, the seat of my trousers scraping across the dirty floor. For many moments I stare at his body. It's like my mind is numb, a void space, yet at the same time a million questions swirl. Who did this? Who is he?

What do I do? Lastly — with a swift look around at the shadows of the room — am I in danger too?

Springing to my feet, I burst from the crypt. I wince as the door clangs behind me. I'm not sure if I should call attention to the crime or walk away, let someone else discover and report this death. Tucking the switchblade and piece of paper into my coat pocket, I slip back onto the path. I scuttle along as fast as my legs can take me but, when passing other people, I drop to a saunter, pretend to admire my surroundings. In this way, I arrive back at the cemetery's imposing gates, with an uneasy smile fixed to my face, raindrops mingling with the droplets of perspiration at my brow.

The caretaker leans on the end of his broom as he chats to another fellow. I almost halt by him, to report the murder but, when he turns his head to smile at me, I just nod and smile back and keep on moving. There would be too much to explain. I could become implicated unnecessarily. I feel for the note in my pocket again, allow for it to crinkle between my fingers.

It's late afternoon before I steal another look at the note that the murdered man shoved upon me. I've kicked off my boots but haven't changed out of my male attire yet, so impatient am I to read the message. Weak light streams through the suite's bedroom windows as I spread out the note on my lap. Really, it's just a stub of paper. I flatten out its creases, revealing the grimy edges where it's been folded. Next to the tear in the page, there are fragments of five words. 'reen's *Court* is scrawled above 'oho. A bit further down the remnant of paper, in bolder letters, is written *28 March* and the year. I frown over these clues for a few moments. March is over half-finished already. Whatever is planned, it is not far away. Folding the note again, I place it back into my jewellery box. I will take it to Somerscale in the morning.

I'm just about to pull the shirt from my body when there is a loud rap at the suite's door. I wait almost twenty seconds, wondering who could be calling. Maybe Hatterleigh forgot his key. Or it might be Violette, returned from her mother's house, come to ask if I need assistance. I don't hear Chiggins answer the summons so, after another peal of knocks on the door, I go to answer it myself. Hatterleigh's man must be off imbibing too much brandy again. I don't know how Hatterleigh puts up with it.

Pressing my moustache more firmly to my upper lip, I grin, imagining the look of surprise on Hatterleigh's face should it be him waiting for the door to be opened. He will wonder if he's come to the wrong suite, or maybe, just maybe, he will wonder who this blackguard is who is visiting his sweetheart.

I fling open the door with a flourish. My grin freezes into place. The blood in my body seems to fall to my feet in one chill rush.

The man in the straw hat.

And he's not alone. Two hefty fellows hover behind, dark shadows in the hallway's gloom.

I almost swing the door shut again, but manage to move my mouth, ask him in French how I can be of service.

80

"Is this where a Madame Heloise Chancey stays? With a . . ." he glances down at a slip of paper in his hand. "Lord Hatterleigh?" he says.

I nod, my lips still fixed in that ridiculous, rigid grin.

"And you are . . . ?" he asks me.

I blink. "Chiggins. I am the valet to the master." I revert to English. "I am sorry. My French . . ."

His bright eyes roam my face — its lack of stubble, the smooth skin, my lips — and I swear that the tips of his whiskers quiver, like he's a fox nosing out some rabbit flesh.

"I am Inspector Mercier, and these are my men," he says, smoothly transitioning to English. He moves to the side so that I can see the men behind him more clearly. One is older, has a grey handlebar moustache, the other one tall, clean shaven and dark. Both wear their dark blue uniforms with the blood-red piping, kepis crammed on their heads, sword sticks angled against their hips. Police.

What are the police doing on my doorstep?

"How can I help you?" I ask.

"Lord Hatterleigh, is he on the premises?" asks Mercier, peering over my shoulder.

I shake my head. Please, please, do not let Hatterleigh arrive home right now. How could I possibly explain this new mess to him? "No, I am sorry. I'm not sure when to expect him home. Please, if you would like to leave a message, I will relate it to him."

Mercier frowns down at me. Glass tinkles on a lower floor and the older of his men shifts his feet.

"I think I should tell him in person," he says, finally.

Rising to my full height, I try to distil my voice with a little of my butler, Bundle's, air of reproof. "Really, sir, I can be trusted to pass on your message to my master. What is it?"

His foxy whiskers twitch again. He gives me a curt bow, but his eyes, when they catch mine, are hard, challenging, even. "Please inform Lord Hatterleigh that we are sorry to inform him that Comtesse Heloise Chancey has been found. Murdered."

CHAPTER
EIGHT

Amah

Amah wraps her cold fingers around the warmth of her teacup. She hasn't slept well at all, and her head feels like it's being squeezed in a vice. She takes a sip of the jasmine tea, willing her scattered thoughts to settle. Leaning her forehead against her bedroom window, she watches the milkwoman make her way down the street, her heavy pails lurching from their wooden yoke with each step. Stooping before the house across the way, she fills a metal can with milk and lowers it to the doorstep. She tramps on to the next house, and her iron-shod shoes tack loudly against the pavement, reminding Amah of the first time she'd been startled awake by their pre-dawn clatter. In Liverpool, it had been. All those years ago. When she had shared a small lodging room with her uncle and nephew, waiting for fortune to change and provide them with work and hearth.

Liverpool. She had spent nearly fifteen long years by the docks. Thinking of it leaves her feeling hollow. For a period, her time in Liverpool had been the happiest of her life but, almost in turn, some of her loneliest, most worrisome times had been spent there too. One of the only things she'd kept safe in that time — she thinks of Heloise's desertion, of her own loneliness — was her mother's earring. Amah smiles as she remembers how, when she was small, she used to imagine the dragons clinging to the golden orbs with their claws as the earrings swayed with her mother's movements. How they dangled from her mother's small, shell-like ears when she bent over to kiss her goodnight.

And now she has the opportunity to reclaim her earring's sister. But at what cost?

Besides the exorbitant amount of money the terrible pair demand from her, Amah wonders if, by recovering the earring, she will be exposing them all to ridicule or shame.

"How do you suppose I could come up with such an amount of money?" she'd asked them the night before.

"That's not my problem," the young woman shrugged.

Amah tried to remember if Heloise had that amount of money stashed in her bedroom safe, but she doubted it.

"I'll need some time," she said.

"A week," said the young woman. "Meet us back here in a week's time."

Amah knew she wouldn't be able to raise that sort of money without help, but she couldn't be sure when Heloise would be home. Sometime at the end of the month? Early April? Amah hadn't taken much notice of what she had told her.

"I will need at least two weeks," she said.

The young woman took in Amah's steady gaze. "Two weeks then." She reached across the table and picked up the earring between her gloved fingers and slid it back into its pouch. Standing up, so that the legs of her chair screeched unpleasantly against the wooden floor, she slapped Joshua on the arm, and told him to move.

Amah sat and stared at the spot where the earring had been for a good two minutes after she heard their footsteps recede.

And now, watching the milkwoman turn the corner out of sight, Amah asks herself the same question again: how did they get their hands on her earring?

She wonders if she should report them to the police, on a charge of blackmail or something similar. But besides their hints of ensuing scandal and the sensation of being extorted, what was it really but a straightforward sales matter?

She turns from the window and re-fills her cup with more tea. The rest of the household still sleeps and Abigail has not yet arrived to light the fires. Amah's eyes are gritty from tiredness and her head feels heavy, dull. Anxiety gnaws at her belly, though. She can't seem to shake the feeling that she may not see the earring again; that she cannot trust that couple to turn up. And what if Heloise does not return in time? How will she raise the £400 then?

Again, her thoughts turn to Liverpool, to a woman named Golda Berman who worked in her father's pawnshop. Amah had chosen that particular pawnbroker because it was far away from where she lived, but close enough to not warrant the expense of a cab. The first time Amah had to use Golda's services, the shame she'd felt had been great. While pretending to browse through the teaspoons and snuff boxes, Amah was thankful that the high collar of her dress covered the blush of mortification she could feel burn across her chest. Finally, when the last customer left and the road through the glass-front door appeared clear, Amah brought out the goods she could spare. Her hand trembled as she handed over a book and a pair of men's slippers. Golda, a mane of bushy, brown hair loose about her shoulders, framing a striking face with lovely arched eyebrows, whistled the tune *cherry ripe cherry ripe* between her straight teeth. She looked up at the toddler clasped to Amah's breast and her lips widened into a smile as she sang, *full and fair ones, come and buy.*

Golda turned the book over, and said, "Thackeray. I have not read this one."

She spoke with a slight accent, familiar to Amah, yet not an accent she heard often around the Liverpool area.

Golda slid the slippers onto a shelf below the counter. She then pulled a copper pot towards herself and poured two short cups of coffee, sliding one across to Amah. "It's very sweet. And hot. Enjoy!" She took a sip from her own cup and nodded to Amah, encouraging her to take up the other.

"No, thank you," said Amah. "I just need my money."

"Of course, of course," said Golda, rattling coins in the pocket of her apron. She plonked down two shillings and a groat. About what Amah had expected. Perhaps a little more. "Now, you drink a coffee with me." Golda pushed the cup further towards Amah.

Amah juggled the child higher onto her hip and with her free hand lifted her veil to above her nose. Wondered what Golda would make of her skin colour.

Golda smiled. "You are like me. You are not from here. Where are you from?"

"Makassar."

Golda's eyes widened. "But I am from Holland. Many years ago. I remember seeing people like you in my country. Golden skin. Beautiful black hair."

Amah tasted the coffee, glad of its sweetness. Hunger was her daily companion, made her heart flutter, her mind spin. But as long as the child received her bread and milk, she was satisfied.

"I'll be back next week to retrieve the book," she'd said to Golda.

"Not the gentleman's slippers?"

Amah shook her head. "Not the slippers."

Amah blinks at a tap on her bedroom door. "Come in."

Abigail pokes her head around the doorway. "You in need of tea, Amah?"

"No, thank you. I was up early this morning. Fetched my own. An egg would be nice, though, if you could ask Agneau."

Abigail bobs her head and withdraws.

Amah stares down into her teacup. Golda. Golda had become almost a friend to Amah after that. Each time Amah returned to the pawnshop to redeem her goods or to pawn a china teacup, a set of cotton handkerchiefs or even her blankets when the weather became warm again, they had exchanged stories of Makassar and Holland, of youthful days, of half-forgotten songs, of dishes and fruit sorely missed. Amah had liked the woman's matter-of-fact manner, her acceptance of Amah's daily existence that spooled to and fro as though she were a bandalore.

Golda. Surely she would give Amah a good amount of money were she to pawn the pearls, the gaudy diamond and peridot cameo brooch Heloise had received from a lover and eschewed, the agate beads and the gold band she used to wear on her ring finger. Combined with her savings, Amah is sure there should then be enough money to pay for her mother's earring.

Amah hesitates as she pulls a skirt over her petticoats. Liverpool's a long way to go to find a pawnbroker, she thinks. A London pawnbroker would do just as well. But Amah shakes her head, decided, as she buttons up her skirt. How could she be sure she could trust the rascal pawnbrokers in this big city? She would have to explain herself, identify herself. Golda knows her already. The exchange would be quick, reliable. And what else is she to do with the next fortnight? A trip to Liverpool will help keep her mind from fretting over the earring.

Her pulse quickens at the thought of returning to Liverpool, to be caught up in the bustle of the docks again, to admire the palatial counting houses. But she does wonder how she'll feel to be faced with the squalor and stench to be found in the courts buried behind the opulence. Will her distance from that time bring her the warmth of nostalgia or the chill of relief?

She wraps a shawl about her shoulders and trips lightly down the stairs. She slips through the front door and follows the sharp odour of straw and manure to the mews two streets over. She hurries across the dirty cobblestones and peers into the third stable along.

"Taff?"

He steps out from behind Heloise's mare, Malani.

"You need the carriage, Amah?"

"Actually . . . Actually, I wondered if it is possible for us to take a trip to Liverpool."

Surprise pleats Taff's forehead. "Liverpool."

Amah nods.

"Liverpool." Taff nudges his cap to the side and scratches behind his ear. "That's a strange whim of yers, Amah."

"It may be several weeks before Heloise is home, and I am tired of sitting around."

"You should've gone with her," he says, taking up a brush. He sweeps its bristles across Malani's inky coat. After five strokes he looks back at Amah. "You'm not serious?"

"Of course I am," Amah replies. She wouldn't have walked around to these smelly stables were she not.

"It would take an age, Amah. We'd need to organise a change of horses and inns along the way."

Amah nods. "We've done it before, Taff. These things can easily be arranged."

"You'd be better finding yourself'm a copy of Bradshaw's and looking for the trains."

Amah stares at him. The thought of travelling with so many strangers and the deciphering of complicated timetables does not appeal. She shrugs. "If you do not have the time or inclination, I can easily travel post or hire another coach and coachman."

Taff returns to brushing down the mare. "I don't know what game you'm playing at."

"It's not a game, Taff. I just have several weeks at my disposal with Heloise away, and thought a visit to Liverpool would be interesting. I have often wondered how much it might have changed since we left."

"Not much, I'd say," he grumbles. "Still the pong of the docks and too many people. London's much better, if you'm ask me."

"But tell me you wouldn't look forward to a tankard of ale with . . . What was the name of that man you used to drink with?"

"Old Holker, you mean?"

"Yes. Wouldn't you like to have a tankard of ale with him and the other brutes down at the Pink Salmon?"

His lips twitch a reluctant smile. "If it still be there."

"We can find out."

Taff wipes his hands on a cloth. "I don't know what game you'm playing at," he says again.

CHAPTER
NINE

I fall back a step. Did Inspector Mercier just say I had been murdered?

My head spins and my trousers and coat feel cumbersome and unwelcome. I almost feel as if my true identity has been spirited away by this silly disguise I wear. Heloise Chancey, dead?

"I'm afraid you're mistaken, sir," I say. My hand slides to my chest. Yes, there is a heartbeat. "What makes you think she's . . . deceased?"

"We have her body, of course," Mercier replies. "A couple of carriers found her slumped in an alleyway in Montmartre."

"But how could you possibly think it is Madame Chancey?"

His expression is baleful as he glares at me, rocking back and forth on his feet. "It's a long story, Monsieur, which I will keep for your master."

There's nothing for it. I will have to tell him the whole, or fabricate a likely tale as quickly as possible. I usher him into the suite, asking if his men could stay behind in the corridor. "I have something to relate to you that is rather private."

He hesitates. Saying something briefly to the others, he closes the door behind himself.

We stand across from each other in the middle of the drawing room.

"What is it?"

Taking the hat from my head, so that my braided hair falls to my shoulder, I say, "I am Heloise Chancey, Inspector Mercier. This is merely a disguise I donned as a jest." His head draws back in consternation as I peel the moustache from my lip. "Therefore, whoever you have found in that alleyway is certainly not me."

"Well . . ." he exhales. "I did think your appearance a little, shall we say, womanly, but I never suspected . . ." He blinks. "What is this jest you talk of?"

I pretend to laugh, tossing the hat onto a side-table. "Oh, just a wager I had with Lord Hatterleigh. I bet that I could enter his gentleman's club undetected by him or the club's staff."

I take a seat and gesture for him to follow suit. "I was so successful, I was in and out of the place before anyone had a chance to notice me."

I listen to the air whistle from his nostrils five times as he considers me. "I'm not sure if I believe you, Comtesse."

My heart skitters, but I force a smile to lift my lips. I watch as he draws his pipe from his vest pocket. Tamping the tobacco with his thumb, he reaches into his other pocket for matches.

"I do not get your meaning, Inspector?"

As he lights his pipe, I notice his fingernails are dirty, ragged.

"You first came to our attention when you left the debtors' prison in Clichy, Comtesse." He puffs on his pipe and peers at me through the smoke. "I had a man follow you home, where he discovered your identity."

"Why would you have me followed when I was simply visiting an old friend?" I ask, flipping open a walnut box on the side-table to take out a cigarette.

"Ah. You must mean Somerscale. You say he is merely a friend of yours?"

"Yes, he is. And I hope you're not insinuating there was more to it than that," I say, indignant. If I act like I believe his line of questioning is to do with sexual transgressions, he might be thrown off the scent. "I really have no idea why you would waste your time in following me."

"I am not convinced it has been a waste of time, Comtesse," he says. "We have had our eye on Somerscale and his kind. We — the Parisian authorities — like to be sure of what is afoot in this great city. We spy upon the spies, especially when they are Englishmen. This type of monitoring is absolutely necessary. It is what the masterful Fouche called high policing." He casts his eyes to the ceiling for a moment, as though he's speaking of his god. He's standing a few metres away, and yet towers over me. I'm at a disadvantage, but feel that I would appear unnecessarily agitated should I take to my feet too.

"Well, this 'high policing' of yours has been a waste of time in this instance," I say, voice flippant. "You have uncovered nothing more than a mere visit of courtesy between two people who are not much more than acquaintances."

"And yet, it proved fruitful when you were followed to a certain establishment in Bocages des Anges."

My hand hesitates on its way to my mouth. I then draw on my cigarette, the paper crackling as the ash recedes. "I don't know what you're talking about."

He pulls a pair of spectacles from his upper coat pocket and places them on his nose, before withdrawing a notebook from his inside pocket. Using the thumb of his free hand to leaf through the pages, he pauses to read, "Comtesse Chancey — purple hat and fur tippet, exchanged striped gown for yellow — exits Hotel Chevalier in the company of one unknown gentleman, short, slight of stature, grey overcoat. Time, eleven o'clock, evening."

I stub my cigarette out into a crystal ashtray. "I don't own a yellow gown. Check if you please."

"Purple hat? Fur tippet?" His lips lift in a quizzical smile, like he knows he's caught me out.

"Well, of course. I have any number of purple hats." I shrug, taking a deep, exasperated breath. "I have one made of purple felt, and two straws with purple ribbon. I even have a very smart riding bonnet with a bunch of lavender. Take your pick, sir."

Purple hat. An uneasy feeling settles in my stomach. Before I can dwell on my thoughts, though, Mercier takes a seat opposite me and slaps his infernal notebook shut. "By the time you arrived at the Dernier Livre, I was on hand to take over from my colleague. During this period, not much after midnight, it was with my own eyes I noted a man shove something into your partner's pocket." His eyes narrow as he puff-puff-puffs on his pipe, his gaze trained on my trousers. When he finally speaks again, his words reach me through a cloud of smoke. "I see. I see. Tell me, why were you dressed as a gentleman last night at the Dernier Livre? It was you *with* the woman in yellow? Yes? This is a habit of yours, is it, dressing up as a gentleman?"

It's my turn to blink. My mind races as I push myself up from the armchair and make my way to the sideboard. "Actually, it is. I like to enjoy the pleasures of the small hours, and it is often only in the guise of a man that I can experience it to the full." I pour myself a finger of whisky. "But I still don't understand this interest of yours in what I got up to last night; what my proclivities might be." I sip my drink. The whisky's burning trail through my chest is welcome. "I can't answer for some scoundrel slipping something into my pocket. Here, check them if you must," I say, drawing out my empty coat pockets. I maintain an irritated scowl on my face, which, hopefully, covers my alarm. I'm not even sure what the penalty might be if I've been caught dealing with a spy. And what of this murdered woman?

My hand quivers so that I have to put the tumbler down. "This body you found? You thought it was me, because of the hat and tippet."

"That is correct, Comtesse. When her body was shown to me, I was sure it was you." His expression is grave. "Now I wonder — in fact, I am sure — it is the body of the woman in the yellow gown that was with you last night. The woman we thought was you."

My hand finds my mouth, pinching my lips together. "How can you be sure?"

He shrugs. "I will need you to come identify her. That is the only way we can know."

I press my eyes shut for several moments. Violette. "She was visiting her son . . . You found her in Montmartre, you say?"

"That is where her body was found. You know where she was going?"

I shake my head, ashamed. I knew hardly anything of the girl. "A friend of mine, Sabine, recommended her to me. I will give you her directions."

Mercier nods as he scrawls the scant particulars I can give him into his notebook.

"Where is she now?" I ask.

He taps his pipe out into the ashtray. "Her body is being kept at a surgeon's place of work near the prefecture." He looks me up and down. "You will escort me there now?"

"I will change. Please wait a few moments."

Closing the boudoir door behind me, I shed my male attire. I hear Mercier give instructions to his men in the next room, and I know I should be hurrying, but I stare at my pale face in the mirror. Please don't let it be Violette.

Her skin has lost the shades of life. Her lips, once rosy, are the colour of paste, and a smear of mud

96

sullies her right cheek. Dark shadows cloud her half-closed eyes.

"Yes. That's her." I shake my head in disbelief as the surgeon pulls the sheet back up over Violette's face. "How'd she die?" I turn to Mercier.

"A powerful knock to the back of the head," he says, still staring at the shrouded figure. "The back of her skull . . ." He tuts. "You are lucky she lies face up, Comtesse."

I grimace. "Did anyone see who assaulted her?"

"No. A young couple came across her body and brought it to the police's attention."

On a bench lies my battered purple hat. The tippet lies not far away, damp and straggly. My jaw loosens and my blood seems to peak and surge.

"Was she robbed?" I ask, thinking of the extra coins I'd given her.

"She didn't have a purse on her."

My eyes find his. "I know that when she left me, she certainly had money. She was going to give some to her mother, and I gave her extra for the carriage ride." I glance back at the shrouded figure. She must have decided to save the coins and walk instead. It's exactly what I would've done in those grim days in Liverpool. Maybe it was nothing more than a violent thief who stole her life, but Mercier voices my concerns when he says, "I do wonder if, rather than a mere robbery, the aim of this heinous act was in fact to attack you, Comtesse Heloise Chancey. Maybe the murderer mistook her for you, just as we did."

It's like a chill slap to have my fears reinforced. "That's ridiculous," I say. "Why would anyone want to harm me?"

I follow him into the corridor. His words are clipped, serious, as he says in an undertone, "Comtesse, I am not sure what you have done, but I would wager that you are in danger. This man who put something in your pocket last night —"

"What? What of him?"

"He belongs to a terrible band of crooks, bent upon heinous acts. They call themselves the Red Brethren. Have you not heard of the bombing of the police station in your own London? Or when someone tried to shoot our own Minister of Finance, here in Paris? The crimes are all related. I am sure of it."

"Who was this man? Describe him for me," I say, thinking back to the tavern the night before. Was it the older man, heavily covered, alone at his table? Or the tavern keeper and his enticing daughter? The American? His friend?

"Tallish man with a red kerchief tied around his neck. His facial hair was as black as coal. Long hair."

My eyes widen.

"You remember him!"

I nod slowly. "I think I do. He stood at the end of the bar?" I lie. I can't remember him at all from the night before, but I remember him from that crypt. "When was Violette murdered? Do you know?"

98

He pulls his watch from his vest. "The doctor thinks she was only newly dead when she was found. That means no longer than three hours ago."

My gaze takes in the blistered paint on the walls, the tiny fissures that peel away from the cornice. I'm almost certain that the bearded fellow in the crypt had expired by then, so he couldn't have murdered Violette. Perhaps the same person tailed and killed both the bearded fellow and my maid.

I shake my head. My thoughts are still a little muddled and I will need to think on this. I say to Mercier, "I'm positive you must be mistaken. I know nothing of this gang you speak of. There is absolutely no reason for them to wish me harm."

As I turn to leave, the Inspector grasps my wrist. "I know you lie, Comtesse. And these people who you are associated with are dangerous, deadly even. Look at what they have done to your maid. I would suggest you walk away now. Leave Paris."

I stare at him for a few seconds before I pull my arm free. I want to answer him with something jaunty, defiant, but words fail me. I nod briefly and walk back out onto the street.

When I arrive back to our suite, Hatterleigh is seated in the drawing room with his ghastly brother-in-law, Cyril Breeden. Despite being the younger sibling of Lady Hatterleigh, he's never shown any sign of disinclination towards my company. The opposite, in fact. Too many times to mention, I've had to avoid his drunken embraces, like we were the leads in a terrible farce. If

99

Cyril were not male and was not of such superior lineage, he could quite comfortably be referred to as a whore.

"It's about time you arrived home," Hatterleigh says as I enter, his voice merry. "Come along. We have a festive evening prepared, haven't we, Cyril?"

I don't feel up to banter. My mind is still awhirl. I consider claiming a headache, but I can see Hatterleigh is in a mood to tease me into whatever revelry he has planned. I lower myself onto the arm of his chair, and take a sip of his brandy.

"Well, you must tell me what we will do so I can dress accordingly."

"We're to take in the early show at the Cirque Napoléon, have supper in the Boulevard des Italiens, and then we thought we might search out . . . Whose ball is it again, Cyril?"

"The de Ferriéres masquerade ball?"

"That's the one!" Hatterleigh pulls out his watch and glances at the time. "Why don't you change your gown, Heloise. Take your time. We don't have to be at the Cirque Napoléon for another hour. And ferret out your mask for the ball. If you forgot to bring one, send your girl out for one."

He means Violette. If only I could call for her.

I hold my carriage well as I sail into the boudoir, but behind the closed door, I slump onto my dresser stool, and sink my face into my hands.

I think of a tawdry bedroom in Waterloo not two years past. Of the golden girl's pallid skin. The blood that was as thick as treacle. Sorrow wrings my insides

100

so that I feel like doubling over. Please do not let me be responsible for another death. If only I hadn't involved Violette. If only I hadn't given her that damned purple hat.

Copious glasses of champagne can't lift my spirits. In fact, with each act — the pretty, dancing pony with a ballerina upon its back, the tightrope walker in his spangled costume, and even when a performing goose lands in Hatterleigh's lap — I sink further into my gloomy thoughts.

Finally, I can't stand it anymore, and I take my leave of Hatterleigh and ghastly Cyril at La Maison Dorée, ostensibly to change my jewelled slippers for a more comfortable pair of dancing shoes. I shake my head as I think of our evening so far. La Maison Dorée is one of my favourite restaurants and, as usual, we were given a private room in which to dine, with gilded mouldings and elegant furnishing, but Cyril's new ladybird, Bluette, had almost spoilt the atmosphere with her lashings of face paint and dockside swearing. Even I know how to rein it in in such a place.

As I leave the restaurant, one of the waiters runs ahead to fetch our carriage. I step close to the road, pulling my fur more snugly around my shoulders against the evening chill. Opening my beaded purse, I'm just taking out a cigarette when I hear a man call out, and someone close by gasps. A buggy careers around the corner. Its two harnessed horses bear down upon me. I catch a whiff of their hot breath, a flash of quivering muscle. I can see the alarm in the horse's eye, which is a mirror of mine, when I'm yanked out of the way. Thundering hooves mount the pavement as the buggy's wheel scrapes inches from where I lie on the ground, before bobbing back down onto the road. At speed, the buggy continues upon its way, disappearing around the next bend.

The waiter runs back to me, helps me to my feet. The heel of my right hand bleeds, and my forearm aches from where it jarred against the cobblestones.

"Madman," the waiter mutters, peering after the long-gone buggy. "Madman. *Mon dieu*. He could have killed you, Comtesse."

I crouch in the armchair, shivering, despite the warmth from the fire I've had the valet make up for me. I'm not sure how long I've been seated here. Hours maybe.

It was only in the cab back to the suite that it occurred to me to wonder who had hauled me out of the way of the speeding buggy. Was it just a bystander, or — I search my memory of those frightful moments — did I see someone familiar? Hear something? And who drove the buggy? All I can come up with is a shadow, a flash of a greatcoat. I shake my head again. It's difficult to remember anything besides the horses' pounding hooves, their hot breaths. The waiter was correct. I was nearly killed.

I have been puzzling over this since I arrived home. Was it an accident, or was somebody actually trying to kill me?

I think Mercier is right. It's time to leave Paris.

Uncurling my legs, I stand. My arm still aches, but the graze on my palm has ceased to bleed. My fingers are stiff with cold as I gather my clothing, jewellery and toiletries and shove them into my portmanteaus and trunks. Amah and Abigail will sort out my things when I arrive back home in Mayfair.

I'm so preoccupied with my packing, I don't realise Hatterleigh's returned until I smell the whisky on his breath as he stands behind me. I yelp.

"Bloody hell, Giles, you scared the wits out of me," I say, picking up the petticoat I've dropped.

"What the hell are you doing?" he asks. "We waited and waited for you. I had to leave Cyril to kick his heels at a tavern in Saint Germain."

"Well, that should suit Bluette, at any rate," I say, my voice sour.

Hatterleigh takes the velvet jewellery pouch I'm about to drop into a portmanteau from my hands. "Heloise, what are you doing? Why are you packing?"

I sweep the rest of my accoutrements from the dresser into a leather case. "I have had word from London. From Bundle, in fact." I fabricate the story as I speak. "Amah is very ill. The doctor's not sure what might be the matter with her."

"You're going back because your *maid* is sick?" he asks.

I stare across at him. I could kick myself. I should have made up an imaginary aunt or some such. Instead, I have to persevere with my tale. "I'm very fond of Amah, I'll have you know," I say, indignant. "We are not all so cavalier with the well-being of our servants as you might be, Giles." But, despite a quick frown, he won't be drawn down this path.

"But this is madness, Heloise. I will ask my doctor to wait upon her. He's the very best in London. He'll have her right as rain in no time. You must remember that we are to go into the countryside the day after next, to that chateau I told you of."

I pause in packing away my brushes. The chateau is far away from town. I might just be safe there.

But then I imagine the rambling mansion, its many wings, devoid of people except for me, Hatterleigh and a few servants; its lonely position amongst sprawling formal gardens, orchards of apple trees and fields of grass. I'd be an even easier target there. A tremor of fear shudders through me. No. I will be far safer amongst the crowds of London.

"I'm sorry, Giles, but I must return as soon as possible." I stare up at Hatterleigh, at his nose, ruddy from drinking too much whisky, at his kind eyes. I feel a prick of alarm. What if I have put him in danger as well? Perhaps it would be best, safest, if we were both to return to London, together.

Lifting his hand in both of mine, I kiss it. "Come, Giles. Join me. I've had enough of Paris anyway. And you'd soon be bored at a fusty old chateau, admit it." I grin up at him, and watch his face soften.

CHAPTER
TEN

Amah

When Amah wakes at the Three Lions Inn in Liverpool she expects the dockyard reek of brine and tar to reach her nostrils, but all she can smell is the polish the boy has used to blacken her little boots and a hock of ham roasting in the kitchen below.

She stretches her legs, luxuriating in being able to lie in for the first time in four days. Luckily rain hadn't held them up on the road and after three uneventful nights in guesthouses of varying degrees of comfort, they'd reached Liverpool. Amah's surprised by the quality of the mattress, which is firm, no lumps. Although not of the first class, the small inn has proven to be a good find. Amah knows that apart, perhaps, for the very grandest of hotels in town — those accustomed to fabulously rich foreigners disembarking ships from far away — she would not be welcome to a room in most. And she is here to gather more money, after all, not spend her savings on fancy accommodation. Therefore, Taff had asked around and found her this modest room, close to the harbour.

Amah places her bare feet on the cool timber floor and tabs across to the window that looks out onto

Northumberland Street. She gazes through a gap between the tall, handsome buildings along the harbourfront to the litter of ship masts that bob in the shoal-grey water. She wants to be down there amongst the shouts of the tide waiters and the flurry of sailors and fishermen. She wants to see for herself if the area has changed much in her absence.

She quickly dresses, wondering how Taff fares. She hopes he and the horses found restful quarters and that he didn't get too 'corned' — as he likes to call it — on Jamaican rum with his old cronies.

The air is crisp when she steps from the inn, its slight fishy odour strengthening into an overwhelming damp fug the closer she walks towards the waterfront. A ship, newly arrived, spews people and cargo onto the dockside. She skirts dock labourers, all brawn and filth, and marvels at the number of vessels that jostle for room in the harbour. She looks to the mouth of the inlet, and her eyes peer further, to the horizon that slices sea from sky. In the direction of her earliest home. She'd sailed in on that body of water so long ago, and had never found her way out again.

Amah stands at the edge of the pier, away from others, and lifts her veil. She closes her eyes and for two full breaths she relishes the feel of the lemony light on her face. She remembers how sometimes she used to escape to the docks here, away from the gloom of encroaching buildings and dark back rooms, so that she could experience just a few moments of space beneath the breadth of a muted sky. Opening her eyes, she turns to stare across at a vast, red-brick building that looms self-importantly above all others. The counting house of a prosperous shipping company. Where her love once worked when she first knew him. Her eyes search the windows just as they used to do, wondering which office was his.

She was standing here, watching a drunken brawl between two scruffy deckhands, when they'd first met. Just as one of the men had pulled a knife from a scabbard, John had blocked her view, said, "Madame, you do not want to watch this." She hadn't worn a lace veil in those days, just a linen bonnet with a broad brim pulled low. When she'd lifted her face to peer up at him, at his fair hair that feathered from beneath his felt hat and the straight nose set in a plain, yet handsome, face, she watched as something like surprise, approbation, lit his grey eyes.

Pulling her veil back into place she turns to her right and continues on her way. Her steps slow as she approaches Henderson Street. The fish shop still stands on the corner across from The Green Horn. As she passes the tavern, she can hear the clink of cutlery that accompanies the chatter of the breakfast crowd. The street is narrow, the buildings huddled close and intrusive. She walks past the rickety house that the spinsters used to live in; is surprised when she doesn't see their pasty faces pressed to the grimy glass. Nasty, smelly old things, trying to catch passers-by unawares with the contents of their chamber pots. She doubts they're still alive. She passes a run-down lodging house, quite sure that most of the occupants renting rooms there in her time would have moved on, although a young man, red-haired, skin ashen with malnutrition and dirt, stares at her as she walks by, and she wonders if he is the same boy who sometimes carried laundry for her for a farthing. She keeps walking, her shoes skidding on manure and mud and, as far as she can see, every second dwelling seems to have turned into a beer-house. A fiddler plays a merry tune to a bleary crowd in the shop where Mr Scout used to mend shoes and fashion belts out of scrap material, and two girls, skinny with rickety legs, lounge outside the hovel where a whole family of eight had died of cholera. Her mouth pulls down as she remembers that time, the boards nailed across the door, the terrible stench that no amount of wadding could keep from slinking through window cracks.

Finally, Amah reaches the row of four semi-detached cottages and stands in front of the one furthest north. Mustard-coloured bricks, arched portico over the front door, large bay window. An attractive dwelling once, although rather shabby by the time Amah lived there. Going by the state of the peeling paint, the crumbling wall and the smashed window covered with newspaper, it appears the owners have fallen on even less fortunate times. She wonders if the Walters still live on the first floor, all seven of them crammed into the two and a half rooms and cellar.

John had arranged for Amah to live on the second floor. She'd had a small scullery, living room and bedroom, all to herself. And it was from that window, the one on the right, that she'd watch John leave of a morning, his long, jaunty gait taking him down the road towards the docks. Sometimes he'd look back, grin and salute her, as though she were his captain. Amah clears her throat to loosen the tightness there.

A glorious time in her life, that had been. Pitched in joy. She wonders how much the property is worth now, decrepit as it is. Perhaps the owners would like to sell. Amah thinks of the lodging house in Bloomsbury that she owns. She could arrange for its sale and invest the money here. She could have the front door re-painted a lovely red lacquer, have the yellow bricks scrubbed. She would hang lovely curtains — blowsy flowers against a black background — and have the floors covered in Axminster carpets. Maybe she would even leave London, leave Heloise, and live here.

And what? Stare out the window for a man who will never return? Desiccate in discontent like that old woman in the Dickens serial? You can't go back, she mutters to herself as she walks away. Past happiness could not be so easily regained.

CHAPTER
ELEVEN

It's almost evening when Hatterleigh's coach pulls up across the road from my home on South Street. Hatterleigh and I parted ways outside his town residence in Piccadilly and I have come on alone. I wonder if he will rush straight into the countryside to his wife and children now that we are returned, but I am feeling far too jittery to care. My mind is a tangle of anxious thoughts and, to be honest, I was very hard put to not snap at his inconsequential prattle, poor fellow.

Poking my head out the window, I glance around. As far as I can gather, I have not been followed. But how could I know for sure? I watch as a cab pulls in at the corner. Behind us, a buggy trots slowly along the road. The groom jumps down ready to open the coach door, but I hold the handle still.

"Just give me one moment, please," I say through the window to him.

As I stare up at my house again, my eyes rest on the window of Amah's sitting room. I wonder if she is at home. I wonder what she is doing. Sewing, perhaps, or writing a letter at her teak escritoire? I feel an overwhelming urge to jump from the coach and run to her side, tell her of all that has happened to me in the last couple of days but, for once, a sense of caution holds me back. I look up and down the street again. A lone man strolls the pavement. The cab still waits at the corner. The buggy has moved on further down the street but appears to be paused outside the house with the Greek columns. I almost choke on the stress of not knowing if my assailants have followed me from Paris.

Light beams through the sidelights by the front door. Bundle has lit the lamps for the evening. I think of him going about his butler business, and Agneau concocting something tasty in the kitchen, and how even Abigail might still be about, getting under everybody's feet. And as much as I long to be inside with them, I am also terribly loath to expose them to the long hand of danger that reaches for me. I call out to the groomsman, still waiting on the pavement, "I've changed my mind, Roberts. Take me to Brown's Hotel."

Traffic is light as we bowl along towards Albemarle Street, and I think of the warm bath I will enjoy as soon as I arrive. I will order champagne, just for myself, and eat a light supper of bisque or, perhaps, that pastry dessert of theirs I'm so partial to, served with the creme anglaise that has a hint of hazelnut liqueur. I feel a twinge of guilt that, while I enjoy such things, poor Violette's mother, her son, will be wondering about her.

I run my tongue across the sharp edge of the chip in my front tooth. Perhaps Brown's is not the best place for me to lie low. Alone. With nobody to account for my presence, perhaps until it is too late. And it would not be very difficult at all for my assailants — if indeed there are assailants after me — to find out that Heloise

111

Chancey often enjoys interludes at Brown's Hotel. Besides the danger, too, how very mortifying it would be if my attackers from Paris were to pursue me to Brown's, causing trouble or ruckus. As much as the good people at Brown's might turn a blind eye to my profession — no doubt due to my wealth and Hatterleigh's prestige — they would not look kindly upon being involved in a scandal, and I would greatly dislike placing my good name with them at jeopardy.

I rap on the hatch again and call out to the coachman. "I've changed my mind again, Roberts. Take me to Derby Street."

"Heloise, how I have missed you." Isobel Pidgeon trembles with emotion as we embrace.

"And you do not mind if I stay with you for a few days or so? I've come home from Paris early, and my household is in an uproar over a gas leak of some sort."

"Of course not, Heloise. Come into the parlour. I have a fire going, and Hitchins will bring us supper shortly."

She leads the way into a cosy side room. Lace doilies, linen tablecloths, porcelain ornaments lift the darkness of the furniture. China plates line the shelves on the wall, and a small grandfather clock ticks above the fireplace. My heart stretches as I gaze up at the one portrait in the room — a timber framed photograph of Isobel's father, Sir Henry Pidgeon.

Isobel takes my hand and leads me to a cushioned chair at the small table. "Let's not talk of sad things,

Heloise. I'm weary of it. I have enough of that from Aunt Adelaide."

"Where is your aunt?" I ask of my old friend, buttering a square of bread to the very edges so that it greases my fingers when I lift it to my mouth.

"We are in luck, Heloise. She is with my cousins in Scotland for the month. She became terribly attached to a set of people she met at a temperance meeting here in Chelsea, I'm afraid, and was quite unbearable." She smiles as she pours tea. "I have another cousin staying with me at the moment. Charlotte. She's taken to her bed with a terrible cold, poor dear."

"The house seems quite full up. If you do not have room for me, dear Isobel, I can easily stay in a hotel until the workmen have finished with my house."

"Well, the thing is, the only room we do have spare at the moment is dear Papa's. It's been cleared out, Heloise, of course. There is no risk of discomfort," she adds quickly. "Or if that doesn't appeal, I can have Hitchins make up a bed in this room, if you'd prefer."

"Of course I don't mind taking Sir Henry's room," I say, leaning over to squeeze Isobel's cold fingers. But the bread and butter sits heavy in my stomach.

After a light supper of barley soup followed by pudding, we retire to bed. It's very early but I'm shockingly tired from the long, hasty haul home. I look out the window briefly, making sure nothing suspicious catches my eye. Then I sink onto the side of the bed. Pidgeon's bed. My fingers follow the pattern of stitches in the blue and white quilt. Isobel was right, apart from a framed portrait of Sir Henry and his late wife on the bedside cabinet, the room has been cleared of his belongings. The wardrobe is empty of his clothes; instead, my gowns hang there, where Hitchins, Isobel's housekeeper, has unpacked them. Only two of the drawers in the chest are full, and that is with my undergarments and trinkets. I glance beneath the bed, pull open the cabinet door. Nothing. Isobel's grief must be strong indeed to necessitate the almost total removal of her father's presence. Or perhaps it's her aunt's hand at work here. She seems the bossy, interfering type who would arrange things thus. Or maybe — I pull a face at the thought — maybe Isobel has gathered his belongings close to her. Does she have his coats hanging in her wardrobe so she can sniff the cuffs for the smell of him? Does she rifle through a box of his things, weeping over the memories each trifle brings to her? I have never known such loss. I never knew my father, and my mind can't even fathom a time after Amah.

I wake at dawn, still fully clothed, lying across Pidgeon's bed. I'd dithered so long over whether I could really sleep in his bed that I must've dozed off. It's a drab morning, the sun buried behind a bank of grey clouds, and through the window I watch a couple of housemaids huddle against the wind on their way down the street. A street cleaner sweeps leaves that gust back towards him again, and an old man walks his little brown dog. Two men seem to be inspecting the street light on the corner while a line of four or five children watch on. Nothing terribly suspicious.

114

I sit back on the bed and wonder what to do with myself. The day stretches out before me. I will wash and find fresh clothes to put on. I will breakfast with Isobel. Perhaps sit with her and her cousin. Sewing? Reading? Playing some parlour game? Do I let Amah and Bundle know I'm in town? What excuse do I give them for coming straight to Isobel's? And then? My foot already taps with impatience. And then what to do with myself? When will it be safe to resume my normal routine, whatever that is? I would've thought being pursued would involve some sort of thrill, but in actuality it is boring indeed.

Shedding my travel dress, I leave off my crinoline but pull on extra petticoats under the gown I had made for me in Paris. It's the shade of treacle with contrasting green, and intricate lace patterns the hem. A matching shawl drapes my shoulders, crossing at my bosom. I'm just fastening a gold bangle around my wrist when Hitchins peeps around the door.

"A guest for you ma'am."

My immediate delight at the prospect of a visitor is doused in the dark realisation that I couldn't possibly have a guest. For nobody, besides Isobel, knows I am here. I shiver as the clasp of my bangle clicks together.

"Madame?"

I close my mouth. "Sorry, Hitchins. Did they give you a name?"

"A Mrs White, I believe."

I rub my arms and my hands are quite cold. Mrs White? I don't know a Mrs White, but she doesn't sound all that threatening, after all. "Perhaps show her into the parlour we dined in last night, Hitchins. Is Isobel up yet?"

"Yes, ma'am. Her and her cousin have already left for chapel."

"Ah. Yes. I forgot that was their plan. Thank you, Hitchins. I will be down in a few moments."

I finish my toilette in a hurry and, taking my pistol from its holster in my portmanteau, I make sure it's armed. Shoving it into my skirt pocket, I wonder if I should instead brandish it as I enter the room. In my other pocket I slip my slender dagger.

When I enter the parlour, an elderly woman turns from where she is inspecting a sky-blue plate that has a boy and cart painted upon it, and roses and peonies entwined around its edges.

"Sévres," she says. Her voice is deep, gravelly, yet she is well-spoken. "A fine piece."

I stare at her, blank. What do I care of porcelain plates? "I am Heloise Chancey. Apparently you are here to see me?"

"Yes, that is correct." She contemplates a small sofa at the end of the room but decides against it and takes a chair at the table, nodding for me to join her. "I have something to discuss with you."

The straight fold of her lips, the pucker of fine lines, seem familiar to me. Her hair, a dusty colour with streaks of white, is pulled back in a hairnet, but her eyes, as dark as currants, twinkle in a shrewd, knowing kind of way. For some reason yellow flowers spring to mind. And the smell of stale beer.

"Mrs White, is it?"

116

"That is correct."

"Mrs White, may I ask how you knew to find me here?"

"We had you followed, of course."

I can't help but look surprised. I change position in my chair, seemingly to rearrange my skirts, but really it is so my fingers can find the ivory handle of my pistol.

"But why would you have me followed?" My stomach tautens, and I feel a bit nauseous. Afraid.

"We've been following you since that night at the Dernier Livre, my dear woman."

I hesitate. It seems silly to deny my presence at the tavern as I had done with the French inspector. "We. Who do you mean by 'we'? Where are these spies of yours?" My eyes dart to the sash window that looks out on the street.

"It wouldn't do for me to give away my people's secrets, Mrs Chancey." She places her reticule on the table and rummages in it. "And before you pull that ridiculous toy you call a gun on me, let me give you this."

She hands me her card. *Mrs H.B. White. Cumberland House. Pall Mall.*

I look at her. I've heard numerous of my gentlemen guests speak of this place. She's from the War Office.

I can't be sure how much this Mrs White knows of my movements. Does she know of my trip to the cemetery? Or of Violette's death? "I really have no idea what interest you have in me." If only it were not too early in the morning for a whisky. And Hitchins. Where is the dratted servant? She should have offered us tea or some such.

"Tell me, my dear," she says. "The good French inspector has told us of your games, but how did you come to be involved in the first place?"

I think back on my meeting with Somerscale. If I am going to sink in this mire of intrigue, he is coming with me. Presumably this woman is from his lot, anyway. "An acquaintance of mine, Sir Simon Somerscale, asked me to contact someone for him."

The older woman nods. "Ah. I did wonder. He's a bit of a fool, but convenient to our needs once in a while. Doesn't help matters when he gets himself locked up, though."

"Yes, he found himself in a pickle and that is why I was at the Dernier Livre."

The yeasty smell of the bar comes back to me, the green of the absinthe, the barmaid's sly eyes. And daffodils. The old lady, with bright eyes, who tried to sell me a bunch of daffodils.

"I remember now," I say. "How extraordinary. You were there, at the Dernier Livre, selling flowers."

A small smile softens Mrs White's features. "You remember. Good girl. What else do you remember of that night?"

I begin to tell her of what I told Somerscale: that I didn't see who his point of contact was; that I didn't know who left the note in my pocket, stealing Hatterleigh's pistol in turn. My voice trails off. Because that's not entirely true anymore. I do know who left the

118

note in my pocket. The man I found dying at the cemetery.

"What is it?" she asks me, her voice sharp.

I stare at her. There's something about her plain countenance, the intelligent expression on her face, how her mouth is set in a no-nonsense line, much like Amah's. I know I can trust her. I tell her of that day at the cemetery when I tried to reach the assignation as outlined in the note. How in the crypt I found the man with the dark beard and red kerchief. The same man that the French inspector had seen rifling my pockets the night before.

"And you are sure he said the word *bomb?*"

"Yes, I am certain. It was the very last thing he said."

"And are you sure he was dead?" she asks.

"Yes. He died before me. There was so much blood . . ." My eyes glaze a little as I look across the table at Mrs White. In my haste to leave Paris I had totally forgotten about the torn missive he had tucked into my hand. Where had I left it? I look about me, as though I might find it to hand in Isobel's parlour. I jump to my feet. "Wait here. I must find something."

I run up the stairs to Pidgeon's room and there, lying neatly beneath two pearl rings in my jewellery case, I find the folded scrap of paper. I pick it up, trying to avoid touching the stain of dry, rusty fingermarks. Bounding back downstairs again, I nearly bowl Hitchins over as she squeezes through the parlour doorway with a tray of tea things. Impatiently, I help her lay out the pot, the milk jug, the little saucer of lemon, the teacups. Finally I lift off the plate of shortbread and bid her leave us.

"Here," I hand over the note to Mrs White. "He gave this to me just before he died."

The older woman unfolds the paper and reads the fragmentary words out loud. " 'reen's Court. Must be Green's Court, surely. Yes, 'oho, must be Soho. Soho . . ." Her eyes wander the room as she thinks on something, and then she gives a little nod. "And the 28th of March. That's terribly soon. It's a pity the full address was torn off. What the devil are they up to?"

"Who?"

"Well, the French would like us to believe there's a group of assassins — rebels of some sort — who call themselves the Red Brethren." Her voice curls with mockery as she speaks. "But I'm not so sure that the people behind these recent attacks are from something as childish as a group who call themselves the Red Brethren."

I think of what the inspector told me. "You mean the bombing here in London? The shooting in Paris?"

She nods. "And just last week there was another bombing not far from the palace. The bomb was concealed in a costermonger's barrow. The explosion quite destroyed a sixty-foot section of the wall."

"What havoc," I say, shaking my head in wonder.

"Yes, it would seem that havoc is the intended goal. That, and a terrible death toll." Her voice is dry. She scrunches up her face and closes her eyes. "Let me think."

I pour two cups of tea, add a dash of milk to each. The tinkling of the teaspoon against china seems to rouse Mrs White, who opens her eyes again and says, "It would seem that this message was to be handed to someone of this group, someone who is central to their plans. Perhaps the note leads to one of their major conspirators, here in London, or, perhaps this is where we will find the makings of the bomb." She pauses, and her eyes widen. "Or perhaps —"

"This is where there will be another bombing," I say.

She scrutinises the piece of paper again. "What are these numbers along here?"

I take the proffered note.

"Can you see?" asks Mrs White. "I think it must be some kind of code. Someone's deciphered those words from a numbered code." She leans back into her chair. "Very interesting. This might come in handy if we manage to intercept any more communications such as these."

"What will you do now? Watch Soho?"

Mrs White stares across the table at me, and her intelligent eyes glitter. "I have an idea. Seeing as you already seem to be embroiled in this mess of ours, I'd like to make you a proposition. It just happens that we've had word that a shady character indeed has arrived in Soho. Surely this cannot be a coincidence. My idea, Mrs Chancey, is that you go into Soho, to this Green's Court, and keep an eye on things for us."

"Be your spy?"

She nods. "Keep an ear out for who might be the criminal we are after. Find out what is planned for the end of the month. Meanwhile I will look into what is happening on that date in parliament, and at the palace."

Excitement surges through my body, buzzing beneath my skin. My immediate enthusiasm falters though, at the thought of being in such close proximity to a bomb.

"You must have any number of spies at your service," I say, cautiously.

"Of course we do. Any number of men. But you must know as well as I do that nobody takes notice of a woman in anything considered important. It's the ultimate disguise, my dear."

I think of poor Violette. Of how someone has already tried to murder me twice.

"I might be recognised, Mrs White. I'm not sure how much the Inspector told you in Paris, but it would seem that I am already in their sights."

"Well, dear, perhaps it is time to stop running and start hunting. Until you — we — know who is behind all of this, you are in danger. And we only have a matter of five days until the 28th of March. You really must get to work as soon as possible."

CHAPTER
TWELVE

Amah

The hotel room is cast in shadow when Amah wakes. She's unsure of how long she's been asleep for, or how late it might be. She lifts her head, and peers out the window. The sky glows with the last light of day. Amah swings her feet off the bed and sits up. She must indeed be exhausted to have needed such a rest.

She washes her face and looks out her window down to the harbour. A man sells baked potatoes on the corner and a boy walks by with a tray of silver fish. Her stomach stirs. She missed lunch, but it's too early for supper. She decides to find something to nibble upon and a cup of tea on the way to Golda's shop.

Opening her jewellery box, she lays the beads and brooch out in a neat row across the bed, mentally calculating how much she thinks each trinket might be worth to the pawnbroker. Gathering them up again, she drops them back into the jewellery box and tucks it into her reticule. She sets out towards the docks, just as she had earlier in the day, but this time she turns left, her stride sure. She passes a number of taverns and eating houses, tobacco shops and bagnios; everything a seafaring man might need from his brief sojourn. A

123

little girl, dressed in a tattered nightdress, her dark hair matted to her scalp, offers Amah limp watercress, while another, not much older, crouches in a doorway, her sharp, expectant eyes on passing sailors.

Amah turns up a road, away from the waterfront. Passing several nondescript buildings, she pauses in front of a squat shopfront squeezed between a butcher's that advertises a 'galore of delicious pork' and a cobbler's, his boots and shoes strung like streamers across his display window. Amah feels a tic of disappointment as she gazes upon the closed door, white and mute. The windows are dark, as vacant as a cold stare. Even before she steps closer to peer inside, she can tell the shop is empty.

"Moved on," says the cobbler, a pipe hanging from the corner of his mouth. "About a year ago."

She had hoped Ping Que and his eating house were still around. She had hoped for a bowl of noodles at the very least, if not for a little gossip.

"Do you know where to?"

"Can't say," says the cobbler, cramming his bowler hat down so low his ears bend under the force. "Bit of trouble, there were. Him taking up with a local girl and all. Some of the people around here didn't like it. No, they didn't. Don't see the problem, myself. One more girl off the streets is what I say."

Amah stares at the shopfront again. Probably just as well. Ping Que would probably put her straight to work in the kitchen again. She rubs her fingers together and, although encased in silk gloves and softened thanks to Heloise's creme, she can almost feel her skin itch like it

124

did in those days, from the daily scrubbing and washing.

She thanks the cobbler and walks on, deciding to go straight to Golda. Perhaps, just like before, she will offer Amah a coffee or tea.

"Well, you've come up in the world, Li Leen," says Golda, from behind the magnifying glass she uses to inspect Amah's jewellery. "Very nice pieces you have here." She picks up the strand of pearls. "These are especially nice." Her eyes, as sharp as a squirrel's, watch Amah, but she doesn't probe, a characteristic of the pawnbroker's that Amah has always appreciated.

"I just need some ready cash in the short term, Golda. I'll return soon enough to reclaim my property." Amah takes a sip of her sweet coffee and places the cup back on the bench.

Golda laughs. "You never missed a repayment, Li Leen, unless you wanted to." Her hair is as woolly as ever, but now white strands streak the brown.

Footsteps boom across the floorboards above. Amah looks up at the ceiling.

"Your father?"

"Passed away, Li Leen. Two summers ago now." Golda looks a little sad. "That's Yosef. My uncle. He's taken it upon himself to watch over the business now my father's no longer here."

They listen as Yosef's heavy steps make their way down the back stairs. His wheezy voice precedes his bulbous stomach as he enters the shop. "If that crook Simpson didn't come back for his fob watch . . ." His

125

eyes light upon Amah and he pauses. "I am sorry, my dear, I didn't realise you had custom." His hair, as bushy as Golda's but far more grey, tumbles from below the brimless, cloth cap on his head.

"This is an old friend of mine, Uncle Yosef." Golda's fingers are deft as she folds the velvet display cloth over the jewels. She pours him some coffee, and says, "She's just leaving some of her things with me for a little while."

Golda tries to pull the velvet towards her but Yosef catches hold of its corner, and flicks the cloth wide. An acquisitive smile lights his face at the sight of the baubles, revealing three missing teeth in his upper jaw.

He beams at Amah. "Fine jewellery, madame. What fine jewellery."

"Yes. I am very fortunate." Amah avoids Golda's eye, sensing the other woman's discomfort.

Yosef's stomach gurgles. Golda stands still behind the counter, a smile fixed on her face. Amah feels unaccountably shy of asking Golda for her money in front of Yosef. Perhaps she'll expose Golda's generosity to the old rogue. Perhaps he will remonstrate, block Golda from giving Amah a fair amount of cash.

Yosef bends to inspect the diamonds, saying, "Golda, let's have some dinner brought over from The Anchor." He glances up at Amah. "You will be our guest."

Amah tries to demur, but Yosef is insistent. He waves her objections aside, striding to the shop's front door, calling for someone named Bert. He stuffs coins into the lad's fist and tells him to fetch them three roast beef meals and a jug — no, make it two jugs — of ale. He

126

glances over his shoulder at Amah and says, "No, make it one jug of ale and a jug of claret."

Amah and Golda keep up a light conversation about people they have known, about life in London, as Yosef noisily pulls a small table and chairs into the middle of the room. He draws a blind down over the front windows and lights candles. But he can't help but peer at Amah's jewellery each time he passes.

Bert arrives back with the first of his deliveries. He slides two jugs of grog onto the counter, the glitter of the brooch catching his eye. Golda tells him to move on, go collect the rest of their meal, and packs the jewellery back into its box.

"Come, come," Yosef waves Amah to the table. "Have a drink with us."

Amah wonders if his plan is to make her inebriated and then . . . what? Swindle her of some of her money? Rob her of a pearl or two?

"I'll have another coffee, if you don't mind."

Disappointment flickers across Yosef's face, but he nods at Golda to fill her coffee cup. The meal is mostly a quiet affair apart from Yosef's slurping of meat and beer, and his prying questions to Amah and her evasive replies. The beef is rubbery and the gravy greasy. Amah sips her coffee while Golda drinks a fair amount of the claret. By the time Yosef's knife and fork clatter onto his empty plate, Golda seems more relaxed; is more effusive than Amah has ever seen her before. She tells Amah of the strange things some people try to pawn, and of the last time the police checked their inventory for stolen goods.

"Oh, I will sleep well tonight," Golda says, her face flushed, her eyelids heavy, as she rises from the table. She walks behind the counter and lifts out a money tin. Amah follows her, a little put out to find Yosef closely behind.

He watches Golda count out notes and coins for Amah. There's almost an imperceptible shake of his head and his finger strokes an agate bead.

Suddenly Amah realises she can't leave her valuables in the vicinity of this man. He might have paste replicas made. Or disappear with them. Anything could happen.

"Golda, I believe I will return tomorrow for the money," says Amah, reaching across to tuck the jewellery back into its box. "I wouldn't want to walk about with such a large amount of ready. I'll come back with my coachman."

Golda and her uncle watch Amah push the jewellery box deep into her reticule.

"But Amah," says Golda, "it's just as risky to gad about with a bag full of gems."

But Amah is quite determined. She needs time to think about what to do. "No, no, I'm quite used to carrying them around."

They walk her to the door. Amah turns and squeezes Golda's hand, saying, "I'll come back in the morning." She will think on it.

She looks to Yosef to say goodbye but his mouth hangs ajar, and all he can do is lift his hand in farewell, his eyes on her reticule.

CHAPTER
THIRTEEN

The cab lurches over a bump and my glasses slip down my nose. I push them back in place, thankful that I don't require them in the normal run of my life. The glass I had fitted into these spectacles earlier in the day is of no actual use to a person with faulty eyesight. The glasses are merely a part of my disguise. My hair is parted in the middle, its length coiled into a tightly arranged braid. On my head is my plainest hat, its floral and cherry arrangement discarded with. Luckily Isobel's cousin, Charlotte — a pastor's daughter — had a rather dull cotton gown I could borrow, and Hitchins managed to procure another like it, secondhand, from a street seller she knows. The part I am to play is sober governess, in between posts, although I rather regret the itchy woollen stockings.

The last thing Mrs White told me of was the suspicious fellow I'm to look out for. A Prussian. All she could tell me was that he answers to the name Ernst — she couldn't be sure if Christian or surname — and he is getting on in age, and tall. Last seen with a fulsome beard, but of course he may have cut it off by now. Apparently the Austrians have had their eye on him for a while, convinced his constant travels around the Continent harbour mischief. And his first port of call when he arrived from France had been Waltham Abbey, suspiciously close to the Gunpowder Mills. My stomach flips again at the thought of being so near a possible bombing.

Peering out the cab's window I can see that we have finally arrived in Soho. There are any number of boarding houses in the area, and I hope to find a vacancy in one. I also know that there is a surfeit of private rooms here, too, used by gay girls, and the occasional Molly-house. We make slow purchase down Broad Street, the cab weaving its careful way around countless people — factory workers, street vendors, beggars — and a long line of buggies. We pass an ironmonger, a grocer and a large building that houses a 'mineral teeth' workshop, whatever that might be. On the other side of the road, signage for a local bonnet-maker vies for room on the wall with advertisements for a furrier and a trimming-seller. I catch a whiff of freshly baked bread and promise myself I will visit one of the two pastry shops beneath the surgeon's rooms. The cab turns right and a costermonger, ropes of onions held high, offers me his wares through the side window.

The driver calls out to me that Green's Court is not much further ahead. I press my forehead to the glass and look for any lodging houses with vacancy signs.

Pinned to a lamppost outside a rather dusty-looking building is a small placard touting good rooms for single gentlemen. Not much good to me. A little further on, a house in the middle of a row of dilapidated

130

dwellings advertises beds for four pence a night, which is not what I'm looking for at all.

The cab pulls to a stop. "As far as I can go, Miss. Green's Court is too narrow for me to squeeze through."

I hop down into the street and turn to haul my portmanteau after me. Green's Court is a cramped laneway. The air is close, has a grimy feel against my skin, from the black smoke that coughs from thin chimney pipes. The buildings are not tall, but frown down upon each other so closely that only a tepid inlet of light breaks through from the sky above. A sandwich-board man waddles by, bids me visit the tavern on Brewer Street for a hearty dish of salted pork trotters and I become distracted, thinking on the pork trotters in Chinese sauce Amah used to cook for us in Liverpool — delicious they were, caramelised and sticky — and I have to dodge a milk cart that swerves around the corner. The lane is quiet, except for the occasional bleat from a nanny goat a boy leads along the dirty paving. At street level, the buildings — brick and unadorned — seem to be taken up with small, dreary businesses — a barber's shop, a tobacconist, a rag shop, the front office for one Baxter Brewery. I can only suppose that the upper floors are occupied by private inhabitants, or by offices perhaps. In the window of a shopfront is a sign — not professionally printed like the others, but rather just a hasty scrawl across a piece of writing paper — that declares 'rooms for let, respectable only need apply'. Entering the dim shop, which is filled with an odd assortment of candles, hats, raincoats, slippers, crockery and even some dusty bottles of cordial liqueurs, I ask the man behind the counter about the room for let. He walks me back outside and points me towards the building to the left, a three-storey brick building, plain, the trim work peeling away. A laundered shirt and breeches drape the balustrade that encloses a tiny terrace on the second floor.

I lug my bag over to the front door which is painted a dapper blue, in stark contrast to the peeling paint elsewhere. Knocking, I watch two young ruffians chase each other towards the junction, and the barber steps out onto the road to peer over at me. Finally, there is a rustle at the door and it swings open into a dark corridor. A woman, older than me, with a dissatisfied look on her face,ushers me through. Her brown hair is pulled into a drab bun, and she wears a bulky, dark blouse, but her skirt is made of taffeta and has the most striking pattern of white shapes against a burgundy background. It's quite a handsome piece of clothing and not one, I should think, acquired close by.

"You are here about the room?" she asks. Her accent is thick. Spanish perhaps? Italian?

"I am indeed," I say, pushing the damned glasses higher onto the bridge of my nose.

She leads the way into the house, which smells like most other cheap housing: of oily fish and cabbage, and mouldy corners. We reach a shabby sitting room that overlooks the lane. It's a rather large space. A round table for four takes precedence in the middle of the floor while a sofa — its saggy cushions not quite hidden beneath a crocheted throw blanket — is pushed close to the fireplace. Cloudy glasses surround a single bottle of ratafia on the side board, which appears to be in desperate need of a polish. Two armchairs reside companionably near the front window, next to which is a footstool, a side-table and a basket brimming with balls of wool.

I drop my bag to the floor, and look about, conscious of the woman's eyes on me.

"What is your name?"

"Julia Charters," I say. The Christian name I used at school, chosen because it matched the cadence of the Chinese name Amah gave me. "And you are?"

"Sofia Modesto." She turns at the sound of footsteps coming down the hallway. "This be my husband."

Mr Modesto appears much older than his wife. His pate is bald, and what hair is left on the sides he keeps long and has groomed to cup his almost skeletal head. A white beard covers his lower face and when he speaks, I see that his teeth are so full of gaps.

"Who is this, Sofia?" he asks. He too has a heavy accent.

"She wants the room."

"That's correct." I move towards the window and look down on Green's Court. This could be a perfect place from which to spy. "Do you still have one free?"

"Can I ask what is your name and occupation, madame? And do you have any reference letters?"

I tell them my story — that I'm a governess, waiting to sail abroad with a French family — and I hand them a rumpled letter of recommendation Mrs White

133

made up for me. Not as herself, mind you, but in the guise of her niece, a young mother who lives in Shropshire.

Mr Modesto's eyes rake over the letter and then linger on my dress, my portmanteau. "All we have is a set of two rooms. They must be taken together. Six shillings for you."

He's bamming me. I pretend to think. "But I'm not really in need of two rooms." I sigh. Look out the window. It really is the best position, but I don't want to look too eager. I have to be careful not to call attention to myself. "I am not sure I could stretch to such an amount. What about five shillings?" I beseech Mrs Modesto.

Mr Modesto gives a nasty little laugh. "No use looking to her. She has no head for numbers." He taps his temple, rolls his eyes. "If I left things to her, our tenants would soon run this place and we'd be thrown out onto the road with the cat." He waves his arms dramatically.

It's lucky I finally accepted both rooms for they are tiny. The main bedroom, that fronts the tiny terrace on the second floor — Mrs Modesto having hastily taken down the drying clothes from its railing — barely fits a single bed and chest of drawers. When I pull out the top drawer, it sticks, and I have to wrench it back into place, inch by wretched inch. The room behind is really no larger than a wardrobe, in which a child-sized pine desk and chair have been crammed.

134

Mrs Modesto places a basin of water on top of the drawers. "Supper will be in twenty minutes, if you care to join us," she says as she leaves me. "The dining room is at the back of the house downstairs. Next to the kitchen."

So early. I feel as though I've barely finished my midday repast. I spend the time I have in washing my face and hands, although I decide to unpack my few pieces of clothing later. I unlock the doors onto the terrace, but I don't step out, not trusting the sturdiness of the narrow platform. I crane my neck to look out onto Green's Court. I've managed to find a perfect spot with a bird's eye view of my surrounds.

Hearing voices, I pull the terrace doors shut and leave my rooms. I follow the noise down the stairs and find myself in a hot room, overcrowded with chairs and people. Mr Modesto is curt as he introduces me to a Mr Beveridge and a Miss Haven. We pull our chairs in tight to the dining table so that Mrs Modesto and the maid can reach over us with plates of cabbage, carrots and haddock. My heart sinks at the sight of the damp, pongy food. There is sacrifice indeed to be made in this spying business.

"Ah. Haddock, again. I apologise, *miei amici*," Mr Modesto says to us, shaking his head, "but one day we will have something different for our dinner."

Mrs Modesto opens her mouth to say something, then closes it again. Then she says, "But, Giuseppe, you told me to serve haddock tonight." She looks a little confused.

"No, I said that we were sick of it, and that you should serve us some fowl. You misheard me. Again."

135

He glances my way, tips his head to the side. He sighs loudly and says in a jesting tone, "Perhaps one day I will taste the flesh of a nice, roasted fowl again."

A blush rises to Mrs Modesto's throat as she stares at her plate.

"Are you new to the area, Miss Charters?" asks Miss Haven. She's very young and mouse-like, with a pretty, elfin face.

"Yes, indeed I am. I have just come from the country. A lovely woman I once worked with suggested that I might find a temporary home here." I gabble on a bit more about my governess plans. I don't model myself on a sensible Bronte or Austen type governess but, rather, one who's more garrulous; more ready to please and be pleased. "And you? Do you work near here, Miss Haven?"

Miss Haven tells me of the draper's shop she works in. Its proximity to King Street. Its genteel custom. Nobody takes up the conversation when she stops talking. All that can be heard is Mr Modesto wetly chewing his boiled vegetables and fish, and the clink of cutlery against plate.

I adjust the glasses on my nose. "And you — Mr Beveridge, is it? — may I ask what your occupation might be?"

Mr Beveridge has sandy, thinning hair. He is covered in gingery freckles; even the skin on the back of his pale fingers has not escaped the caramel spots. He lifts his head, mutters, "I work for the London Omnibus," and returns his attention to his meal.

"He drives the 'bus," explains Miss Haven. "And sometimes even a horse tram, in Westminster, isn't that right, Mr Beveridge?"

"Oh. Very interesting." I am seated at a table with a bus driver and a draper's assistant. Probably the most respectable people I have ever taken a meal with, really.

Positioning my fork and knife together across my plate, partly in order to cover what mush I cannot stomach, I say, "I think I will take a turn around the court. I'm a true believer in the importance of exercise," I lie. I peer over my spectacles, as I look from one to the other. "I always take my wards out for a brisk walk after each meal. After each meal, I say. Nothing better to fortify one's spirits and vitality." This way, if these people notice me prowling about, they will hopefully put it down to a strict adherence to this ridiculous system.

Green's Court is rather dark when I set out. Two of the tallest people I've ever encountered saunter towards me, and it's only when they're close, bathed in the light from Mrs Modesto's sitting room, that I see that it's just a couple of coster-women, piles of empty fruit baskets stacked high on the top of their heads. I walk past them, in the other direction to the end of the lane. Apart from the brewery, the shutters are down on the other businesses and all is quiet. Candlelight blinks from a number of the upper windows, and a woman pops her head through one, calls out to someone named Will. Where would this Prussian be hiding away if he were here? I frown, my eyes searching the dark windows. Or is something else afoot here, in this nondescript little lane? What would be of worth to bomb here? Turning, I make my way towards the other end. The shops on the corner are rather smarter than the others. The grocer's walls are covered with green tiles, while the white columns outside Jackson Bros and Wilty, an establishment that seems to specialise in walking sticks and umbrellas, are very handsome indeed. I step from the dark lane to where the main road is illuminated by street lights. To my right the shops and buildings look rather similar to those in Green's Court. Glancing to my left, though, I see a throng of people gathered outside a corner building, so I decide to walk in its direction.

Once close, I see that it's an establishment called the Horse and Clover Inn, and men are gathered on the pavement sipping their evening pints. I peer into the crowd, trying to discern a familiar face. I move slowly, listening for a Germanic accent, but all I hear are the usual gripes and small talk and, often, the lilting burr of an Irishman. A menu is tacked next to the front doors that lead into the inn's restaurant. I push my way in.

A waiter leads me to a table that, although in the middle of the eating house, is in a booth divided from others by panelling that rises close to the ceiling. There doesn't seem to be any other table free. I slide into my seat and ask for a cup of tea to start. Straightening my spectacles, I pull my book from my bag and pretend to read. Only occasionally do I look up, quickly taking in the other custom. Across from me is an older couple, who concentrate on their pigeon and spinach. At the next table along are four noisy clerks, well and truly into their cups. On the way through I saw that the table in the booth before me is occupied by two elderly men but, unfortunately, I cannot see into the booth behind me, due to the panelling. The waiter returns with my drink and I hesitate over what meal to order. It's not like I am full up after that watery meal at the Modestos'. Although tempted by the omelette, I settle on blackberry pudding.

Gaskell's Margaret is quite fascinating and it's difficult to not become totally engrossed in the book, but I must keep an ear out for the Prussian fellow. I'm savouring a mouthful of pudding when I look up to see Mr Modesto glaring down at me.

"You dine alone, Miss Charters? Or should I say . . . you dine again?" His eyes linger on my dessert. "How very strange."

I let out a foolish whoop. "Ooh, you've caught me, I'm afraid, Mr Modesto. I do have a very sweet tooth. I couldn't resist the urge to indulge when I walked past this inn. And you? Are you here to indulge in something sweet, too?"

He shakes his head. "Sometimes I come here of an evening to sip an aperitif. That is all. To escape the tedium of the domestic, you understand." He gives a small bow and moves on.

As Mr Modesto walks away I catch sight of a man entering the inn. He's tall and, for some reason, faintly familiar. His clothes are well-cut and he wears a wide-brimmed hat, very exotic in these parts of bowler hats and caps. He saunters past and I hear the waiter usher him to the booth behind.

"Thankee, kind sir. Get me one of them ales my pal here has, would you?"

My eyes widen, and I almost wrench around in my seat to gape.

I'd know that drawl anywhere. It's the irritating American from Paris. From that night in Bocages des Anges.

CHAPTER
FOURTEEN

Amah

The air is chilly and a tacky mist drifts up from the waterfront. Amah pulls her shawl about her shoulders more firmly, her reticule clasped snug to her chest beneath. She's in a puzzle over how she can trust Golda with her jewellery without her uncle having access to it. Surely the woman understands Amah's reticence. Indeed, didn't Golda seem uncomfortable in his presence, herself? Before she drank those four glasses of claret, in any case.

Amah glances around for a cab but there are none. She decides to walk a little way towards the harbour in search of one and as she passes the tavern, she notices Bert lounging against its front wall. He catches sight of her and tugs his cap. "Missus."

She nods back at him and continues on her way. She knows that a little further on she will come to a road that will take her towards the harbour and to her inn. But the mist seems to thicken with each step, muting everything around her. Fellow pedestrians remain invisible until they are almost upon her; trees and buildings merge into a muddle of grey shapes; twice she slips into the gutter. She hears others' conversations drone in and out towards her like the buzz of a roving fly, but mostly all that reaches her ears is the occasional passing carriage and the tapping of her own footsteps across the cobblestones. And perhaps their echo a little way behind? Amah's fingers press against the hard corner of her jewellery box.

She walks at a more careful pace than her usual trot in order to avoid bumping into lampposts or knocking her shins on the edge of the odd pedlar's cart, but she has an uncanny feeling that the slower she moves, the closer someone looms up behind her. She pauses for a moment, hears a faint pulse of footsteps. Her heartbeat quickens, its whoosh surging her eardrums.

Stupid. She'd been stupid to drink that extra cup of coffee. It's made her jittery. She can feel the beverage hum in her fingertips, stir her nerves.

But Amah can also sense the gap shorten between herself and whoever follows. She shivers, as though a feather tickles its way up her spine. Probably just a hansom cab, she reasons, the driver moving through the soupy mist as carefully as she does. Her heart flops in her chest like a fish landed on deck. Flops again. She tightens her hold on her reticule, annoyed with herself. The coffee has left her behaving as foolishly as one of the simpleton heroines in Heloise's novels. She glances over her shoulder, knowing it's futile, that it would be impossible to see anything by this murky light. But is that the crown of a black hat? Hovering through the haze? A cap? A cap, not unlike Yosef's.

Turning left at the next crossroads, Amah finds herself on a familiar street, where she used to work, at

Ping Que's. A street she had walked countless times, by moonlight, by sunlight.

"Excuse me, ma'am." She starts as a man brushes past her, closely followed by two more. They hurry on until they're swallowed up by the mist.

Amah follows them. Heading towards a row of bleary lights, she decides she will settle in a tavern or eating house and pay some boy to scamper down to the docks and fetch Taff and the coach for her. She comes to pass one of the beer shops, a larger establishment than most, yet not as spacious as a tavern. She hears a clacking sound and yelling, followed by laughter and the sound of clapping. Peering through the plate glass, she watches as a man stoops and rolls a black ball down the length of the wooden floor.

Skittles. They're playing skittles. Amah shakes her head from side to side. Skittles.

She hasn't seen the game played in years. And all it brings to her now is a memory of her girl, Heloise, absconding from home with that wayward Walters girl, to set up skittles in the filthy back lanes for a farthing a go.

A roar goes up as the ball smashes through the nine pins. A farthing a go from a bunch of rowdies like this. Amah's mouth tightens. The beginning of the end, that had been. But to be fair, Amah can't be certain of who led who astray, perhaps Heloise was the wayward one, not the Walters girl, after all.

A tussle breaks out between two of the players. One holds fast to the ball while the other tries to pry it from his fingers. A third joins the fray, who's shortly joined by five more men who surge into the middle of the room, throwing punches or wrenching opponents apart; kicking skittle pins to the side and stumbling back against tables. The crowd spills through the doorway and tumbles about the narrow pavement. Two men thrust another onto the road so that a horse and cart have to rear to the side, the squeals of the horse and driver rising above the groans and swearing of the combatants. Amah backs away and, unsure of how successful she'd be at circling the mob, she decides to duck down the alley beside the beer house, hoping it's a shortcut through to the next street over. Just as she steps into the alleyway, a pale face catches her eye, and she's sure it's Bert, loping down the road towards her.

Weak moonlight cuts through the mist for several moments and, as she walks, Amah strains to see how far it is until the end of the lane. She's only five steps in when she hears voices behind her and, looking back, sees that two, perhaps three, people are hard upon her heels. She picks up pace. It could be that they too are intent upon avoiding the fight. She clenches her reticule tight. Or maybe they want to snatch her bag, taking all her jewels.

Amah lifts her skirt and runs along the narrow path. She can feel the jiggle of the beads and brooch in their box as her reticule swings against her side. Relief loosens her breathing when she sees the street ahead. A hansom cab passes the mouth of the alleyway and she's just raising her arm to summon its driver when she's grabbed from behind by her shoulders and slammed against a wall. Something heavy and hard crashes

144

against the side of her head and she slumps to the ground. Pain rings in her ears, and she moans with each ragged inhalation.

"I said to knock her out."

"What do you want me to do? Cave her head in?" someone whispers back. "She'll die."

Beneath the thumping ache, Amah's head whirls. She rocks on her haunches, tries to drag herself to her feet. Her voice croaks when she tries to call out for help.

"Give me her shawl."

Amah's so dizzy she's sure she will vomit. She collapses against the wall.

"Bind it tight around her mouth."

Strong hands wrap the woollen shawl about Amah's head, tying it tightly at the nape of her neck. She tries to push away but the knock to the head has left her feeling weak, disorientated. With a grunt, her assailant grips her around the waist and slings her over his shoulder.

CHAPTER
FIFTEEN

I lean right back into the cushions of my seat, trying to listen to what the American — what was his name again? — has to say. He is seated with his back to me and, although I can hear that twang of his, I can't make out actual words. And whoever sits opposite him speaks too low for me to catch anything. What the hell is he doing in Soho? It's a bit of a rich coincidence him being here. He must be connected in some way with what happened at the Dernier Livre. I scrape and scrape at the last of the pudding with my spoon as I puzzle over the possibilities. He wasn't Somerscale's secret contact, because that was the man with the black beard. But there must be some connection. Why else would he be here?

I think of the way he stuck so close to Violette and me. What had he known? What was he up to?

I cock my head, trying to drown out the rowdy clerks, the rumble of conversation, the clinking of cutlery against crockery. I strain to hear what the American is talking about. And who is he talking to? But the damned panelling is in the way and I can't exactly poke my head around the side to look.

Once the waiter whisks past with a tray of dirty plates, I stuff the book back into my bag and prepare to leave my booth. I will follow him, ostensibly to pay my bill, and I will have a good look at the American's 'pal' on my way.

Taking to my feet, I straighten my skirts and edge a step closer to the partition between the American's booth and mine. A step further again. But the bench seat opposite the American is now empty. Damn. I sidle towards the back of the restaurant and find my waiter. I'm very tempted to look over my shoulder as I wait for my change, but I resist. Once the bill is settled, I turn and make my way sedately towards the street. As I pass the American I glance his way, and my eyes snag on his. I look away quickly, but not before I see a grin of recognition light his face.

When I enter my temporary home in Green's Court, I peep into the sitting room on the way to my rooms. Mrs Modesto is seated in one of the chairs, reading.

"You seem to be very busy there, Mrs Modesto," I say from the doorway.

She looks up. "You may join me, if you please, Miss Charters."

On my way to the armchair next to hers I peer out the front window. I scan the laneway to see if anyone — the American in particular — has followed me home. Across the way I can see directly into someone's living room: the lamp on a side board, an overstuffed sofa, square table and chairs, barren grate. A man enters the room and I take a step back behind the curtains.

"That is our neighbour." Mrs Modesto doesn't look up from her knitting. "We do not know his name. I think he is something secret. A — what you call it? — a man who does science."

"What makes you think that?" I ask, glancing out the window again. The man has taken a seat on the sofa. The bald spot on the top of his head shines by the light of his lamp as he leans low to read from a thick sheaf of paper on his lap.

"Our charwoman sometimes clean for him too. Says he has a room full of bubbling things in glass. She says he is foreigner too. Like us." Mrs Modesto closes her book, and I catch a glimpse of its title, *Biblia Sacra*. The Bible, perhaps?

I stare across the lane at the man again. Could he be the Prussian I am searching for?

He looks up and I draw back quickly, but it's a knocking at his front door that has caught his attention. Someone stands down in the shadows. After a few moments, the front door opens and the dark silhouette slips inside.

Mrs Modesto pours something from a small jug and offers the cup to me. "Please. Drink with me."

I take the chair next to hers. "Warm milk?"

She nods, a small smile lilting her lips.

I take a sip and almost splutter. Warm milk and gin. Not a favourite of mine. "Ooh, Mrs Modesto. You have tricked me."

The smile slips from her face at the creak of the front door, and she gathers together her needles and wool. Mr Modesto walks in and, arms akimbo, says,

"Knitting again, my dear? If you are so bored, why don't you find the time to clean up this pigpen we live in? What Miss Charters here must think of us."

I look about the sparse yet well-ordered room. "Oh, Mr Modesto, I beg to disagree. This house is as neat as a new pin."

He ignores me. He runs a fingertip along the mantelpiece and tuts. "Don't stay up so late, will you, Sofia? Perhaps you can get something useful done tomorrow."

What a detestable man. I want to tell him that perhaps if he didn't spend time drinking aperitifs at the Clover, he might find time to do some dusting himself. Which makes me think of when I saw him earlier in the evening. Not that much before the American entered the restaurant. Could it be . . . ?

Mrs Modesto frowns over her knitting, but I think there is a slight quiver to her fingers.

"What is it you are knitting there, madame?" I ask her.

She holds up a blue bootie. "I make them for the — how you call them — babies back home. Babies with no parents."

"Orphans?"

She nods. "There has been much unrest where I am from. It is very unsettling. Many orphans."

"Unrest? Where is that?"

"I am from Venetia. My husband is from there too."

"Ah, yes, there has been trouble in your parts, I understand. Quite a spate of rebellions, so I've heard."

Mrs Modesto knits in a peculiar style, yarn in the wrong hand, the nose of the needles held low. Not at all like how I was taught back at school when we girls would cluster around Miss North, listening to her stories of the princes in the tower or poor Lady Jane Grey. I wonder what happened to the lopsided scarf I knitted, the one that seemed to become wider and wider the longer I worked on it.

Mrs Modesto ties off the bootie and tosses it into the basket on the floor by her chair. She takes a sip of her milk and gin. Someone shuffles above us, blows their nose. Several soft raindrops tap the window.

"Well, I might take this delicious nightcap with me and head off to bed. It's been a long day." I smile at the other woman, who murmurs goodnight but does not look up from where she loops fresh wool onto her knitting needle.

I grimace as I place the dreadful drink on the chest of drawers and rummage through my portmanteau for my flask of whisky. I also lift out my writing accoutrements and carry them into the tiny back room. Taking a seat at the desk, the chair is so low to the ground I feel like my knees are up about my ears. At this awkward angle, my writing is no better than a scrawl as I pen a report to Mrs White. I write of the man across the way, and how, apparently, he is a secretive scientist. I will have to find out if he is Prussian. I lift my head and look towards the road. His room, where he performs his experiments, might be directly opposite, and if something were to combust . . . I imagine the glass in the terrace doors blowing in,

150

vicious shards lodging into the furniture, the walls, me. I shake my head and return to the letter. The biggest news I have regards the American. Mr Ripley, I now recall. Of course, I can't be sure if this is his real name but this information will be of great interest to Mrs White. And for good measure I add the redoubtable Mr Modesto to my list of suspects. What does he do when he's not mocking his poor wife? I seal the letter and slide it beneath the inkwell, ready to send in the morning. Not a bad start at all. This spying game suits me.

Turning my lantern low, I open the doors onto the terrace. Careful to not step too far, I light a cigarette and blow smoke towards the night sky. I puzzle for a few moments over Mr Ripley. What the hell is he doing here? I am quite certain he recognised me at the inn tonight, yet I am equally certain I must have imagined it. At the Dernier Livre he knew me as a man. Didn't he?

CHAPTER
SIXTEEN

Amah

Amah jerks awake. She has to blink three times, firmly, to confirm that her eyes are open but that she can't see anything. She is almost totally immersed in darkness as though she has been lowered into the depths of a well. Only after several seconds do her eyes adjust so that she can discern a faint glimmer to her right; a very dim line of light across the floor, beneath what must be a door.

She rotates her head, side to side, trying to stretch out the painful crick in her neck. A cloth gag cuts into the corners of her mouth. Her shoulders and waist are bound to a hardback chair, her ankles tied fast to its legs. The side of her head still aches from where the man clubbed her and a sharp little headache pokes at her right temple. How could she have fallen asleep at such a time? Where was she? What time of day was it?

Amah had spent a good amount of time huddled on the floor of the buggy the man had thrown her into. She can't be sure how long she'd lain there as the buggy trundled along. An hour? Two? It was difficult to be clear about time with the shawl muffling her eyes, her ears, although she could sense when the buggy's wheels left the town's even road surfaces to bump their way along dirt. Her assailants had kept her pinned to the floor with their feet, like she was a spaniel of some sort to warm their feet upon. And one had pressed the icy flank of a blade to her temple, told her to lie still.

Amah's hands lie numb in her lap and she rubs them together. She pinches her fingertips, relieved when a wiry prickle signals the return of sensation. The rope tied about her wrists itches her skin and a cramp tightens her left thigh. The room is as chill as an icebox. As a coffin. As a graveyard plot.

"Don't be so fanciful," she says out loud, testing her voice.

When the buggy finally pulled up — Amah presumes in the middle of the previous evening, although she can't be sure — and her assailants pulled her to the ground, she waggled her head so that the scarf slipped. Not that she could see much. The half-moon was hidden behind cloud, and a bramble, huge and gnarled, reached across the sky, screening all else. Her assailants marched her towards a low-set lodge. No fire or gaslight glowed from its windows and a cold draught swept through the hallway as they walked her towards the back of the house. She had tried to wrench herself free, to run out into night's dark refuge, but the stern tip of the dagger was again pressed to her throat. They half carried her down the stone steps to the cellar and, after they tied her to the chair, left her alone. Amah doesn't know how long ago. She finds it very disorientating being buried so far below, away from the sun's regulating light or even a candle's reassuring flicker.

She feels terribly exposed, pinned to the chair like a moth mounted in a glass case. She wonders where her bag is, where her jewels are. Was she attacked for her belongings? And if that were the case, why take her too?

It's as black as pitch in the cellar and the dank air whispers against her throat, tickles the hair at the back of her neck. She shifts in her chair to break the silence that hums in her ears. The darkness presses in on her, flutters against her skin until her heart matches its beat. Something in the corner makes a faint scratching sound and Amah wonders if it's a mouse. A memory — something her Chinese grandfather had once told her when he was in his cups — creeps into her mind, and the harder she tries to shut it out, the more surely it slips into her thoughts like a serpent into its nest. He'd whispered to her of ghosts that could transform into small creatures, into insects, into vermin. Ghosts that could slip through tiny crevices, scuttle up great heights before they transformed back into spirits that were hungry, for flesh, for life, for one's soul. Amah lifts her feet as best she can from where they are bound, imagining the same spectre of her childhood — a faceless black void dressed in pale rags — crawling across the ground, brittle arm reaching for her.

Amah's panting now, and it takes all her will to wrench her thoughts back to somewhere safe, peaceful. She closes her eyes and pictures an expanse of ocean, azure and calm, warmer than the leaden waters of Liverpool. She can smell the salt in the air, the sweet stink of overripe mango. Birds squawk and trill. And it's sweltering, so warm her skin feels sticky, her limbs are

154

heavy. Her mother strokes her cheeks, soothes her tears away with her thumbs.

Opening her eyes again Amah stares into the shadows. Is she alone in the house? Should she try to call out? From the little she could take in the evening before, the house seemed to be isolated, far from others. Even if she were to shout, would anyone hear? Perhaps she would only attract the attention of her kidnappers. Perhaps they have forgotten her existence and left her here to expire. Her tongue is dry against the cloth gag and her stomach feels hollow. She must find a way out. She can't just sit here waiting to perish one way or another.

Twisting her hands, she tries to wriggle them free from their bind, but all she achieves is a slight loosening — not enough to slide free — and terribly chafed wrists. She strains against the rope, wondering if it is blood or sweat that dampens the back of her hands. She gives up, vexation rubbing hot against her chest. She catches sight of the faint glimmer under the doorway again. She'll get herself to the door. Then decide what to do.

Amah clenches her calves against the chair legs and, with toes pushed to the ground, eases the chair forward. With each short scrape, she waits, listens for a response from overhead. It's not until she's halfway across the space that she hears footsteps cross the floorboards above. Her heart quickens as the footsteps pause. A pang of nauseous dread sweeps over her as the footsteps descend the steps towards her.

CHAPTER
SEVENTEEN

First thing the next morning I slip out to send my letter to Mrs White, which means I am a bit late to the breakfast table and have missed both Mr Beveridge and Miss Haven. This is of no matter to me as I've decided to spend the morning watching Mr Modesto and the house across the way. It's quite awful having to sit through Mr Modesto slurping up egg yolk and herring, so much so that I only manage to nibble on a piece of toast myself. I notice Mrs Modesto doesn't eat anything at all, only sips from a cup of coffee. She is knitting again. A striped bonnet this time. I don't admire how she's mixed the lilac, black, grey and green.

Mr Modesto rises to his feet. "You still have your list of tasks for the day, Sofia?" he says to his wife. "I am just checking, you see, because often you forget. I will use Miss Charters here as my witness that I have reminded you."

I smile up at the detestable man, wondering if I could possibly slip something in his tea at some time. Not to kill him, mind you, just cause maximum discomfort for a night or two.

Standing too, I say, "Yes, I believe I have had enough. Thank you, Mrs Modesto, for breakfast." I

156

make my way slowly up to my room, keeping an ear out for Mr Modesto's movements. Once in my room, I pull gloves and a bonnet on and listen to the household through a crack in the door. Mrs Modesto murmurs instructions to the housemaid as they clear the dining room, and water slops in the bucket as the charwoman climbs the stairs. It's not long before firm footsteps approach the front door, and keys clink as they are drawn from a pocket. Slipping onto the landing, I race down the stairs and reach the front hallway just as the front door clicks shut. I wait four toe taps and then I too open the front door and step out onto the pavement. Mr Modesto heads off in the direction of Brewer Street.

The day is clear, yet quite chilly and I wish I'd brought along a shawl. Too late to turn back now though. I maintain a good distance behind Mr Modesto, ready to fling myself into the closest shop should he turn and see me. I pass an organ grinder who tips his hat to me. The monkey on his shoulder wears a red coat and a tiny captain's cap, and I am sorely tempted to stop and pat the dear creature but Mr Modesto has already turned right at the next corner. One more turn to the left and he makes his way to a rather scrappy-looking park. He follows a dirt path that meanders through the middle of the grass and takes a seat on a bench. I hurry across the road to watch him from the shops that line the road opposite to the park entrance. When I look over at him again, he's just pulling a folded newspaper from his pocket, which he spreads out to read.

Well. That would be right. He's taken himself off for some nice peaceful reading time, while he's left all the chores to the missus. I keep an eye on him as I linger over a haberdasher's stall. I've chosen two rolls of pink ribbon, some lace edging and five faux-shell buttons when a woman, garish green skirt swaying, makes her way up the park path towards Modesto. He hails her, tucking the newspaper under one arm and taking her hand in his other. Hastily paying the stall keeper, I run across the road and follow them through the park. They step briskly and seem to be keeping up a lively banter. Even when she glances up at Modesto, I can't see her face for all the brash flowers and furbelows that decorate her hat. They walk through the gates on the other side of the park and turning right, they cross the road and disappear into a tall, rather ugly, building. As I approach, I read the sign above the doors. Supreme Hotel.

"The likes of you don't want to stay there, miss," a paperboy says to me from where he squats in the gutter. "Not if you don't want no room for no more than an hour or so."

I stare at him over the rim of my fake glasses and then back to the hotel. The entrance hall is dingy and I've quite lost sight of them. Thanking the boy, I drop a couple of pennies in his hand.

Damned if I'm going to stand around and wait for Modesto to finish up with whoever his ladybird is. I'm nearly at the park again when I realise my mistake. What if Modesto is up to something that is not simply carnal? What if that woman holds the key to a future

158

bombing? Turning reluctantly, I walk back towards the hotel. I'll have to wait.

By the time I return to Green's Court several hours later, I am feeling very annoyed indeed. That blasted man, Modesto. True to the paperboy's word, my quarry had re-emerged not an hour after they had entered the hotel, blinking at the light and straightening their clothes. Mr Modesto turned towards home while the woman took off down the road in the opposite direction. I decided to follow her, see where she would lead. By the time we arrived in Covent Garden, outside her dwelling, which was clearly a doxy house, my shoes pinched my feet and my temper was quite frayed.

As I enter the house on Green's Court, I curse myself for squandering half the day. Although, perhaps it had not been a total waste of time. Perhaps I can now discount Mr Modesto as a suspect. He's certainly despicable, but most probably not caught up in a possible attack.

I pause with the front door still open. Voices — hushed, clipped — come from the sitting room. A muffled thump against the wall. A squeak.

A rush of anger rings in my ears. Not for nothing did I spend years in bawdy houses. I would recognise the furtive, threatening echoes of menace anywhere.

I slam the door shut and call out, "Is anyone home?"

Mr Modesto steps into the hallway from the sitting room. He looks a little flushed. "Yes, Miss Charters. But Mrs Modesto is resting. You must not disturb her.

159

She is very feeble and if she doesn't get her rest, she is of even less use than usual."

Stretching a smile across my face, I promise myself that before I leave this place, when this is all over and done with, I will lace his milky coffee with a good dollop of boracic acid.

I pace the floor of my bedroom, torn between going to Mrs Modesto and offering assistance and letting things lie until I find out who is planning to bomb innocent people in a matter of days. Realising my fingertips tremble with not just anger, but with hunger as well, I snatch up my bag intent upon finding a late luncheon somewhere.

As I leave the Modestos', I pretend to tackle a recalcitrant parasol so I can scrutinise the house opposite. The number eight has been painted in the top right hand corner of the door. All the curtains are drawn, and nobody seems to stir within. Perhaps I will find out who this charwoman is that Mrs Modesto shares with the 'scientist' across the lane, question her about him. Turning right onto Peter Street I have a meal of fritters and mince in a passably clean eating house and, replenished, I stand on the pavement. Down the road I can see the Horse and Clover Inn. I will saunter that way, see if there is any further sign of Mr Ripley.

I don't go into the restaurant this time, although I do peer in the side window as I pass. The dining room seems to be quite empty, and as far as I can see, the American isn't seated there. I come to the door to the taproom and poke my head in. A group of five or six hobbledehoys, dressed in greasy cords and pea jackets, gather around an upright barrel, sharing three ales between them. And two men sit at the end of the room on high stools at the counter. I'm almost positive it's Mr Ripley's straight, broad back I look upon. And next to him, someone who looks terribly similar to dastardly Cyril, Hatterleigh's brother-in-law. But it could not be . . .

"Miss Charters."

Swinging around, I make my foolish whooping sound in Miss Haven's face. I straighten my spectacles. "Oh, you did startle me. I was just peeping in here to see if it were a coffee room but, alas, it seems it is an ale room for the men."

I step away from the doorway; I don't want to be seen by either of the men. Miss Haven points out a coffee stall across the road.

"Let us have a coffee from there, and then I must be on my way," she says.

We walk past the taproom again and I glance in. I see the American has disappeared, but the other fellow, the one who looks strikingly similar to Cyril, remains seated on the high stool, his head tilted back as he swallows the last of his beer.

As we pay for our coffees, Miss Haven says, "I'll be moving on soon from the Modestos'. She's nice enough, but he keeps the purse strings tied too tight." She holds up her coffee. "I should be able to have a nice cup of tea when I arrive home, but he makes it very difficult. And that show last night about telling

Mrs Modesto to get some fowl in, what an untruth that was. Mark my words, most every meal you have in that household will be herring, or mackerel, when it is in season, later in the year. We are always served cheap fish, although sometimes we are lucky enough to get boiled mutton of a Sunday." Miss Haven draws breath and leans in. "You know, he never lets her out of the house."

"Mr Modesto?"

She nods. "Never lets his wife out. It's a wonder the poor thing's bones haven't turned to mash. Can you believe it?"

Yes. I can. We sip from our pannikins of coffee. "How was work today?" I ask her politely.

"I don't mind the work," she says. "I don't even mind when my boss expects long hours of us. I am luckier than the others, because I don't live in. Mr Munby allows me to start at seven in the morning and leave at five in the evening. And I get half Sunday off. But the pay, Miss Charters, the pay, it is not enough for a person to live on." She shakes her head. By the bleached light of dusk, I see that she is not as young as I had earlier supposed. Her skin is covered in faint lines, like watermarks on brittle paper, and her eyes are tired. "Look at us here. Reduced to taking a hot drink in the middle of the road, with all the bonnetless women and the shoeless children, when everybody should have the means to feed themselves and house themselves comfortably."

"You work at a draper's, I think you said?"

162

She nods, swirling the remnants of her coffee. "Very lucky, I was, to get the work. My mother, before she died," Miss Haven swallows, pauses a moment, "she was a very good needle-woman. But the hours she had to work! By the light of a candle. Quite ruined her vision it did. I think that's what killed her, you know? She couldn't get around no more, couldn't do anything, until she just waited out her final days on some straw bedding." Miss Haven returns her cup to the coffee stall owner. "Of course, some young puss on one of them sewing machines would have replaced her by now. Yes. Lucky I was to get work in a shop. What about you, Miss Charters? You happy with your employment?"

I scan the street for Mr Ripley, or the man who looked remarkably like Cyril, as we head towards Green's Court. "I can't complain. Although I agree, a more generous wage would be most welcome." I think of the restrictive life a governess is expected to lead; the lack of possessions and privacy. My tone is more grievous when I add, "I mean, we are expected to watch over people's precious offspring; to care for them more vigilantly than even their parents do." I pull a face. "Although, perhaps we are to be thankful, for one day we might very well be replaced by a machine too."

Miss Haven halts and gazes up at me. "I see that you feel like I do about these things. You should come to a meeting with me tonight!"

I think of the temperance meetings that Isobel talked of. I can't imagine sitting amongst a bunch of prudes prosing on about whichever virtue or offence that has

163

taken their fancy. "What meeting would that be, Miss Haven?"

"One of our delivery men introduced me to them." Her eyes glisten a little when she speaks of him. "It's a place where men — and some women too — can protest their treatment at the hands of their employers."

"But why? What does that achieve?" I ask.

"Oh, they don't just sit around and grumble, Miss Charters," she says, taking me by the elbow and steering me past Green's Court. "They speak of ways we can rise above those who are determined to keep us down."

We walk for twenty minutes before Miss Haven guides me down a muddy alley, littered with broken bits of glass and one soleless boot. We come to a narrow building, its pale façade grimy in the dreary evening light, and follow a line of men down a set of steps that lead into the building's basement. The stench from a public privy nearby makes my eyes positively water. We shuffle in, shoulder to shoulder with factory workers and the like, sweat and grime etched into their every furrow. Miss Haven waves to the one other female in the room, a tall, forbidding type.

"We might need to wait a little for some of the workers to finish their shift for the day," she tells me.

I look about me and calculate that perhaps thirty, forty, people are crushed into the basement.

"Mr Beveridge," I hear Miss Haven say. "I've never seen you here at one of these meetings."

I turn to look at the bus driver. He appears to be as reluctant to converse as he was the night before in the dining room. He mumbles something about usually missing the meetings due to his work and, tugging the brim of his hat, he moves away, squeezing through a knot of men.

At the front of the room, a rough-looking fellow, black stubble with several missing teeth, turns over a wooden fruit crate and stands on it. He calls for everyone to "Bloody shut your yaps, would you." He says he's a representative of something called the Reform League, the words whistling through the gaps in his gums, and from what I can tell he demands more political rights for the working class, he wants a time of manhood suffrage. He goes on and on and my damned shoes start to pinch my toes again. Industrial system . . . dismantled . . . exploits workers . . . The old man next to me, his gnarled knuckles clamped over a short pipe, mutters, "Aye," once in a while, while a group of men to my right shout, "Hear, Hear!".

Next, a short man takes his place on the box. He's much more charming than his predecessor, with a pleasant Irish accent. Miss Haven becomes still beside me, her hands clasped in front of her breast.

"Is that your delivery man, Miss Haven?" I tease.

"Yes, no, not my delivery man, Miss Charters. But yes, that is Mr Connolly."

Mr Connolly beguiles us with his lilting voice, urging us to demand less hours, to insist upon better pay, to learn self-respect. There's a low rumble of agreement from his audience. Mr Connolly's tone slowly climbs until he bellows something about doing away with

165

piecework altogether and Miss Haven squeezes my hand, no doubt in memory of her dead mother.

"And if they won't give to us what is rightly ours," he shouts, "we will take it. By force if need be. We will show them we mean to have our way."

The men around us cheer and stamp their feet, and Miss Haven claps her hands. It comes back to me that Mrs White had told me of a group calling themselves the Red Brethren. My eyes scan the gaunt men who mutter amongst themselves. Could they be here? Could this be a cover for their more covert activities? As the crowd disperses, I ask Miss Haven what she thought Connolly meant when he said he'd use force if need be.

She shrugs, but someone behind drawls, "I suspect they mean to cause trouble, like them Fenians in Ireland or them Frenchies across the channel."

I turn slowly, already aware that it's Mr Ripley I will encounter.

He smiles down on me as if we are old mates while I manage to maintain a blank stare.

"Are you two acquainted?" asks Miss Haven.

I say no, but Mr Ripley says, "I am sure we have met before, ma'am. You look remarkably familiar. I spied you last night in the Clover and I said to myself: Sean Ripley, where in the name of Sam Hill have you seen her before?" His eyes narrow like he's trying to place me but I can see that he is funning. His fair hair is tucked neatly behind his ears and he's clean shaven. Not at all like when I first met him in Paris when he fell all about the place, drunk as a lord. I glance up at him, wondering if it had all been an act. He's still smiling

166

but there's a gravity about him that is unsettling. My heartbeat picks up speed. If he's the bomber and he does suspect that I was at the Dernier Livre that night, I am in great danger.

I go to walk past him but he bars my way. "No, wait, ma'am. It's coming back to me. Could it have been in Paris that we met?"

"I'm sure we did not."

"Actually, now I remember." He slaps his forehead. "You look uncommonly like a — sorry if this gives offence — like a fellow I met in a saloon in Bocages des Angels or some such place. What a screwy idea! There is no way a lady like yourself would be in a seedy saloon like that. Looked uncommonly like you, though. You have a brother I might have met?"

I shake my head, jamming the spectacles more firmly onto the bridge of my nose. "I doubt it, Mr . . . er?"

"Ripley. Sean Ripley, at your service, ma'am."

I smile widely for him and say, "Won't be needing it."

Again I try to move on but he's joined by the second speaker, Connolly, and Miss Haven won't budge.

Connolly clasps the American on the shoulder and thanks him for coming.

"Very interesting business, Pat. Gave me a lot to think on," says Ripley.

"Meet me tomorrow, Sean, and I can give you a lot more to think on," Connolly says, a hard glint to his blue eyes.

Connolly and Miss Haven peel off together leaving me to follow with Ripley. Once outside, I fold my arms against the chill breeze that has picked up.

"You staying close to here?" he asks.

"Not far."

"A bit of a coincidence us meeting up like this again, wouldn't you say?" I turn to remonstrate, but he holds his hand up, skirts an old lady pushing a barrow of green walnuts. "Didn't want to wear that moustache again? Looked like a black grub ready to march right off your lip, it did."

I can't quite make out his expression in the dark alley.

"All right, you have me," I capitulate. "I had a great desire to have an adventure in Paris, so I dressed up in my master's clothes and sneaked out with the chamber maid. Please don't tell anyone of my indiscretion. It would cost me dearly."

"You in these parts for work too?"

"I'm between stations." I point towards Miss Haven. "I'm currently staying in a boarding house with Miss Haven not far from here. And you?"

"Much the same."

I roll my eyes when he doesn't volunteer further information. As we stroll along, I think hard. It really is too much that he is here in Soho so soon after that night in Paris. And I think of how close he stuck to Violette and me. I feel a pang at the thought of poor Violette. Could this man have something to do with her death? A shudder of fear passes through me. Could Ripley be the man who had tried to kill me, even? Tried to mow me down with that carriage? There is only one thing for it. I think of Mrs White's words. I have to stop being the prey; I must be the hunter. Although I'll have to be very cautious indeed. Removing my glasses, I pretend to wipe them clean between gloved fingertips.

"Where are you staying, Mr Ripley?" I gaze up at him by the light of a tailor's shop. It's all about eye contact when trying to beguile a man.

"At the Clover Inn. Where I saw you last night. You should swing by sometime and share another absinthe with me." He smiles, and I'm the one who has to break eye contact, stomach flipping, because I can't tell if it's with admiration or if he wants to stick a knife in my gullet. I'm glad of my velvet bag, the bulk of my pistol giving it a reassuring heft.

We say our goodbyes to the men at the corner of Green's Court and Miss Haven whispers to me of a possible assignation the next afternoon.

"Perhaps a picnic, Mr Connolly said. Do you think . . ." She breaks off as we come across Mr Modesto, standing in the middle of the court, lamp held high.

"Miss Haven. Miss Charters. You missed supper."

"Oh, I do apologise, Mr Modesto," says Miss Haven. "We were caught up looking in shop windows, were we not, Miss Charters?"

Modesto waves his free hand in a very foreign manner. "I have asked you before, Miss Haven, to please inform Mrs Modesto if you are not to join us. All that food wasted!"

Wasted? No chance. I'm just thinking of how he'll probably serve it up re-heated for our breakfast, when I catch sight of an old man rapping at the door of number eight with talon-like fingers. A skinny thing, he is, quite engulfed by his overcoat, top hat pulled low over his ears and in his right hand he carries a portmanteau. The glass in his pince-nez winks in the light thrown from Modesto's lamp. I glance back to the main street again and, standing on the corner, hands deep in his coat pockets, is Mr Ripley. When he catches me looking, he tips his hat and moves on.

"Miss Charters? You will join us?" says Mr Modesto from the steps of his house.

As I turn to follow him into the boarding house, the man raps on number eight's door again, calling out, "Is there anybody home? It is Ernst here!" and I almost stumble.

There is no doubt that his thick, guttural accent is German.

CHAPTER
EIGHTEEN

Amah

The key rattles in the lock, and the door swings open. Amah tenses as a draught washes over her. One figure, then another, silhouetted against the shadowy staircase, make their way into the cellar. The first person holds a lantern to Amah's face and she squints against the sudden light.

"She looks hearty enough," he says.

Amah strains to see the planes of his face by the lantern's light. Yes. Just as she thought.

"Ugh," a woman's voice responds; a voice Amah recognised immediately the night before. The woman with the big eyes. "I almost wish she had perished."

The young woman steps forward into the light. She bends down and gives Amah a nasty smile. "Surprise!"

Amah glares at her.

"Ooh, it's cranky," she says. "We've rattled its cage." She moves in closer, inspecting Amah's face, her attire.

"What shall we do with her, my love?" asks a man Amah now knows to be Joshua.

"Undo the tie about her mouth," she says, hands on hips. "I don't want to touch her." She shudders theatrically.

Joshua crouches and pulls the cloth from Amah's mouth. His fingertips brush her cheeks as he removes the gag, and he looks at the back of his hand with surprise. "Her skin is surprisingly soft, actually."

The woman gives him a withering look. "Go fetch the ink and paper, numbskull."

He bounds from the room and they listen to his footsteps scrape up the steps.

Amah tries to lick her chapped lips but her mouth is dry. "What am I doing here?"

"Well, we might ask you the same thing. What were you nosing around Liverpool for?"

"I was trying to raise the money to buy that earring back from you."

The woman smirks as Joshua returns, carrying an inkwell and notebook. "That's what we surmised when we went through your reticule and found all your gewgaws and that nasty little dagger. But when we first saw you, down by the docks, my poor Joshua panicked and thought you'd followed us with that bully boy of yours."

It takes Amah a moment to realise she's speaking of Taff. Taff! He doesn't know where Amah's disappeared to. Has he even noticed yet? Surely, surely. Perhaps he is on her trail right now. But Amah's rising hopes fade quickly. How could that be? He knows nothing of this repugnant pair and Amah herself doesn't know where they have brought her.

"Why am I still here then? Keep the jewels if you must."

"We will. You have a nice little hoard there." She tilts her head as she considers Amah. "How did one such as you acquire such riches? Did you steal them from your mistress? Or perhaps, just perhaps, they were given to you in return for your silence?"

Amah's fury uncoils slowly. "I think if we are to speak of blackmail, you might need to look to yourself."

"Ooh, she's ahead of us, Joshua. Untie her hands and shoulders but keep her legs bound tight." She disappears into the gloom of the cellar for a few seconds and returns, dragging a dusty side-table behind her. She sets the ink and book down upon it. "Now, all we want from you is for you to write us a little letter, and we will let you go."

"A letter saying what?"

"We'd like you to write down who you gave that earring to and why."

"I don't know what you're talking about. Perhaps you should tell me who you had it from yourself?"

The young woman frowns and her mouth screws into a mean pout.

"I'll give you a name," she says. "What about Jonathan Anthony Crewe? Have you heard that name before?"

Amah doesn't move a muscle. John Crewe. Her own John. So these terrible people did get the earring from him. Her heart hurts a little at the thought.

The woman holds the lantern to Amah's face again. "I can see that you do know who I'm talking about." Her voice becomes cajoling, whiny, almost. "Come, just write a note to that effect for us. Admit that you knew him and that you gave him the golden earring. And then you can be on your way." She kneels close to Amah and whispers theatrically in her ear, "Even better. Write about the child you had together."

Amah looks away, the chair creaking beneath her. Joshua scratches his head; the air whistles in and out of his nose. Finally, the woman climbs to her feet again.

"Fine. I thought you'd be stubborn about it. But there is no hurry after all, so we will leave you. Give you time to come to your senses."

She tells Joshua to tie Amah up again and, as they make their way to the door, lantern in hand, Amah says, "Can I have a drink of water, please."

"Demanding old trollop, aren't you?" she says, as she closes the door.

Amah's back aches like it never has before, and she can barely feel her bottom where it is pressed into the hard chair. Every so often a spasm of pins and needles shudder up from the soles of her feet through to her thighs. Closing her eyes, she tries to shut out the fustiness of the cellar, the gloom of her surrounds and wonders if John ever thinks of her anymore. Wonders about her, like she does him. He might not even realise the earring is no longer in his possession. This sorry thought pierces her deep.

What about their rooms above the Walters' on Henderson Street? Could John really have forgotten? The fragrance of the lilies he brought home to her mingled with the smell of Mrs Walters' boiling mutton below. The baskets of handkerchiefs and linen Amah embroidered for the ladies and gents of Liverpool. And the cracks in the ceiling left behind by the damp and blistering paint. They used to gaze up at them from their bed, and John traced shapes with his finger in the air, making up stories about the patterns of cracks like they were constellations in the night sky: the blob that was actually a cheerful butcher — see his big ears, wide mouth — who stole children the same size as piglets to roast on the spit; and the stick-men — legs as tall and thin as a winter oak tree stripped bare — who could wade through rivers, saving village folk from terrible flooding. Most evenings, too, John sipped Irish whisky, so that when they kissed, she would taste its fire on her own lips.

John. How did these people know she'd given the earring to John? And how did it come to be in their hands? A frostiness takes hold of her chest, slowly, thankfully, replacing the melancholy, the foolish nostalgia, she has been feeling for the last few weeks. It's the same frostiness that had fortified her against John's desertion so many years before. Of course, at first she had been distraught, bereft as only she had been when her mother had died, but with time . . . with time those tender edges had hardened, had toughened like a piece of buffalo hide.

Amah opens her eyes and breathes in the dank air. Cocks her head towards the door. Footsteps shuffle their way down the basement steps and, again, the rattle of a key in the lock and the door swings open.

She knows from the silhouette that it is only Joshua returned this time, lantern in hand.

"A drop of tea, madame," he says, raising a teacup to her mouth. "I'm afraid it's rested in the pot a long while now. It's become cool, and you might find it a little strong."

Amah drinks greedily, her thirst forsaking good manners. Some of the tea trickles down the middle of her chin, drips onto her bodice. Only after a moment does she taste the tannin on her tongue, the awful bitterness.

Joshua leaves her for several minutes before returning with another cup of tea. He holds the lantern over the side-table. Nods towards the ink and notebook. "Any chance you would like to pen that letter for us? For another drink?"

Amah gives a tight shake of her head. Keeping a stony expression on her face, she pretends to avoid looking at him by sliding her gaze about the room. She wants to make the most of the feeble light to take in her surroundings. Apart from the doorway, there doesn't seem to be any other way in or out of the basement. A barrel stands in one corner, covered in cobwebs, and a stack of portmanteaus clutter the other. She glances behind, but the light doesn't extend but a foot or two across the dirt floor. She's swift to banish the thought of her spectre — tattered rags, brittle bone — that flashes across her mind. But what if the spectre — that spirit that haunted her childhood — was reaching out to her for help? What if he was benevolent, after all? Amah slumps lower in the chair. What if the spirit was a she? Amah's puzzled as to why this has never occurred to her before. It takes some effort for her to swing her gaze to the front again, and her head lolls a little as she focuses on that man.

Amah struggles to remember what she was thinking of. John, probably, her beautiful John. He's no longer with her. How sad. She can't feel the anger anymore. Joshua is not such a nasty-looking fellow, with that kind smile of his. Not handsome like John was though. Pity this man's nose is so pointy. Amah smiles. She never smiles. Why doesn't she smile more?

Joshua unties her hands. "There. That's more comfortable, isn't it, madame." He pulls the table close. "Perhaps you are now in the mood to write that letter? Just tell us of how you came to know Jonathan Crewe. How he came to have that earring."

Amah's thoughts drift back to John, to placing the dragon orb into the palm of his hand. Curling his fingers — lovely hands he had; fine, yet strong — over her treasure. She'd lifted his fist and kissed it. Binding them together forever. So she had thought.

"Here you are," Joshua says, offering her the pen. The slick of ink on its tip glints in the lamp light. "Tell us."

But Amah can't even lift her arm, even if she wanted to. She feels like she is melting into the timber of the chair, like hot candle wax into a saucer.

"You gave her too much, you stupid man," comes a woman's voice from behind him. Amah didn't notice her enter the cellar. Her voice seems far away, as though Amah hears it through a thin wall. "Joshua, can I not trust you to do anything right? Is this how it will be forever?" The woman's voice rises in frustration.

"I'm sorry, my love." He runs his hands through his thinning hair and Amah feels a mellow delight at the sight of a fine strand floating to the ground. "I gave her the same amount as you take of an evening to find rest."

"Well, clearly the old cow isn't used to it. Tie her up again. We'll return to this in the morning."

CHAPTER
NINETEEN

I lie in my hard, cold bed, and sleep's a long time coming. I rub my feet together, willing them to warm.

My mind skips back and forth through the events of the last couple of hours, and I wonder if I've left any of it out in my letter to Mrs White.

When I heard the Prussian man call out at number eight, I'd had a hard time of it to not stop and gawk. Instead, I hurried into the house after the others and, after swiftly wishing the other two good night, feigning a sudden need to slumber, I locked myself into my bedroom. Without lighting a candle or lantern, I flitted to the terrace doors and looked across at number eight. The two men — the occupant of the house and the Prussian — entered the living room I spied upon the night before, but almost immediately Mrs Modesto's 'scientist' whisked the curtains shut.

I kept a sharp eye on the front door of number eight, waiting for the Prussian to leave. I knew it would have been better to watch from downstairs, but I could still hear the Modesto's or the maids moving about. The court seemed even darker with the light from number eight's living room cloistered behind curtains. A fishmonger paused on the corner, hollering his discounted sprats to the dwellers of Green's Court, waiting a minute or two before continuing on his way. The sorrowful notes of a barrel organ pressed against the night air, while two women, perhaps even the same two I had encountered the night before, sauntered past, baskets piled high atop their heads. I only had time to take two sips of whisky from my flask when the front door to number eight opened again, and the Prussian stepped out.

Rushing out of my room, I ran down the staircase to the bottom landing. I unlatched the front door and poked my head out onto the street. He wasn't to my left. Looking to my right, I could just see his figure move through the shadows onto Brewer Street. Closing the door silently behind me, I pursued the Prussian at a smart trot. By the time I arrived at the crossroads, I was quite out of breath. I stood, panting, my eyes searching the length of Brewer Street. A shoemaker stood before his shop, taking off his leather apron. Several stragglers seemed to be making their way home, probably from the hat factory on the next road. A woman stepped down from her carriage outside the veterinarian's, a spaniel clasped in her arms. But I couldn't see the blasted Prussian.

I cursed myself all the way back to the Modestos'. I'd lost the Prussian.

It went against the grain having to explain myself to Mrs White in my nightly report. My pen squeaked across several pages as I described the labour meeting Miss Haven had taken me to, and how the American was there. Could these people be the Red Brethren, I asked. And although news of the Prussian — Ernst — should really have been my *coup d'état* of the day, having to admit that I had lost him fell rather flat.

And now, in my rather uncomfortable bed, my mind keeps flapping between possibilities. Excitement worms through my belly as I think back on the evening, and I have to admit I am rather enjoying myself. Even amongst all the discomfort associated with these detecting jaunts, the thrill of the investigation is almost — perhaps more — satisfying than the gilt-edged life that preceded this period in my life. Not that I would ever give that up either. It's just that I now have less time, less inclination, to wallow in the envy of other ladybirds who have landed richer gentry or live in fancier homes. I can't even find the time to feel that twinge of jealousy for the proper young women who enjoy easier, more sheltered, upbringings than I have experienced.

I try to burrow deeper into the unyielding mattress. I must find sleep because on the morrow I will need to watch number eight again. Keeping my ear pricked for any suspicious noises from across the way, I close my eyes and let my thoughts go where they will. Did the American see where I reside? I must be careful of him. And where exactly had Modesto been tonight, with his lamp held high?

A dull clunk from below wakes me. Morning light streams through the glass of the terrace doors, for I haven't drawn the curtains. I sit up, swinging my legs over the side of the bed, wiggling my toes against the cold floor boards. Scrambling into my gown, I glance across at number eight but, just as the day before, it's shut away from prying eyes.

I skip down the stairs. I've thought this through and decided I will watch out for the Prussian from Mrs Modesto's sitting room, if possible. It's closer to the front door and will give me more time to chase him again, if need be. I catch hold of the maid and ask her to take my letter for Mrs White to the nearest receiving house as soon as possible, giving her an extra shilling for her trouble. Peeping into the sitting room I see that it's empty, so I make my way to the back of the house where the breakfast things will be laid out in the dining room. I've missed Haven and Beveridge again and, to my relief, Mr Modesto isn't present either. Only Mrs Modesto is seated at the table. Her left hand crumbles a piece of bread while her right hand is lightly clasped about a teacup.

"Good morning, Mrs Modesto," I greet her. "I have a terrible headache. Do you mind if I —" My speech is cut short when she turns to look up at me. The left side of her face is crimson and the flesh across the tip of her cheekbone is quite swollen, encroaching upon her eye.

"But what happened to you?"

"I hurt myself," she says. Her face is expressionless. "It is nothing."

I think of the clunk that had woken me. I also remember the pounding I'd heard the day before coming from the sitting room. I swear, before this case is through, I will stab that man right through the heart. Well, maybe not the heart — but into the fleshy part of his thigh or buttocks or somewhere else satisfyingly fleshy.

Her dark eyes are still on me.

"I have a terrible headache, Mrs Modesto. Would you mind terribly if I rested by your fire in the sitting room with a nice cup of tea?"

She pushes her chair back and slowly takes to her feet, careful with her movements as though her bones ache. "Yes, Miss Charters. That is fine. I join you soon."

"Where is Mr Modesto this morning?"

She shrugs. "He went out. I do not know where."

As she clears plates and dirty cutlery, I pour myself a cup of tea and carry it into the sitting room. Standing by the window, I gaze out onto Green's Court, which seems to be simply crawling with people. I frown to see the organ grinder loitering by the steps of the rag shop. Strange to see him so often in this part of London. I have heard organ grinders quite haunt the streets of Clerkenwell, but this fellow seems to spend much of his time here. A stream of factory girls walks past, followed by a youth lugging a basket of live poultry. I position one of the armchairs at an angle so I can keep a lookout.

It's not long before Mrs Modesto joins me, bringing a saucer of bread and butter that she sets on a little table next to me.

"Thank you," I say. "You're very kind."

She shakes her head imperceptibly, taking a seat in the other armchair. Picking up her Bible, she scans a few lines, flips through to another page. Her lips move as she reads to herself.

She's just gathering up another stripy bonnet — yellow, brown and green this time — when the Prussian man wanders past the window and knocks on the door of number eight again. Springing to my feet, I lean against the window sill and say, "Looks like it might rain, Mrs Modesto." I pretend to gaze up at the sky but, really, I keep my eyes on Ernst until the 'scientist' opens his front door, ushers his guest in.

What can they be doing? I try to think of some excuse to beat on their front door — I could declare that I'm searching for a pet dog or cat, perhaps? Or can I say I am selling something? Something that necessitates me entering the house. My eyes dart from the closed front door to the dark windows.

"I believe fresh air might help relieve me of my aching head," I say to Mrs Modesto, who leans over to read a sentence from her Bible. "I might just try a gentle stroll of Green's Court." She nods, returning to her knitting as I leave.

I step out onto the front step, tying the ribbon of my bonnet. Heavy clouds press down on the street. My heart jumps as number eight's front door yawns wide, depositing Ernst onto the front mat. In the ashen light, he appears younger than I first supposed. His cheeks are sunken, and I can see by the angularity of his wrists and neck that he is skinny indeed, and yet his oversized overcoat makes him seem of more heft at first glance. His eyes are hidden beyond the reflection in the glass of his pince-nez.

He fastens the overcoat buttons at the front, and that's when I realise that the bulk he encases there

184

could not possibly be from his own thin frame. He has placed something underneath the fabric. Something bulky. Something hidden, nestled carefully at his breast. My pulse quickens. My mouth goes dry.

Could it be a bomb? But what else would he be concealing beneath his coat after a visit to the 'scientist'?

I cast about me for … what? Mrs White? A policeman? What would I say to him, in any case? My eyes follow Ernst as he walks in the same direction he took the night before. And I wonder just how far behind him I need to travel to not risk being torn to pieces if he were to explode?

I settle on roughly ten yards. My steps are skittish because I'm pretty sure that I am still not far enough behind, but any further and I might lose him again. An icy shower catches me without my umbrella, and my shoes slip against wet cobblestones. Trailing behind him for a good twenty minutes, I need to keep up a smart trot to account for his wide, yet steady, strides. Soon, I am exhaling cloudy puffs into the cold, damp air and, although my fingers are freezing, a flush of heat warms my body.

The Prussian doesn't seem to be in a hurry, although it does appear as though he has a goal in mind. We pass Leicester Square, rather sordid and soiled this early in the morning. Sodden food scraps, several not-so-gay girls and a drunkard or two strew the rain-soaked paths outside the slumbering music halls and theatres. It's at night, with its glitter of artificial light and the delightful anonymity of shadowy comers, that the area is truly alive and alluring. However, the Alhambra, which the Prussian treads past with nary a glance, remains majestic. I hope today goes well so I can enjoy more evenings there in the future.

We reach Holywell Street and Ernst slows down, glancing up at the numbers above the storefronts. As usual, the street is horribly congested with men leering into shop fronts and sooty gables that pitch towards each other over the narrow road. From a distance, the shops look no less innocuous than any other bookstores to be found in London yet, closer up, titles such as *The Lustful Turk, Part the First* and *The Seducing Cardinal* reveal the true nature of the shops' wares. It seems the Obscene Publications Act hasn't quite found its mark here in these parts. A fat fellow wheezes up to Ernst, flaps his coat open for him to look at something, but the Prussian waves him away. The fat fellow then tries two more men idling ahead of me, but when he turns to me, he claps his coat shut. Not before I see the flat packages within, wrapped in brown paper. I try not to grin. How shocked he would be if I were to demand to buy one of his dirty little books, but I don't have time for such funning.

Ernst crosses the road and pauses outside a shopfront that advertises *Books Bought* under a neat sign that says *John Oates Bookseller*. He looks from right to left to right again before he pushes the door open and disappears into darkness. I linger outside another second-hand bookstore above which hangs a crescent moon with a disgruntled expression on its golden face. The alleyway behind me reeks of piss and

186

God knows what else. I know I should follow Ernst, see what he's up to, but what if his aim is to blow up the shop? Perhaps he is a moralist. Perhaps his aim is to destroy this sordid row of shops.

I fidget with my reticule for a full minute, as though searching for something. I buy chestnuts from a passing costermonger, distractedly peeling and nibbling on three before I realise the flesh is rubbery and stale. Despite the scholarly air I've tried to cultivate, what with my spectacles, sober clothing and severely plaited hair, one man tries to lure me into the alleyway for a suck and, not much later, another asks me to stroke his cock. A steady glare and a reference to Jesus's healing ways moves them each along swiftly.

And still no Ernst.

I'll have to go in.

Waiting for two horse and carts to squeeze past, and four horsemen, I walk across the road. Tension grips my throat tight and it's as though everything is magnified, in sharp relief — the glistening bristles of the chestnut that passes close, its rider's boots in desperate need of a shine; how when he kicks the horse's flank, there is a billow of dust; straw-like manure caked between the pavers; a trolley's wheels creak as a delivery boy runs past — and all too soon I am at the entrance to John Oates' bookstore, staring down at the litter of books that fill a trestle table on the pavement. I push the door open. A bell tinkles and my hackles prick, almost in anticipation of an exploding rush of air and destruction.

All is hushed, though, inside the shop. As I look about me, at the neatly stacked bookcases and the teetering piles of books on the floor, I breathe in the dusty air. I doubt a fresh draught has ever touched upon the contents within these dark walls. A shiver shudders through me, I hope because the rain has left my bodice quite drenched and chill.

It seems I am alone. Moving towards the back of the shop, where I am sure I can hear the murmur of voices, I scan the titles on the spines of books. Harmless enough, inoffensive books, as far as I can gather. It's not until I reach a glass-top counter at the end of the room that I find items of interest, including a generous array of Paul Pry penny weeklies fanned across moth-eaten velvet, and two publications, mysteriously unlabelled and bound in green leather, which sell for the eye-watering amount of a guinea each.

I straighten up as a woman enters from a back room, which is cordoned off by nothing more than a length of curtain across the doorway. She catches me looking at what's displayed in the front counter and pulls a black piece of fabric back across the glass from where it is ruched to the side.

"How can I help you, madame?" The shopkeeper is a plump woman probably not much older than me, yet there is a shock of grey in her wiry hair. As far as I can see, she wears no stays or corset or undergarments of any sort beneath the white bodice that stretches over each roll and rise of her body — although this state of undress does not seem to be in any way salacious in aim, but more indicative of a slovenly manner.

188

The tone of her voice is helpful, yet there is a wary look to her. I realise that she is probably either suspicious I am from some moral group ready to report her more illicit doings to the authorities, or maybe she even worries I am a spy for the police. Well, I am spying, I realise, but not to uncover her trade in pornography.

"A dear friend recommended I come to you," I say. Something clunks to the floor in the room behind, and a male voice growls 'careful'. I can't make out if it's the Prussian's voice or not. What did they drop? Sweat dampens the palms of my hands, and I swallow before I continue. "I've been trying desperately to obtain a copy of a certain book. A book I have had a terrible time finding. I am quite sure I caught a glimpse of it here, before you pulled this sheet over." I tap the glass top with my finger and glance over my shoulder, as though afraid I will be heard. I turn to stare at her, pretending to be as chary of implication as she is. I lower my voice to a whisper. "I believe you have a copy of this book, *Anti-Justine?*"

A smile widens her lips, so much so that she resembles a toad. Her hard little eyes slowly trace my figure and I have to stop myself from cringing. "Where did the likes of you hear of such a thing?"

"Like I said, a good friend told me of it."

"Ha. A good friend indeed." She's still smirking as she sweeps the black sheet aside. Pulling down a panel at the back, she lifts out the book I happened to notice before and hands it to me. I run my fingers over the coarse, brown cover. Its title is etched in black. I flip it

189

open and see that it's written in French and I'm not even sure if my French is up to reading it. Some of the pages seem to be gummed together too; at least I hope it's gum.

A baby mewls from the back and footsteps shuffle across the floor. The woman looks to the doorway. I hope she'll go in, check on what's going on, so I can have a peep too. But she faces me again, so I ask, "How much is this?"

She takes the book back from me and pretends to peruse the front page for a pencilled price, meanwhile taking in my gown, the state of my reticule, the simple gold earrings in my lobes.

"I think my husband has it priced at £1 3s," she says, and I'm surprised she doesn't blush with the audacity.

I can't help but laugh. "My dear woman, that is far too steep. Why, the book is written in French." I rifle through the pages again. "And there are not even any illustrations."

Because I've been listening keenly for noises from the back of the house, I fail to hear the racket from the front of the shop until the shopkeeper's eyes widen and she gapes over my shoulder. Stamping hoofs, pattering footsteps, raised voices reach my ear. I too turn to gape when a wave of men — police constables clad in woollen uniforms as dark and forbidding as midnight — quite ten in all, burst through the shop entrance, shattering the glass of the door, knocking teetering towers of books to the floor. Two of the constables corral the shopkeeper into the corner, while a youngster, his helmet slipping forward over his brow, asks me politely to stay put. The rest of the men rip through the dividing curtain into the back room.

"There's a bomb," I say quietly to the young constable. "There's a bomb. Tell them to be careful. Tell them to stand back." He responds to the urgency in my speech but seems to hesitate at the words.

"A bomb?" he repeats.

I nod vigorously. My heartbeat hammers now and it's with anguish that I watch the back room, half expecting an explosion to decimate the policemen. To destroy me. I try to wrench past the constable, try to flee, but he takes hold of my arm, "Sorry, miss, but you can't go anywhere. Sorry miss."

I'm stopped in my tracks by a familiar voice.

"What on earth are you doing here, Mrs Chancey?"

Relief washes over me, almost dousing the panic. Detective Inspector Hatch. His pale eyes gawp at me and he looks a little aghast to see me in such a place. Comprehension finally settles over his nice face. "You must be on a case," he says in hushed tones, so only I can hear him amidst the shopkeeper's screeching and the yelling and crashing furniture that come from behind.

He is curt when he tells the constable to unhand me and ushers me towards the bookcases that line the side of the room. I cling to his arm as we walk.

"There is a Prussian back there," I say. "I think his name is Ernst. He carries a bomb from a place in Green's Court." I'm not making much sense, but I need to put forward the most salient points as quickly as possible to the detective inspector.

Hatch looks baffled. "Ernst? What makes you think he has a bomb?"

"Well, I've seen him . . ." Seen him what? Visit the Green's Court 'scientist'. Leave there with something bulky hidden beneath his coat? "I am on a case for some War Office people," I whisper to him. "We're investigating a threat of some sort planned for tomorrow."

Amusement lightens Hatch's features. "And you think Ernst is implicated?" he says. The incredulity in his voice gives me pause.

"Yes. I am sure of it." Although, of course, now I am not.

Hatch looks over his shoulder to the back room, where a number of constables still teem. "Come with me, Mrs Chancey."

He leads the way, and the constables move to the side as he enters the back room. We stand in a poky, squalid room. The walls are covered in a horrendous wallpaper; it's difficult to see where the brown pattern leaves off and the grime picks up. There is an objectionable smell and, as I edge closer into the room, I realise it comes from the baby who squalls in the corner, from where it lies on a bed of filthy sheets in a drawer placed on the floor. One policeman holds Ernst fast, his hands pinned behind his back, while another two policemen grasp each arm of, I presume, John Oates, proprietor of this charming bookshop.

"What have we got, Detective Wilson?" Hatch asks of another man who, like Hatch, doesn't wear a uniform.

He leans over the round table in the middle of the room.

"Thousands of indecent photographs, Detective Inspector," he says, flicking a couple towards us. Glancing up, he sees me and quickly tries to withdraw them again, but not before I catch a glimpse of two couples enjoying a parlour orgy, and a woman cupping her ample, bare bosom. "Begging your pardon, Miss."

"And what has Ernst here provided for us today, Wilson?" asks Hatch.

Wilson pushes forward two large tomes. One purports to be a book of natural history for children, while the other is an illustrated book of birds. However, lifting open the sumptuous cover of the bird book, Hatch reveals a neatly cut-out space within. And nestled in this void are tens, perhaps hundreds, of further erotic photographs and pictures.

Hatch looks to the owner of the shop. "Did Ernst bring you these this morning?" But John Oates keeps mum. Doesn't even lift his eyes from the floor.

Hatch turns to me. "Mrs Chancey, did you see Ernst bring these books into the shop?"

My eyes search Ernst's body. His overcoat hangs open. I can only assume that these large books — these secret caches — are what he actually hid against his skinny frame. Damn it!

I nod.

Pornography! I've been chasing this damned man around Soho over some bloody pornography.

Hatch escorts me back out into the shop. "We've had our eye on Ernst for a while. We thought he was bringing in obscene literature from the Continent. He stores it or sends it to a man in Soho."

"In Green's Court?"

"Yes," he says, surprised. "How do you know that?"

"That's where I first encountered him. I thought . . . I thought, seeing as the people on the street think that the man in number eight is a scientist, that perhaps he was the maker of the bombs that were used near the palace and the police station just lately."

Hatch shakes his head. "No. He's no scientist. I left more of my men at his place, which we raided on the way here. I think you'll find he's nothing more than yet another snake oil man, concocting serums to trick the poor and less knowledgeable people of London."

We stand back as the constables march Oates and Ernst through the shop. The bell on the door tinkles as they leave. Damn. I've wasted my time chasing someone with a few rude pictures under his belt.

Hatch instructs the others to allow the woman to collect her baby, and then follow on to the police station.

I feel a bit sorry for the proprietress as she walks past, the baby pressed to her breast. I admire Hatch, I really do, but surely there are more worthy criminals for him to chase down. The woman throws me a resentful look as she leaves the premises and I feel like calling after her that I had nothing to do with this. That I have better things to do than report a few salacious photos.

CHAPTER
TWENTY

Amah

Amah stirs from a heavy sleep and rolls onto her back.
Stretches her legs out straight.

Her eyes spring open. She can stretch her legs.

She turns her head and sees that she is lying on the
hard ground. Feeble light flickers from a tallow candle
that's been placed on the little table, and the ropes that
bound her are now draped across the arms of the
wooden chair. Her fingers press into the cool dirt floor
and she pushes herself up into a seated position. She
feels dizzy and holds her head in her hands. She can just
remember Joshua untying her sometime in the night
and helping her to the ground where she thankfully
sank into a deep slumber. Slumber. Amah's mind might
still feel foggy, but her guess is that they added a
generous dose of laudanum to that cold tea she drank.
The teacup still rests next to the bottle of ink and
notebook on the table. Amah's mouth is furry with
thirst and her stomach quakes with hunger, but she
knows not to drink whatever those two have left behind.

Her legs tremble as she pulls herself to her feet with
the help of the chair. She wonders why they've untied
her.

195

Her eyes fly to the door. Perhaps she is free? They have given up on her and left this place.

She totters to the door and rattles its handle. It holds fast. Her hopes and her legs give way and she buckles to the floor. She beats the flat of her hand against the doors' splintery timber, and her voice is hoarse when she cries, "Let me out! Help! Let me out!" Resting her forehead against the door, she gulps in three large breaths, fights the tears that press at the back of her eyes.

The fury she felt the day before — was it the day before, or another day? How long has she been cooped up here? — the fury she felt is almost doused, grey and weak in a cold grate. She doesn't even have the energy to be angry with John anymore, for his desertion of her and their cosy life on Henderson Street.

She sits with her back to the door and allows her mind to wander, picking through the memories she usually shuns: the scent of him, caught in the cleft between his jaw and collarbone; how he pressed his ear to her growing belly; how amber Heloise's eyes were when she was born.

What was that song he used to croon to the baby, seated in front of the fire? Nonsense words come back to her. *Follol, diddle diddle dol.* Something about an old woman and the market and a pedlar and her dog? She can't remember, but the tune comes back to her. She hums it, a little glumly. Stupid song.

She scrambles away from the door when she hears footsteps descending the steps. Grasping the wall, she pulls herself to her feet, panting, her eyes searching the gloom for anything she can use as a weapon. The chair? She feels she might be too weak to brandish it around. The ink? She can throw it at Joshua's eyes, momentarily blind him. She's half way across the room when the door swings open.

The woman stands there, with that malicious smile Amah dearly wants to slap from her face. In her hand she carries a pistol, which she aims at Amah. To Amah's untrained eye, the gun looks a little antiquated, but she would never doubt the dastardly woman's determination to use it.

"So you're awake. Finally." She moves into the cellar, closely followed by Joshua. "Take a seat, please." She gestures towards the chair with the pistol, and Amah thankfully sinks into it.

Joshua nudges the ink and book aside and places a plate of sandwiches and a jug of water on the table. The woman tosses the remnants of the cold tea onto the ground and fills the cup with water. Amah's throat convulses when she hears the water's splash. But she can't trust it. Can she? What does it matter if they ply her with more laudanum? No. No, she won't take it.

"Drink up," she says. "You must be famished." She holds the cup below Amah's nose but Amah turns her head away.

"Are you afraid we've poisoned it with something?" she asks. "Joshua, she's afraid we've poisoned it. Here, watch, foolish woman."

Amah glances up to watch her sip from the cup. She slides the cup back onto the table and shrugs. "Suit yourself. I'll leave it here in case you want some later."

She tilts her head, her eyes goggling at Amah. "Have you changed your mind about the letter, though?"

"Of course not." Amah is adamant. Nobody knows about that time in her life. Not even Heloise. She certainly won't be sharing her secrets with these two.

The woman shrugs. "Suit yourself. But the longer you take to write that letter, the longer you'll be trapped in this delightful cellar." She turns on her heel and leaves the room, closely followed by Joshua. He closes the door behind them, and Amah hears the lock click into place.

Amah's hand trembles so much when she picks up the cup, some of the water slops over the sides. She downs the water in three long swallows and fills the cup again. The second cup she sips more slowly, conscious of a pang high in her stomach from guzzling so fast. She slumps back into her chair. Closing her eyes, she wonders how she will get herself out of this mess. Maybe she will just have to write that letter, admitting to her connecion with John. A little of the cold anger seeps back into her soul. Perhaps it would serve him right, to see this terrible pair wield whatever mischief they had in mind.

But she's better than that. Revenge has never been part of her armour. It's as useless as regret. She reaches over and picks up a sandwich. Cold beef and mustard. She tears off a corner with her teeth.

CHAPTER
TWENTY-ONE

I'm feeling pretty cranky as I find my way back to the lodging house. Cranky and foolish.

The sun has decided to make an appearance, banishing the grey clouds. I pause at the end of Green's Court and gaze down its length. If the note I found on the body of that man in the Parisian cemetery had nothing to do with the occupant of number eight, or with Ernst, then who here is responsible? My eyes linger over the barber's, the tobacconist's, the shop filled with odds and ends. What excuse would I find for entering the barber's, for goodness sake? I peer further towards the grocer down the other end of the court. A small crowd of people have gathered outside number eight, no doubt agog to find out why the place is swarming with police. But my eyes rest on the Modestos' house. The organ grinder stands by the front door, the monkey crawling from one shoulder to the other. I'm used to his presence now, but I'm surprised to see Mrs Modesto leaning towards him, giving him a hessian bag of something or other. It's the first time I've seen her outside the house, and her skin is luminous in the weak sunlight, pale as a pearl. How very interesting. What is she handing over to the organ grinder? I take a step towards them when I hear someone call my name.

Turning, I see Mrs White staring at me through the window of a stately, black carriage. "Step inside, would you?" she says.

I'm hard put to not cast my eyes to the sky. I'm going to have to account for myself. Hauling myself into the carriage with the help of a footman, I take a seat opposite her.

"What have you found out?" she asks me.

"Well, I've found out that the Prussian has nothing to do with any planned attack," I say, rather tartly. I describe my morning to her. When I finish, she nods slowly, a frown puckering the papery skin of her forehead.

"Our information is not always reliable, unfortunately." She watches a buggy clop by, filled to the brim with children. A man leads a very large dog from the veterinarian's. Three lads stroll past the carriage, the closest one leering cheekily in at the window, which seems to break Mrs White from her reverie. "Is there anything else you can tell me?"

I slump back into the cushioned seat. "Have you considered the local factory workers? The ones I wrote to you about?"

She nods. "Yes. These labour movements can certainly become volatile. As can the Irish."

"And the American? Have you found out anything more of him?" I ask.

She shrugs. "I don't think we need worry about the Yank."

I'm not so sure. I think of his lazy demeanour that is offset by the keen gleam in his eye. He appears to be relaxed, friendly, yet I sense a constant watchfulness about him. "But he was in Paris and he is here now. This sounds nonsensical, but I am almost sure that it was him who tried to do away with me in Paris."

Mrs White's brows lift infinitesimally, but enough to make me feel fanciful indeed.

"We too have been doing a little investigating here, Mrs Chancey. One of our men went through Green's Court, pretending to be from the gas company. I can tell you that apart from number eight and your boarding house and a slender building that houses two young families, the rest are housed by the staff of the shops to be found at street level."

"Nothing suspicious?"

She shakes her head. "It would seem that they all keep such long hours in the company of each other that it would be very difficult indeed for any of them to concoct some diabolical plan or build an incendiary device."

"Which leaves . . ."

"The people who live with you at the Modestos'. Tell me more of them."

But, of course, there is not much more I can tell her, that I have not related in my letters.

She frowns out the window. "Now that I think about it, there has been much turmoil in the country where they are from. It's the seat of anarchy, after all, and as there is no rhyme or reason to these bomb attacks in

London . . . Perhaps you should keep a very sharp eye on them, Mrs Chancey."

I think of the boarding house. I have not had a good look around it — my focus was too much fastened on number eight, damn it — but perhaps Modesto has a secret room he disappears to during the day.

"And keep an eye on the Miss, too. What did you say her name was?"

It takes me a moment to think of who she could mean. "Miss Haven?"

Mrs White nods. "Yes. She seems to keep company with an interesting lot. Disgruntled, Irish factory workers. Sounds very much like the type who might be behind these attacks. They're also the type to be silly enough to call themselves the Red Brethren." She looks contemptuous.

I prepare to depart the carriage when her fingers press my wrist.

"And you must hurry, Mrs Chancey. You only have today to find out what they have planned for tomorrow."

I change into a dry, fresh gown, thinking of Mrs White's last words to me, telling me of the timeline being compiled of all the more important events and appointments to be held on the morrow; of how they would add further security to the Queen's circle and ministers. I asked her if they could just cancel all state activities, but she shook her head, said they were not in the business of alarming the citizens of London. Struggling to button up my bodice, I think of how she's not too bloody shy to alarm me, though, and I wonder if I am just one small cog in an unwieldy machine, its tentacles snaking through both back-alley slums and the more noble households of this gargantuan city. I hope so. I really do hope so. The responsibility of discovering what deadly plan is afoot jangles my nerves, leaving me feeling a little nauseous.

On my way downstairs to visit Mrs Modesto in her sitting room I am intercepted by Miss Haven.

"Miss Charters, I am so relieved you are in. I tried your room this morning, but you had already stepped out, much to my disappointment." Her little mouse face looks eagerly up at me.

"Can I assist you with something, Miss Haven?" I have to work hard to keep an impatient note from my voice. I really do not have any time to waste.

"Oh, I do hope you will," she says, wringing her hands together. "Patrick — I do mean, Mr Connolly — has invited us to a picnic this afternoon, should the weather hold true. It will hold, won't it, Miss Charters? The skies seemed positively blue when I looked out just this moment."

I concede that the day seems to have brightened.

"It's just that, dear Miss Charters, Mr Connolly has invited the two of us to accompany him and some of his closest friends on a picnic. And I really do feel . . . I really do feel that perhaps it would be more . . . more *discreet* if we were to act as escort or companion for each other."

The poor dear. If only she knew she was asking the notorious Heloise Chancey to lend her some decorum.

"I'd be delighted to join you at this picnic, Miss Haven. I was just going to ask you when I might be able to attend one of those rallies again that you kindly took me to the other day."

Miss Haven clasps her hands together and beams. The rosy blush of her cheeks seeps into her ears. "Thank you, kindly, Miss Charters."

She races up the stairs, no doubt to rummage through whatever ribbons, flounces and powders she owns, while I continue on my way to Mrs Modesto's sitting room where I find her seated, knitting her interminable stockings and bonnets. The blow to her cheek and eye has deepened in colour, taking on the shade of an aubergine.

"May I join you, Mrs Modesto?"

"Of course, Miss Charters," she murmurs.

I glance out the window at number eight and my eyes narrow with resentment as two men leave the premises, paper bags tucked under their arms. A constable stands guard by the front door. The ogling crowd has thinned down to two bedraggled women and a number of children.

"What is afoot across the way?" I ask.

"I am not sure, Miss Charters," she says. "No doubt the charwoman will inform us when she returns later today." Her indifference is so complete she doesn't even look up.

She opens her Bible to a certain page, runs her fingertip down its length, and murmurs a word to herself. She then turns back to her knitting, changing the wool from black to a length of green. I pick up a finished stocking from the basket, my eyes taking in the uneven rows. It's inordinately long. Surely too long for an orphan child. Her basket is positively overflowing with skeins of wool. Why such irregular patterns and colours?

"I was surprised to see you earlier with that organ grinder. I've seen him about here quite often. Does he come from your part of the world?"

Mrs Modesto's needles pause. When she resumes, the clack of the needles seems less sure, less fluid, yet her voice is quite level when she explains that the organ grinder takes the woollen clothing to Clerkenwell for her. "There is a . . . what do you call it? . . . a mission there; it can send my socks and bonnets to orphans in Venetia." She finishes the line she is working on and lets the knitting rest in her lap, but doesn't look at me again.

Miss Haven's heels clack across the timber floors above us and the housemaid hurries past the doorway, carrying a broom and pan. I take a seat in my usual armchair and puzzle over Mrs Modesto's quite awful creations. The way she alternates briefly between her Bible and the stockings reminds me of a bank clerk, cross-referencing numbers in ledgers. It's almost as though . . . as though her knitting is guided by the book. My eyes follow the rhythm of her hands: the slide of the needle, the loop of the wool, the stitch slipping into place.

A book as a guide. A book as a guide? Didn't Mrs White mention something when she pointed out the numbers along the edge of the message I found in the dead man's fingers?

A code. Could Mrs Modesto be using the Bible as the key to a code?

I stare as she again turns to the Bible, and it feels as though an icy draught rushes against the back of my neck, forcing me to arch my back.

"Are you comfortable, Miss Charters?" Mrs Modesto's dark eyes find mine.

I squirm a little further into my chair, pretending to change position. "Quite comfortable, thank you."

She leans over her knitting again, a red stripe this time. Her lips are pale, chapped, and her brown hair, oily with specks of dandruff, retains the rows left by the teeth of her comb.

Could it be possible that this woman, who is beaten by her husband and who never seems to leave the house, is a part of some terrible conspiracy? It doesn't seem likely at all. Although, perhaps it is at her husband's instigation.

"May I have a look at this book of yours, Mrs Modesto?" I ask, reaching for it before she can reply. I close the cover over so I can have a good look — the title, the colour — but before I can, she places the palm of her hand upon the cover and presses it back to the table.

"Please, Miss Charters, it is very precious to me. Perhaps leave it."

"Of course. I totally understand. I too have a Bible that is of great value to me, not because of its monetary worth, you understand, but because it was my

206

grandfather's. Has your Bible been in your family long?"

"Mr Modesto. He gave it to me when we married."

"Oh, what a charming gift." That man just gets worse and worse in my eyes. "And where is he today?" I ask.

Mrs Modesto drops a stitch. Bites her lip as she retrieves it. "I am not sure, Miss Charters. Most days he is either in his study writing to friends back home, or he is out. I do not know where."

The maid carries a tray into the sitting room, knocking it against the doorjamb so that the bottom of the tray is aswim with spilt tea by the time she bangs it down on the side-table. She titters a little but leaves without mopping it up.

"You will join me, Miss Charters?"

I see my chance to poke around while she is preoccupied with her tea. "No, I think I'll have a little rest in my room before I venture out with Miss Haven."

I climb the stairs to the next floor. My room is to the right and to the left I can hear Miss Haven humming as she prepares for her afternoon outing. The stairs creak beneath my tread as I make my way to the third floor where I assume Mr Beveridge and the Modestos' reside. If I am to come across either of the men, I will act flummoxed, as though I am searching out Miss Haven.

I cannot be sure which door leads to the Modestos' rooms. I know from Miss Haven that Mr Beveridge is out of the house, driving his bus, strictly between the hours of 8a.m. and 7p.m. every day except Saturday.

I press my ear against the first door. Nothing. I try the handle, but it is locked. Crossing the cramped landing, I listen at the next door, which I think must be the Modestos' as it seems to traverse the front of the house. I knock very lightly, but there is no response. Pushing the door open a crack, I peep in at a bedroom. Pushing a little further, I step over the threshold, glancing once behind me, to make sure nobody follows. The room smells of musty sheets and clothing in sore need of laundering. The bed is made, but only in the sense that the top cover has been pulled roughly up over the pillows. The dresser's surface is positively cluttered with bric-a-brac — dusty lavender poking out from the top of a chipped vase; an assortment of pipes, two broken, one still stuffed with tobacco; cheap cufflinks; one potato, sprouting; a haggard ball of navy wool; one brown glove — absolutely nothing of interest.

I move a little further into the bedroom. I hesitate, check the staircase over my shoulder again, make sure nobody sees me. Peering into the small side room, I see that there is a desk and chair, not unlike in my rooms, yet this desk is much larger, made from handsome oak. The desk is strewn with paper and bottles of ink, two pens left carelessly to the side. I tiptoe closer, my heartbeat quite tripping over itself. The spidery scrawl upon the paper is in another language. I take up the uppermost page, however, and quickly fold it. Shoving it down the front of my bodice, I skedaddle.

CHAPTER
TWENTY-TWO

Amah

Perhaps it is just the damp of the cellar closing in on Amah, moving up through the soles of her shoes, leaching into her bones. Her throat feels tight and she shivers uncontrollably. Another wave of nausea rolls through her body and she hacks into the bucket Joshua has left her in place of a water closet. She pants, resting her head back against the stone wall. Stares across at the bowl that held the soup she ate for supper. After the sandwich Amah had felt an uncomfortable cramping, but only after eating the barley soup had she vomited.

That wicked woman is poisoning her. Arsenic probably. Amah has read in the newspapers of its lack of taste, how simple it is to procure. To what end, though? Were they trying to break her? Scare her into writing that letter? And all for an earring? Amah is afraid that if she doesn't capitulate soon, she won't survive this ordeal. But if she does write the letter, who's to say they will allow her to crawl from this hellish cellar alive?

CHAPTER
TWENTY-THREE

Miss Haven tries to cover her impatience with a tight smile as I dart into the shop to send my letter to Mrs White. I have written to her of Mrs Modesto's Bible and how I think it might just be the key to a code of some sort. I also enclosed Modesto's page with mine; she should know of someone who can decipher his scribble.

When I come back out onto the court, the day seems positively bright compared to the fustiness of the shop. I follow Miss Haven to the corner. Although the weather is quite mild, she wears a woollen stole thrown about her shoulders, which has a trim of rather moth-eaten fur. Perhaps she imagines her little mouse face is nicely framed by the ... What is it? Cat fur? Rabbit?

"Oh, there they are," she says, pointing across the road to where Mr Connolly buys pork pies from a street vendor.

Next to him stands the dratted American. Ripley. Tipping his blasted hat at me. Mrs White said he need not be any concern of mine, but I am not so certain. It's suspicious indeed how he seems to pop up at every turn.

"That's a dapper hat you have there," I say, when we reach them. I smile but can't keep the sour note from my voice.

"Newfangled, these are. Like them cavalry hats back home," he says, taking his place next to me as we walk.

We follow Connolly, who carries a large basket. There's a skip to Miss Haven's step as she chatters away, looking up at him once in a while.

"Do you know where we are headed?" I ask Ripley.

"Green Park," he says. "Dang lot of factory workers will be there, I believe. With their families."

"Pleasant," I remark, but I'm also thinking how a gathering of families would actually be a clever way to cover up another meeting. Keep any secret deeds away from the police.

"How'd you come to meet Connolly?" I ask him.

"Met him in America, I did. Good man. Very passionate."

"Passionate about what?"

Ripley halts to choose five apples from a cart. As he pays the vendor, he says, "About many things. Mostly about what is fair and right for the working man. You heard his speech."

"I did. And will the same people be at the picnic today?"

"Probably."

It doesn't take us long to reach the park. We join a straggle of people who also make their way along the path.

"Constitution Hill, Miss Haven," says Connolly, turning to include Ripley and me in what he has to say. The pleasant burr of his accent doesn't quite take the chill from his words. "It's seen three attempts on the Queen's life, you know. And the death of one prime minister. Not a poor record at all. Pity it were only attempts, though, not successes." He winks at Ripley, and I can't help but look sideways at him too.

Ripley nods at the Irish man. "But I'm afraid you've shocked Miss Charters, Connolly. She's probably a staunch royalist." And I wonder if there is the slightest note of warning in his voice.

"Not at all," I murmur, hoping to further the conversation, but another fellow joins Connolly and in not many more moments we arrive at the picnic spot, nestled beneath several oak trees. The grass squelches underfoot as I tread, still a little sodden from the earlier shower. How I hate a picnic. The flies, the ants, the uncertain weather. Perhaps as many as twenty families sprawl across interconnecting blankets and, standing about, there seems to be the same number of single males again. Some of the men only wear vests over their shirts, while most of the women have warm, woollen shawls, of chequered or paisley design, drawn over their grey gowns or white bodices. Connolly chooses a space next to a buxom woman, her giant of a husband and their four children. The woman slaps the eldest boy over the back of his head so that his cap falls to the ground, tells him to go find somebody named Ralph, fetch their quart of milk back from him.

Connolly flaps the blanket wide so that it settles across the grass, a spray of woodpigeons rising into the air, landing on the branches of a nearby hawthorn.

212

I make the excuse of procuring bread rolls from a coster I can see in the near distance and, weaving a slow path past chattering circles of people, I keep my ears pricked for news that might be of interest to Mrs White. It very soon becomes clear to me that most of the picnickers are Irish, and while they seem to be bent upon a merry time, I clock at least two small clutches of men who, mugs of ale in hand, speak to each other in low voices. I pause by one such group, ostensibly to look about me, but they stop talking, wait for me to move on.

By the time I return to the others, Mr Connolly's tea things — three large pork pies, a jar of pickles, two green bottles of wine, a chunk of cheese and Ripley's five apples — are spread across the blanket. I add my offering of bread and lower myself to the ground and, as I lean my palm and fingers against the blanket, I can feel damp rise through the thin fabric. Ripley sits with his back against the gnarled trunk of a black poplar, his long legs stretched out before him. He peels and slices an apple with a short, sharp knife.

"I still think it's mighty amusing that we met up in Paris like that, and then bang straight into each other here as well." His drawl sounds lazy, relaxed, but I can tell he's alert. I'm not sure what his game is, but I might as well follow suit.

"Indeed. Especially as that tavern in Paris, and the workers' meeting in Soho, are not my usual haunts."

His eyes narrow, but he smiles too. "Is that right?"

"Not my sort of places at all," I say firmly. "In fact," here is my chance, "I found Paris terribly savage. Would you believe I was very nearly run down and killed?" I think of how poor Violette did not escape being murdered. I watch Ripley's face closely, but he gives nothing away.

"No kidding?"

"No. I do not jest. Very alarming, it was. I returned to London directly after that."

"But you were saved?"

I nod, picking up a piece of the pared apple.

"Perhaps someone shoved you away in time?"

I stare at him. Lucky guess? Or witness?

I chew slowly, and then say, "That's exactly what happened."

"Dang lucky, you were then." He jumps to his feet. "Come on. Get up. If you insist on frequenting rowdy areas, then you need to learn some ways of protecting yourself." He walks a short distance to a maple tree, a little way from the others.

Standing, I brush leaves and crumbs from the hem of my skirt. The buxom woman on the next rug pours some wine into a cup, while her baby kicks its bare heels in the air.

Beneath the silvery leaves of the maple, Ripley shows me how to drive the palm of my hand into an assailant's nose; how to stomp on his foot, or kick in his knee. I'm surprised at how seriously he takes his task. The teasing smile is gone, his wide jaw quite set.

"Now, turn around. I'll show you what to do if you are attacked from behind."

I feel his presence at my back. I wonder if it is his breath or a gentle breeze that tickles the hairs at the nape of my neck. My shoulder blades tighten.

214

His large hands circle me, and I flinch, despite the park being so full of frolickers he could not possibly try anything here.

"Now, if anyone ever happens to try and grab hold of you like this . . ." He lifts my left arm, high, so it snakes between his hold and my ear. "And step back with this leg," he taps my left foot, with his. "Now turn! Quick. Push against me as hard as you can as you turn."

I give it a tentative go.

"Nice one. Try again, with more force."

This time I put my bodyweight into it, but my movements are still too slow to make a true impact. We try it a third time, and this time I thrust so hard, I fall against his chest.

He laughs as he steadies me, says, "All right. No need to get spooney."

Spooney! I grin too, but give him a look.

Fourth time goes more smoothly, and after I break free from his hold, he grins and says, "And then you poke him in the eye. Or run."

My smile fades as I catch sight of a familiar face. Could it be Cyril again, slinking past the small crowd who cheer on an unruly game of football? I'm sure it's his lank hair and pasty skin I can see.

"Is that your friend over there, Mr Ripley?" But by the time I point, Cyril has bobbed out of sight.

Ripley gazes far into the crowd, shakes his head. "Can't see anyone familiar."

"I thought I might have glimpsed him seated with you in the taproom of the Clover the other day."

"Spying on me, were you?" But before I can remonstrate, he continues, "Nah. If it's the guy I think you're speaking of — pale little rooster? — I don't know 'im. He was just having a snifter on his own, as far as I can remember."

I peer around for Cyril again, but seem to have lost him. I can't understand why the frightful little beast keeps popping up. Although, maybe I am mistaken. Perhaps there is a working-class Cyril doppelganger roaming Soho. Frowning, I walk back to our blanket and kneel down.

"What actually brought you to London from so far away, Mr Ripley?" I ask, pouring myself some of the red wine Connolly has brought.

"Just trying to find my way home, like everyone else in this life." He smiles, but it's half-hearted, nothing on his usual cocky grin.

"But surely you have left your home to come here."

"Nah. I was born in Ireland, you know. County Mayo lad."

I'm surprised. There is nothing of the Irish brogue in his speech. "You must have travelled to America at a very young age."

"Yep, indeedy. Long ago now. My pa couldn't feed us in Ireland, you know, back then. Terrible famine. Do you know about that?"

I nod, too ashamed to admit that no, I don't know a lot about it.

"I remember my gran dying. Took her ages and ages too. You know when a fresh cob of corn starts out plump and pearly, but left on the shelf too long turns

216

dry, thins out to hollow husks. Like that. It was just like that." There's a tautness across his mouth as he empties the bottle of wine so that it sloshes over the edge of the cup onto his fingers. "And when Ma started to go the same way, Pa upped sticks and moved us to Boston." He gulps down half the cup. "Too late for Ma though. She died on the boat over."

"I'm so sorry, Mr Ripley."

"Yeah. Well. That was just the beginning of our troubles." He takes his place next to the tree trunk again. "We swept our way through dirt and manure across the country to the east until Pa found some work in a copper mine. Lost his eye, then his life. You haven't lived if you haven't worked in one of them mines, I can tell you. Drenched in copper, you are. Breathe it, eat it." He rubs the fleshy part beneath his right thumb. "Worked there until I were about fifteen years old, I reckon. Had copper sores for years."

"That's truly terrible, Mr Ripley." I have nothing else to offer. I know as well as anyone the bitter taste that comes with memories of hardship. And how inconsequential another's sympathy can be. I don't know if it's his story, or if it's the wine, but I feel myself softening towards him. I could become fond of his brash ways, his constant humour, his almost brutish physique.

"So, yeah," he continues, "I guess you could say I am in sympathy with Connolly and his friends." He leans back against his tree, pulls his hat low over his forehead, as though ready for a nap, so I suppose he has decided he has revealed enough.

217

I'm not sure where Miss Haven has disappeared to, but Connolly is standing in a group of five fellows, their heads bowed in towards each other as they talk.

"I wonder what they talk of so earnestly," I say, sipping my wine. "Poor work conditions?"

"Never know with this Irish lot. Perhaps it is some Fenian business they speak of," he murmurs.

"Fenian?"

"You haven't heard of the Fenians?" The brim of his hat still shadows his eyes, but I am quite sure they are trained upon me. "Irish Republican Brotherhood."

Brotherhood? Republican Brotherhood?

I shake my head in wonder. "Never heard of them. Who are they?"

Ripley pushes his hat back again, sits up straighter. "They want a free Ireland. You've never heard of them?" Incredulity sharp in his voice.

Again, I shake my head, while scoring this information into my mind for Mrs White. Fenians. Republican Brotherhood. I watch Connolly and his mates, remembering his words about Constitution Hill. What would they be willing to do to achieve a free Ireland?

"And do you consider yourself a Fenian, Mr Ripley?"

But before he can reply, Miss Haven returns, telling me it is time to go back to the lodging house if we are not to face Modesto's ire again. She seems to be a little put out, and I wonder if she's feeling sore that Connolly has snubbed her in favour of his more political cronies. As I toss back the last of the sweet wine, Ripley insists on escorting us home, but for once he's quiet as we walk, perhaps caught up in memories of being buried deep below the earth's surface, with the dust heavy in his lungs and the stutter of his young, frightened heart.

A starling, its feathers a spangle of gold and black, twitters in a branch above. Its handsome plumage reminds me of my favourite ball gown and I console myself with the thought that it won't be terribly long until I can resume my usual life filled with theatre, sumptuous dining and revelry. Not terribly long at all. But instead of feeling consoled, I feel a little bilious, uncertain of what the morrow will bring.

CHAPTER
TWENTY-FOUR

Amah

The tallow candle gutters low in its saucer, losing its struggle against the gloom of the cellar. Amah has no way of knowing if it is day or night outside. Her stomach has been scoured of any nourishment, leaving her feeling heavy with fatigue. She remembers things she hasn't dwelt on in years, things that used to form a hopeless, repetitive loop in her mind, driving her to the very brink of her senses. The hardship she faced when what little money John left with her dried up. How sultry the day was — bringing the pong of rotting fish and clammy sea water — when she finally realised he would never return to them. The mewling of a baby's cry; the weary chore of keeping their clothing and faces clean, so they didn't look like the pathetic waifs that haunted the dockside slums. Amah rubs the back of her hands, remembering how dry and papery they were from washing dishes in Ping Que's scullery; the sting of a torn fingernail quick when she helped Mrs Walters wash the sheets and shirts of the merchants' families for a few extra shillings. How Heloise was thrown together too often with the Walters' eldest daughter. How enamoured she became with the Walters girl's golden

220

hair, her freckled skin and her pretty, fairy ways. Heloise — always so foolish — whose head was so easily turned by anything that sparkled or held the promise of adventure.

Joshua enters the room, interrupting Amah's glum thoughts, with a fresh jug of water and another plate of sandwiches. Amah turns her head to face the wall. She won't look at him or the food. He leaves the cellar, closing the door behind himself and she listens to the sound of his footsteps fading as he climbs the stairs.

Amah frowns. Something bothers her. She tries to remember what she was thinking of before Joshua entered but, shaking her head, she realises that's not what troubles her. It was something to do with Joshua. Her eyes take in the ink and notebook that still rest upon the table, and the food — surely poisoned — that he has left behind. She stares at the door. Joshua walked from the room, shut the door, walked up the stairs. But she hadn't heard the key rattle in the lock.

The muscles in her weakened legs ache as she stands and makes her way across the cellar. Taking a deep breath, she grasps the door handle and turns. Keeps turning. No resistance. She pulls the door open an inch, and a cool draught of air sighs against her nose and lips. Opening the door wider, she peers up the staircase into the cavernous darkness.

Night time.

Amah fetches what's left of the candle and returns to the doorway. By its flickering light, she gazes up the flight of stairs. Her heart gallops. A wave of dizziness sweeps over her but is immediately snuffed by the force

221

of her determination to escape. She will not allow her weakened body to hamper this opportunity to flee her cellar prison and that dastardly couple. First, she slips off her left shoe, then her right. She wonders if she should just leave them behind, but decides she'll carry them, use them as projectiles if need be. With one stockinged foot, she tests the bottom step, resting her weight upon it. No creak. She tests the next step with her other foot. Again, no creak. Only the fifth stair bows a little, emitting a slight squeak. Amah freezes. Waits. Her ears pricked for any trace of movement or voice. When nothing happens, she continues up the remaining stairs, until she finds herself in the hallway. A rug, the colour of port, runs its length, leading from the front door through to the back. She moves further into the hall and looks above. On the second floor, gentle lamplight flows from a room towards the back of the house. She hears a low voice murmur something, and the shrill notes of the woman's response, but they are too far away for Amah to know of what they speak.

Amah tiptoes to the back of the house. She holds the candle aloft and sees that the room to her right is a cramped, old-fashioned kitchen. A length of wood barricades the back door. Amah gently places the candle and shoes on the floor and, cursing the trembling of her feeble arms, she inches the bar upwards, out of its brackets. By the time she lays the bar on the kitchen table as quietly as she can, perspiration prickles her hairline.

She turns back to the door. Please, please don't be locked too. She doesn't know how she would begin to search for the key. Her hands shake as she reaches for the handle and when it unlatches, she almost cries out loud in jubilation. Peeping over her shoulder to check that all is still clear, she slowly pulls the door open. The first puff of air blows out the candle, but that is all right, for moonlight bathes the garden. She picks up her shoes and backs out through the doorway, closing the door softly behind. She doesn't pause to put on her shoes but runs as fast as her jittery legs will take her across a raggedy patch of lawn and into the surrounding woods.

Twigs and prickles jab the soles of her feet through her stockings, and low-hanging branches twist in her hair and scratch her face, but she's heedless. She just wants to put as much distance between herself and those two as she possibly can before they notice she is gone. She keeps up a quick pace and, before long, her laboured breaths wheeze from her chest and she clutches at a tight stitch in her side. She stumbles into a rut, twisting her ankle, which is already weakened from a bygone injury. Falling to her knees, she has to clamp her hands across her mouth to stop from gasping with the pain of it. She rocks a little as she massages her leg just atop where her ankle throbs.

She drags herself towards the closest tree and leans against it. Leaves whisper in the slight breeze and she wonders if she can hear the trickle of a stream not too far away. A low rustle in the undergrowth nearby reaches her ears, too bold, too light, to be from a person. Perhaps a hedgehog, or even a fox. Her eyes search out what they can in the darkness. A thick canopy of foliage blocks most of the moonlight and she can just discern the silvery night sky through the skeletal silhouette of branches. She thinks her shoes lie near where she fell, perhaps three metres away, but she's too sore, too exhausted to crawl across the scrubby forest floor to check. She leans her head back against the tree and closes her eyes.

It takes more than a minute for her breathing to slow down. She pulls her knees up to her body. She wants to curl up as small as possible, be invisible, in case the couple come searching for her. The woods seem extensive though; it would be difficult for them to know where to start. And if they do come looking for her this night, Amah's sure she will see their approach by the light of their lamps which will, she fervently hopes, give her time to scramble away and find another hiding spot.

Amah's not sure how much longer the black night will conceal her. She's uncertain as to whether there are several hours available to her in which she can hobble to a safe haven, or only an hour or two until the pale dawn reveals her whereabouts. She rotates her aching ankle and then places her foot flat on the ground and pushes, as though to stand, but a sharp pang spirals up her calf and she collapses back again. Her body is taut with pain, and she has to will herself to relax. She will rest a short while. And then she will manage somehow to climb to her feet and hop her way out of the woods, if need be.

She is almost dozing, the tips of her nose, her feet, her hands cooling with the night air, when a noise, distant and muffled at first, moves closer, becomes clearer. Footsteps. Treading through the brushwood, crushing dry leaves. But she's almost certain the footsteps are not coming from the direction of the house in which she was held captive. She stares to her left, her eyes straining against the blinding darkness. Scraping the palms of her hands against the rough bark of the tree trunk, she tries to pull herself to her feet, but her hand slips and she jerks to the ground again. The steps come closer. She can't be sure how close because her heartbeat crashes in her ears. She grunts with fright when something — pale, with raised hand, like that spectre, the spectre of her childhood — lurches out from the forest's gloom and descends upon where she crouches.

CHAPTER
TWENTY-FIVE

I lie back on the hard mattress and my eyes take in how the moonlight pools through the glass doors into my dingy room, touching its ghostly fingers to the chest of drawers, my portmanteau, my little boots that I've kicked off in the middle of the floor, the dark timber of my bed's footboard. A strong wind has picked up, rattling the doors, making the terrace railings creak. I wouldn't be surprised if one day soon — tonight perhaps — the whole thing falls to the ground in one loud, deadly crash, wrenched from the front of the house like a crusty carbuncle. In the grate, orange flames, tapered and weak, lick hungrily at the black edges of two pieces of coal. The sudsy aftertaste of yet more herrings for supper lines my mouth, despite a good scrubbing with my toothbrush.

Instead of donning my nightdress, I've changed from my picnicking gown — still damp and muddy about the edges — into the one I wore earlier in the day, and although I haven't worn a crinoline since arriving in Soho, my thick petticoats and skirt flow over the side of the narrow bed. It is not only because I know I will find no sleep that I remain attired in a morning gown, but also because I want to be ready if anything should happen. I want to be prepared to leap into action.

I know why I keep an eye on the terrace doors. They have troubled my sleep each night I have spent here. Although not made of sturdy stuff, that terrace would be easy enough for a strong man — or robust child, actually — to swing himself onto. And although I think, if someone were to spy on me or try to break into my room in such a way, that they would surely fall through the splintered flooring or topple the whole structure, I can't help but watch.

My heart jumps as the doors shake again, the strong gust of wind whistling through the cracks. The firelight leaps for a second, then returns to a low crackle. Truth be told I have often wondered if whoever tried to kill me in Paris would find me in such a way, finish off what he couldn't in Paris. Somehow jemmy the terrace door open when I sleep, slip across the floor, slide the keen edge of a knife across my throat. I reach across for my reticule and hug it to my side. My fingers trace the hard outline of my pistol.

If you'd asked me the day before, my money would have been on Ripley as that fellow. But now I am not so sure. That whole defence lesson rigmarole. What was that about? And he hinted that he was the one who pushed me out of the way of that careening carriage. It was a hint, wasn't it? In my letter to Mrs White tonight, I wrote everything I could remember of Connolly and what Ripley told me of the Fenians. RB. Instead of sending the letter through normal channels, I paid the barber's boy to run it straight to Pall Mall. Surely this is the break they are searching for. Hopefully they will halt whatever disaster is in store for tomorrow.

From the corner of my eye I see a shift in the gloom. I turn my head, the rest of my body tense. I peer towards the door that leads from the hallway into my rooms, and I catch the slightest movement in the darkness. As though the brass door handle is being turned. I know the door is locked, though, and the key lies on the chest of drawers. But perhaps there is another — of course there must be another! — and my heart thrums so hard I press the palm of my hand to my breast-bone. I stare and stare. Nothing. The handle remains still. My eyes fly to the inch-wide gap at the bottom of the bedroom door, and the shadows there seem to me to be irregular. Two black shapes, like feet, wait on the other side of the door. Someone listening, in the darkness, for me.

I must be imagining it. But I watch until my eyes dry, film over, and I have to blink. When I re-focus, the shadow under the door is uniform again. No black shapes. I wait, my heart pounding so loud I'm surprised I can hear the stair creak or the moth that flutters its way across the ceiling. Rain falls so forcefully the iron railings seem to hum with the pressure. Finally, I sit up, wincing at the hollow groan of the bed's frame. I tiptoe to the second room and bring the desk chair out. I pause in the middle of the floor, clutching the chair to my chest like a weapon. Perhaps whoever waits has not left at all. Perhaps they linger to the side of the door. Ready to burst in. Pounce.

Regardless of the loud scraping sound it makes, I jam the back of the chair beneath the door handle. Wedge the damn thing in place.

And then it occurs to me afresh: if Ripley didn't try to murder me in Paris, who did?

CHAPTER
TWENTY-SIX

Amah

"Madame," a low, male voice says to her. He drops to a knee beside her. "What are you doing out here so late in the evening?"

His voice. Something about his voice stops Amah short. John? Could it be her John? She knows it can't be so, is sure it can't be so, but her heart smarts to hear this voice so like his.

A match flares and the man lights a small lantern. He holds it between them, and she can see that he is young — early twenties, perhaps — and his hair is dark, his eyes blue, unlike John, who was fair with eyes the colour of an overcast sky.

"Please. You must help," she says to him. "They might come for me." She peers into the darkness behind.

"Who will come after you?"

"I don't know their names. A young couple. In a house through the woods. They've held me captive these last few days."

The young man takes in Amah's face, her unkempt hair. A light frown puckers his brow. "Come, take my hand and I will assist you." He holds his hand out to her. "My name is Christopher. I live nearby."

230

"I'm afraid I've twisted my ankle," she says.

Christopher hauls her to her feet, where Amah gingerly tests her foot against the ground. By the light of the lantern, Christopher searches for Amah's slippers and helps her slide them on.

"This way," he says, gesturing in the direction from which he came. "It was lucky I decided upon a walk tonight, or you might have frozen, I feel."

"Are we on your land?"

"We are indeed. Know these woods like the back of my hand. Been scouring them since I was a young lad. I often go for a walk of an evening like this when I've had nothing more to do than read the news and stare into the fire." His stride is unhurried, so that Amah can keep up.

"Where are we?"

Christopher pauses for a moment, looking down at her. "You don't know where we are?"

Amah shakes her head. "I'm afraid I was brought here against my will."

"You must tell me of it as soon as you are recovered," he says, adding, "You'll find we are near the township of Eccleston, madame."

Not terribly far from the Liverpool harbour then. Amah is familiar with the area despite never having visited before. They continue on their slow way. Amah's fingers clutch the young man's twill sleeve as she limps along.

"And tell me, just what time is it?" she asks.

"Close on midnight, I should think. I say, would you like me to carry you?"

Amah shakes her head, 'No, thank you,' she says even though she has to grit her teeth against the ache in her ankle. But she much prefers the pain to the indignity — the uncomfortable intimacy — of being lifted into this young man's arms.

At their sluggish pace, it's a good half an hour before they set foot on a neat, pebbled driveway, pale against its verdant surrounds, that leads to a sprawling manor house.

"This is my home. Crewe Hall," Christopher says.

Amah halts, her hand falling from the young man's arm. "Crewe?"

"Yes. I am Sir Christopher Crewe." He sounds a little pompous, but then, by the light of the moon Amah sees a glimpse of his teeth when he grins. "Still not used to saying it, to be honest. Not so long ago when my poor old pater passed away."

But Amah doesn't ask. Won't ask. Keeps walking, listening to the crunch of their footsteps as they follow the driveway.

"Describe this pair to me," Christopher asks her.

He's ensconced her in a soft armchair by the fire and wrapped a blanket about her shoulders. The housekeeper — sniffing with disapproval — has brought her tea, and Amah's fingers are curled thankfully about the teacup's heat. But she's not wholly relaxed. Her eyes dart to the row of four windows that extend from ceiling to floor. She's worried her kidnappers might burst in through them and whisk her away to that dark cellar again.

232

"The man was perhaps of five and thirty years. Sharp features, you know, almost like a rodent. I heard the woman call him Joshua a number of times. She was much younger than he, and quite pretty. Very large eyes. I don't know what her name was."

Christopher takes a seat across from her and his gaze is solemn. "Why were they holding you against your will, do you think?"

By the tender light of the fire, Amah can see it now. The lines of his jaw; something about the hair that curls onto his temple. "You're John's boy, aren't you? Jonathan Crewe."

Christopher's eyebrow lifts, but he doesn't look terribly surprised. He nods. "I am. And I believe that perhaps — before my time, before he married my mother — my father knew you. Knew you quite well." His voice is gentle, understanding almost. She has to look away, blinks as she stares into the fireplace.

She allows bitterness to snuff the hurt. "Yes. We did know each other quite well." Her eyes find his. "But how do you know of this?"

He leans back in his chair. "I wasn't of age when he died, so my uncle took control of the estate. It was only a year ago that I gained access to all my father's papers. I found a modest annuity, made out to a Li Leen Chan, that my father had organised after my younger sister was born."

Amah thinks of that long ago visit from the lawyer, Mr Villin, one afternoon when she was feeding Heloise a supper, yet again, of bread soaked in a little milk, and how he told her of the allowance she was to receive from an anonymous source. Amah has always wondered, suspected even, that the money was from John, and as much as she would have liked to toss it back into his fainthearted face, she was thankful. It allowed for them to move away from the docks, from the house on Henderson Street that had become increasingly slovenly with each year. In a bid to prise Heloise away from the Walters' girl and the Liverpool back-alleys, Amah moved as far as the first instalment of money could take her, to Chester. But Heloise never did settle. Hated the school Amah enrolled her into, hated the staid town with its neat, quaint buildings.

"I also found a single earring and this ..." Christopher stands and makes his way to a side board. He takes an envelope from the top drawer and hands it to Amah. Her mouth drops open as she slides out a photograph of Heloise, of when she was perhaps eleven, twelve years old. She is dressed for school and her smile is coy, secretive as she peers into the camera's lens. Amah has never seen the photo before.

"This is very odd," she says. "This likeness was taken several years after we last saw your father. I really don't know how he came to have it." That little scamp, Heloise. Amah never did know what she was up to, but she readily believed that the girl willingly posed for the stranger's photograph in exchange for what? Ribbon, a silk handkerchief, money?

"But the earring is missing," Christopher says.

Amah nods. "The dreadful couple who kept me imprisoned have it. I think they had the idea that they could blackmail you in some way with it, with the knowledge of who it came from."

Christopher shakes his head. "My careless sister and her wastrel of a husband, no less. I suspect they kept you captive in the old dowager's house, which is located on the other side of the woods. My foreman mentioned to me that he thought he saw smoke coming from the chimneys there yesterday." He sighs. "My sister and her husband are always trying to come up with ways of making money out of me. They must assume I have no idea of your existence."

"How did they track me down? They obviously found the earring . . . but then?"

"We still have the records of where the annuity was sent. The trail leads from Liverpool to Chester to London."

To South Street. Amah nods. Thinks of how the money helped pay for that house in Bloomsbury.

"My sister, Lilian." Christopher shakes his head again. "I'm afraid Father spoilt her too much. She's run through her own inheritance, her husband's riches and now is bent upon tapping into what is left of mine."

"Her name is Lilian?"

"Yes. Father named her. After you, I suspect."

Amah takes a moment to digest this. Li Leen. Lilian. The young woman was named after her? She gives a huff of laughter at the thought.

"He must have been very fond of you, madame," Christopher says.

Amah stares into the fire again.

235

"He must have been. He told me of you once, you know. He was pretty far gone on a bottle and a half of claret, not long after my mama died. He talked of our duty to this estate, of carrying on the line and so forth. That's when he mentioned a lost love and how he inherited all of this quite unexpectedly. His uncle and three cousins had died in a scarlet fever outbreak. He was terribly glum when he spoke of the difficult decision he had found before him: whether to take on the responsibility of this baronetcy or to continue on with his happy, simple life."

Difficult? It shouldn't have been a difficult decision. How could he desert their sunny child with the dimple in her cheek? How could he leave Amah's arms, when her skin was still fragrant and soft? Christopher is not helping his father's case. It makes Amah sad to remember John as a weak man, but there it is.

Christopher leans forward. "Forgive me, but I feel I should ask ... this girl ..." he nods towards the photograph. "She's my half-sister, isn't she? My father's illegitimate child?"

Amah's eyes narrow as she contemplates him. A coolness settles over her. She could be fond of this boy, with his kind eyes like his father's, his sympathetic smile. But how could that ever be so?

She thinks back to a blustery day, when the wind tried to whip the bonnet from her head, its force like a hand in the middle of her back, propelling her towards the docks. John wore a white carnation pinned to his cravat for the occasion, and Amah carried a single lily. The chapel was poky, used sporadically by returned sailors and those far from home, and the vicar had deep lines etched into his face, a map of his seafaring days.

Heloise is many things, but illegitimate is not one of them.

CHAPTER
TWENTY-SEVEN

My eyelids flicker against the grey dawn that filters into my room. I had spent most of the evening so rigid with anxiety, it felt as though my bones fused together as I lay in my bed; I thought the rhythm of my heart would race for evermore. Again and again I ran through the possible culprits, the possible scenarios. The Italians, the factory workers, those Fenians of Ripley's. And what did they have planned? My ideas of what might happen on the morrow started out whole, as rounded and awful as a scene in a play. As the night deepened, the images fragmented and intersected, like the jagged pieces of a smashed mirror. And somehow, amidst my waking nightmares, I must have fallen asleep.

Closing my eyes again, I succumb to the heaviness of my mind, my limbs; I feel sleep's gentle shroud settle over my skin, my ears, my face, deep, deep, the morning light almost extinguished, when a terrible wail heaves me fully awake. I sit up, listening for a repeat of the terrible noise. But all I hear is a high-pitched chattering, the sound of a man shouting.

Hurrying over to the terrace doors, I look out and spy the organ grinder sprawled across the dirty cobblestones of the court, his monkey hopping about his head, screeching and clutching his little captain's hat. Mr Modesto comes into view, and he dashes the barrel organ to the ground, a mangled confusion of wood and twisted wheel, so that it wheezes out that horrible, rising wail that woke me up. The organ grinder scuttles to his knees, his feet, grabbing hold of the organ by its handle, dragging the broken machine across the ground behind him as he runs. The monkey chases, catching onto the organ grinder's coat tails, climbing up his back until he can clasp his tiny hands around the man's neck.

What was all that about? I watch for a few moments more. Two natty shop assistants stand outside the umbrella shop, looking the organ grinder up and down as he rounds the corner and disappears from sight, closely pursued by a gang of three young lads in tattered breeches, who look like they might cheerfully take up where Modesto left off. The tobacconist's wife calls over her shoulder to someone within the shop, before shrugging and turning back inside.

Hearing the Modestos' front door bang shut, I cross to my bedroom door and open it, listening for what I can from below. Miss Haven peeps out too, a wet flannel pressed to her face as though she's been frozen in the act of washing. I place my finger to my lips as I step towards the stairs and peer down. Mr Modesto's shadow crosses the hallway as he makes his way to the sitting room.

Mrs Modesto's voice is high-pitched, cajoling almost, as she says something in Italian to her husband.

239

He shouts at her in their language and then, in English, "I never said you could meet with that man. Never." The sound of a slap, sharp against bare flesh, reaches us all the way upstairs.

My stomach curls into a sick knot and Miss Haven gasps. She bites into the flannel.

"But he just take stockings, Giuseppe, the bonnets ... To the mission ..." Her voice has deepened, lengthens out into a moan. She lets out a short scream when he slaps her again.

Then we can hear a scuffle of some sort, something overturned, fallen to the floor?

"You ... oof ... better ... oof ... not ... oof ... go ... outside ... again ..."

That's it. I run down the stairs in my stockinged feet, and swoop into the sitting room, with nothing but my rage as armour. Mrs Modesto lies on the ground near her chair, curled on her side, forearms covering her face. Her husband's foot pauses when he sees me. A light sheen of perspiration on his forehead, as he tugs at his collar with the exertion of beating his wife.

"Get away from her, you fucker." My voice is low. I almost choke on the anger I can feel coursing through me.

"This is none of your business." He goes to push me out of the sitting room, close the door. I grab an ugly brass candlestick from the tabletop, brandish it at him.

"Get away from her or I will hit you," I say slowly, through gritted teeth.

With all his niceties peeled away it is as though each knobbly contour of Mr Modesto's ugly skull has been

240

thrown into sharp relief. His ears protrude from his head, crimson, and his eyes bulge. He reaches for me, curling his thin claws about my upper arm and I tug free, swing the candlestick across his face.

Clapping his hand to his cheek, he growls something at me in Italian as I back towards Mrs Modesto, still waving the candlestick between us. I've seen that look before, in the eyes of men and animals. It's a murderous look. If he runs from the room to procure a knife or other weapon, I'll have to try and barricade us in somehow.

"Come, Mrs Modesto, get up. I will help you," I say. Help her to what? All I can think is I need to get her away from this man, to her room, outside, anywhere. If only I had my pistol instead of this silly candlestick to threaten him with. And where is that Miss Haven? Mr Beveridge? The maids? I could do with some bloody assistance.

Mrs Modesto pushes herself into a seated position on the threadbare carpet. I'm just helping her haul herself into the armchair when she shrieks, cowers to the floor again. Mr Modesto grabs me by the hair and tugs me towards the door, still cursing in his own language. I twist around and try to swipe him with the candlestick but, in avoiding it, he pulls me into a bear hug. I try to remember what Ripley said about this. I stomp on his toes, but what harm can my bare foot do when he wears leather boots? Pulling away, I kick at his knee, but he just keeps frogmarching me towards the hallway.

241

Somebody raps furiously on the front door, and in the moment that Modesto pauses, listens, I take my chance and raise the candlestick as though it's a bat in that ballgame I've seen the grubby little imps play in the back-alleys, and I whack it across the side of his head. He staggers, knocking over two of the spindly table chairs, crashing to the ground. I'm satisfied to see a split in the skin above his ear spill a thin line of fresh blood.

Modesto groans like a beaten dog, while his poor wife whimpers in her chair. I stand, candlestick still clasped to my side, rubbing where my scalp smarts from when he yanked on my hair. Panting, it's only on the sixth inhalation that I recall the loud knocking on the front door.

Moving swiftly to the window, I glance out onto the lane. Two, perhaps three, carriages block the entrance to Green's Court, and a number of men, three of whom are uniformed policemen, make for the lodging house. I'm puzzled. This is a very unusual turn-up. I have never heard of such a response to a case of wife-flogging.

I hear Miss Haven's hushed voice out in the hallway talking to someone through the front door, and I'm just crossing the room when Mrs White sails in, her eyes narrowed as she gazes from the husband, still prone on the floor, to the wife folded over in her armchair.

"I see you have things in hand, Mrs Chancey." Her voice is dry. She points out Mr Modesto to the two burly men who have followed close behind her. "Is this him?"

242

I nod. Mr Modesto squints at Mrs White, tries to protest as the two men haul him to his feet. He gesticulates, pointing at me, all the time switching between English and Italian. He looks as scrawny as a scarecrow between the two men, with a face that shows he might cry. The lily-livered creature has crumbled all too swiftly.

"No longer the big, strong man, Mr Modesto? Is it only with women you can bring out your fists?" I want to say the words with scorn, but instead my voice still shakes with anger.

I watch as they drag him from the room. Two more men enter, a constable in tow.

"I won't need you just yet," Mrs White says to them. "Make sure the others keep searching the court for anything suspicious. I'll wait here having a word with these ladies first."

She looks at me, mild surprise on her face. "What happened here?" Her eyes take in my appearance. My hair now a mess, the rent in the stitches between bodice and skirt.

Blowing a stray lock from my face, I dislodge a couple of pins, and smooth it back from my forehead, pressing the loose strands into place as neatly as I can. "That b —" I nearly say *bastard*, "That brute was raising his hand to his wife." And kicking the life out of her, I want to add.

Mrs White walks across the room to Mrs Modesto, who still has her head hidden in her hands. She takes a seat next to the woman in the other armchair, nodding for me to follow. I lift one of the chairs from the floor and pull it close.

"Madame, look at me," Mrs White says. "Look at me."

Mrs Modesto takes her hands slowly from her face. Her skin is blanched with tears, and her left cheek is fever red from where her beast of a husband has slapped her. She turns damp eyes from Mrs White to me. "Who is this, Miss Charters?"

"You may call me Mrs White." She takes a folder from a Gladstone bag. Her initials HBW are engraved upon its side in gold lettering. "I have here some information on you and your husband, Mrs Modesto." She rustles through several pages, before pulling one to the top. "Or perhaps I should refer to you by your true name, Mrs Marchesi."

The Italian woman — Modesto? Marchesi? — grows still. "You can call me Sofia," she says, finally, wiping her nose with the back of her hand.

"Sofia, I am afraid you and your husband are in a bit of trouble."

Mrs Marchesi shakes her head. "I have nothing to do with my husband's work."

"And what do you know of his work, Sofia?"

"I know nothing. Nothing." Her thin fingers fidget and she looks to her basket of knitting.

Mrs White brings two pieces of paper forth from her folder. "I have here a portion of a letter written by Mr Marchesi, and its translation. Do you know what the letter contains?"

244

Mrs Marchesi shakes her head, her eyes sliding towards the paper and then away again. "No. I know nothing of my husband's work," she repeats.

"Well, then let me explain. He writes to someone of an uprising, of gaining unity, freedom, through violence of some sort." She cocks her head as she gazes at the other woman. "Mrs Marchesi — Sofia — what can you tell us of this?"

"Nothing, nothing at all." With shaking fingers, she plucks up her knitting needles from the floor, pulls up a line of wool.

Something clanks in the kitchen, and I wonder if the household is still going ahead with their breakfast. A constable opens the door and pokes his head in, before withdrawing again swiftly when he receives an annoyed glance from Mrs White.

"Mrs Marchesi, listen to me." Mrs White leans forward in her chair. "There is something planned for today. Something terrible. If you are to help us in finding out what the dreadful deed might be, we can offer you assistance, perhaps even keep you from prison."

Mrs Marchesi gapes at Mrs White, her mouth hanging open like a baby blackbird begging a worm. "Prison? But we came here to escape going to prison in our own country." Her hands start to tremble even more. At first I think it's with fear, but when I search her face — the heat that suffuses her glare, the rigid set of her jaw — I realise she's furious. "What has he done?"

"We fear there will be a bombing somewhere. Today."

"A bombing?"

Mrs White nods.

Mrs Marchesi sinks back in her chair, the knitting falling to her lap. She lets out a soft hoot. She looks genuinely amused. "A bomb? You think Giuseppe will bomb something today? In London?"

"That is what we are afraid of, yes. Perhaps even here in Green's Court."

"Ridiculous." Sofia's face grows solemn again. "Giuseppe would not know how. He is a man who can write many letters, not a man who takes action. And anyway, if he were to do anything, it would not be here. It would be at our home."

Mrs White waits for more, but when nothing is forthcoming, she slips the sheaves of paper back into her bag. I go to the side board and pour a glass of wine for us each. Maybe a little ratafia will loosen Mrs Marchesi's tongue.

"Perhaps Mr Marchesi has no idea of what is afoot here," I say, handing a glass to the Italian woman. "But someone has been plotting something for today. Someone who uses a code to communicate with others in their circle. Do you know anything about a code, Sofia?" I make sure she sees my eyes linger over her pile of wool.

"I know nothing of a code. What is this code?" Mrs Marchesi brings the wine to her lips, takes a small sip, then one more; chokes a little, her eyes watering, when I pick up her Bible and hand it to Mrs White. The older

246

woman takes it from me, gets to her feet, straightening the creases in her gown with her free hand.

"If that's the case, then, I am afraid we will need to take you along with us, Mrs Marchesi. You will be detained with your husband."

Sofia clutches the cushioned arms of her chair. "But I do not want to be detained with him. I do not want to see him again."

"I've told you our terms, Mrs Marchesi. If you cannot assist us, then I am afraid I cannot assist you."

The Italian woman hangs her head for a moment. The silk of Mrs White's skirts rustle as she bends to pick up her bag. A man calls to another outside. I glance out the window, watch as a constable moves on a neat tinker, his metal wares winking in the dull sunlight.

"All right," Mrs Marchesi says, finally. "I tell you all. Perhaps you have ruined all my plans and I have nowhere to go."

Mrs White drops her bag to the ground and takes her seat again. I lean against the window sill.

"My husband was part of a secret society back home. He, along with the others, were trying to arrange a revolution, but before they could, most of the others were arrested. Then they were executed. So we fled here."

I think of the meeting I attended with Miss Haven. "What did they want? Better work conditions?"

She shakes her head. "No. They want a unified Italy, away from foreign control. But of course our government is against this, as are the Austrians. They would lose power and influence if our lands were to unite."

"And your husband still wants this?" prompts Mrs White.

Mrs Marchesi nods. "More than ever. He cannot return home until all is organised, or else he will also be arrested and executed. Which is why he tries to organise things from here."

I think of Modesto's — Marchesi's — almost immediate collapse when the police had arrived. Of the fear in his face when strangers turned up to drag him away. But he is lucky, I think, that it is the British authorities who have him in hand, not his own countrymen, after all.

"By 'things', Mrs Marchesi, you mean he is trying to organise another rebellion."

"I believe so."

"Tell us more of this code of yours." Mrs White taps the cover of her Bible. "How do you contact these compatriots of your husband's?"

"Me? I do not have anything to do with my husband's stupid ideas. Nothing. Everybody knows he would not include me, and that I have little interest, which is why . . ."

"Why what?"

Mrs Marchesi lifts a stitch of emerald wool between finger and thumb, and gently pulls it loose from the knitting needle. "Which is why they asked for my help."

"Who asked for your help?"

She picks up the next stitch and loops it over the top of the needle. "One morning they came, here, when

248

Giuseppe was out, doing whatever he does during the day. They slipped in without the maids knowing. Two men. They'd heard of me through a friend of mine, a friend who knows of my hardship. They tell me, if I do this thing, they will help me with money. They will help me return home. Without him."

"What did they ask of you?"

"They want me to tell them who my husband contacts. He writes many letters to people back home, trying to form another secret society."

"These people who came to you? Were they from your government?"

Mrs Marchesi shrugs. "I think they were Swiss. Or maybe Austrian. They suggested a code, from that Bible there, but he is jealous, my husband, a paranoid man. I cannot write letters to anyone. Imagine if he were to find them? Or if he were to come home and I am away, trying to send them? He would beat me. You saw this!" She turns to me. "You saw this! He pays the shop man next door to spy on me, the maids too. You saw what happened today? The shop man told him I passed something to the organ grinder this morning."

I glance at her basket of wool again. It's empty of stockings and bonnets. "And did you pass on something to the organ grinder?"

"Yes. This is how I tell them who Giuseppe is in contact with." She slips off one more stitch, so the length of wool has three kinks where it unravels. "We decided upon page thirty-eight in my Bible. The letters correspond with the number of rows I knit. And only the stockings. Never the scarves or bonnets."

Damn. No wonder those baby woollens were so haphazard in design. And long.

"The organ grinder works for them too. He pretends to take my woollens to a mission, but he takes them to these people to solve. I am not allowed to write or send correspondence, but this I can do. Of course, in the beginning, I asked my husband's permission, and Giuseppe approved of me giving these things to the poor orphans, but this morning he was already angry about something . . ." She presses her lips together against their quivering.

Mrs White contemplates the other woman for a few moments. "So perhaps he did have some sort of violence arranged for today? Perhaps he was nervous, out of sorts?"

"No, not a bombing," says Mrs Marchesi. She seems adamant, and a spiteful note creeps into her speech. "That man will bleat like a sheep about taking action, but really, he is a weak man, better at running away than doing anything useful." She turns anxious eyes from me to Mrs White. "What will happen to him now? You will keep him, won't you?"

Mrs White stands again. "I will see what we can do, Mrs Marchesi. I am not sure of your story, after all. Perhaps I will track down these Austrians or Swiss people you speak of. They may help you. In the meantime you will need to go with my officers." Noticing the scared look in the Italian woman's face she says, her voice kinder, "I will make sure you are not detained with Mr Marchesi. We will arrange something suitable. Do not fret."

250

CHAPTER
TWENTY-EIGHT

Sliding the soft bristles of my brush across my head, I peer into the speckled mirror above the chest of drawers, trying to neaten my braid without re-doing it. I just need to find a cab home, and Amah can wash and set it again. I cannot wait to tell her of all my adventures. We'll sip cups of hot chocolate and I have no doubt my sitting room will smell pleasantly of lilies or peonies or whatever other flowers Hatterleigh will have sent from his hothouse. I almost feel refreshed just thinking of it.

I can hear furniture scraping across the floorboards above, where Mrs White's men are still searching for anything untoward.

"So, Marchesi is not one of these anarchists, as such, like some of his countrymen with their senseless violence and attacks," she said to me, once they'd taken Mrs Marchesi from the sitting room. "But we can't be positive he doesn't still mean trouble. And we can't be sure of her word either." We watched as the woman was escorted to one of Mrs White's carriages and driven away.

Mrs White looked troubled. "I wish I knew what was planned for today." She took a small notebook from her bag and it flipped open to a page she had obviously pressed open many times before. "The Queen's family is having photographic portraits taken in the afternoon, but the photographers have been thoroughly scrutinised. Nothing much in parliament. The Home Secretary has already boarded a train for Edinburgh, and Thomas is visiting a Brazilian businessman in Audley Street."

My ears pricked at Audley Street, which was terribly close to my home, but she didn't elaborate.

"Perhaps if someone means to meet the man I had the note from — you know, the man who died in Cimetiere du Romilly — perhaps they are waiting for someone to be wearing a red and white kerchief, like I had to when I went to the Dernier Livre. If one of your men is to don a red and white scarf of some sort, that might lure the contact to us."

Mrs White looked at me. "A red and white scarf?"

I nodded. "Yes. Somerscale told me that's how they would recognise me as the contact."

Her eyes widened and she nodded, slowly. "A red and white scarf," she repeated. "I see. Mrs Chancey," she gathered up her notes and bag and made for the door, "I will take my leave of you now and look into this. You return home and I'll be in touch. Good day." She bustled from the room, calling for someone named Harold to take her back to Pall Mall.

And now, as I place my hairbrush into my toiletry case, I think again of how Mrs White mentioned Mayfair, and I feel a peak of alarm. What if something were to happen near my home? Or Amah is on her morning walk nearby or visiting one of the local shops

252

when there is an explosion? I must return home as soon as possible, make sure everyone stays safely indoors for the rest of the day. I sweep the rest of my trinkets into the case, which I shove into my portmanteau above the bundled gown and drawers. I force my slippers into a side pocket and step into my boots. Standing upright again, I glance out the terrace doors to see Mr Beveridge skip-run down the lane towards Brewer Street. Digging around in my velvet reticule for my watch, I look at the time. It's just on 9.20 a.m. Much too late for him to be departing for work. I press my forehead to the cool glass and watch as he turns abruptly away from a passing constable and pauses outside the tobacconist's. I spy a flash of red at his neck.

What is he up to? Beveridge, who Haven and I had encountered at the workers' meeting; who sometimes works in Westminster; who is, unaccountably, not at work. Beveridge, who lives in Green's Court.

Still clutching my velvet bag, I rush from the bedroom and clamber down the stairs. By the time I reach the court Mr Beveridge is hovering at the comer, looking left and right. I walk towards him, just as he turns to his right.

I reach the end of Green's Court, and I just catch him hooking right again, almost immediately. I spin around, and spin again. Where the hell have all the blasted policemen disappeared to? A girl circles me, like I'm a mad person. An older woman passes, observes my lack of bonnet.

I pause for the count of five beats before following. My footsteps slow as I approach the alley Beveridge turned into. The soles of my shoes scrape against the dirt on the ground. A black bird caws from the branches of a scraggy elder tree. A Clydesdale clops past, pulling a dray full of barrels, the driver and the horse equally laconic, ignorant of any danger. My fingers trail the rough, gravelly texture of brick, tracing the scratchy line between the blocks. I wonder if the wall will stay true, unyielding, if Beveridge does indeed detonate a bomb. Inching closer to the turn, I feel about in my bag for the cold handle of my pistol, nestled in its special pocket.

"Madame, may I be of assistance?"

I nearly jump out of my skin, pressing myself against the wall. "Damn, you gave me a fright!" I say to the young constable staring down at me. He's a bit startled at my swearing, and he doesn't have the brightest countenance I've ever come across, but he'll have to do. I grab hold of his sleeve. "Have you been searching Green's Court?" I say.

He nods, his helmet jiggling with the movement.

"I am terribly afraid that the person you are after might have turned down here." I point towards the alleyway. "I'm very much worried that . . ."

The constable's face takes on a scared expression. "You think he's hiding a bomb or somethink on 'is body?"

He's a little sharper than I had thought.

"Exactly," I say. "We must follow him."

We creep closer to the mouth of the alleyway, and peep around. Mr Beveridge has disappeared. The narrow lane widens into what I think must be the yard of Baxter's Brewery, which backs onto Green's Court. As we steal into the lane, the odour of manure, hops and cat piss is almost overwhelming. The horse and dray plod into sight again, approaching from a road to the east, and two men come out from the brewery to help unload the barrels. Smoke billows from large smoke stacks, and a brown dog barks at us in a desultory manner.

I walk a little faster, anxious that I've lost Beveridge, and the constable shadows me so closely I'm pretty sure he clings to my skirts like a child with his nanny. The dog joins us, nipping at my petticoats in a playful manner; licks the constable's trouser leg. We are not halfway down the lane before Mr Beveridge swings around the corner towards us again, coming from the same direction as the horse and dray. He has his head down and rushes right past us, but this time he is not empty-handed. He grips a square, hard-case satchel stiffly at his side.

I poke around in my bag for my pistol. I nudge the constable with my elbow, and hiss, "That's him. Apprehend him! Can't you see what he carries?"

Mr Beveridge slows down and looks back at us. His face is so blanched of colour, the freckles on his face stand out like sprinkles on a Dutch cake. He takes to his heels abruptly and his bowler topples to the ground behind him.

I start to run too, still trying to dislodge my blasted pistol from its holster, when the constable, more game than I had anticipated, gives chase with a long-legged lope, easily outrunning Beveridge. Between the constable and the dog, Beveridge is driven up against a dilapidated fence, which bows under the man's weight, splinters of wood crumbling from the palings.

"What's in the bag, sir?" the constable asks him. He tries to take hold of it, but Beveridge snatches it away. "Easy now, sir. Easy now." The constable's eyes are a little wild when they catch mine, his arm outstretched to the other man.

We both instinctively take one step back. The dog pounces again and again at Beveridge's shoes, growling, sending little clouds of dust in the air. Still thinking it is all a game.

If the policeman stays with him, keeps guard while I run for help, Beveridge won't have an opportunity to escape, or light whatever is concealed in that bag. "Constable, I think you should . . ."

A loud report cracks through the air. I flinch, covering my ears, and a scarlet poppy blossoms at the base of Beveridge's throat. Except it's no poppy. The petals trickle red and Beveridge's mouth yawns wide with disbelief. He claps his free hand to his throat and falls onto one knee.

I turn at the sound of footsteps, freeze when I see a man running towards us, a cocked gun ready. He halts once close, although he doesn't lower the gun. And there's something about that gun, but I can't think straight, and a grunt draws my attention back to

256

Beveridge. He's sunk to the dirt, and blood seeps through his fingers in a steady stream. The constable catches him from behind, gently lowers him onto his back.

My gaze finds the gunman again. I manage to drag my eyes past the muzzle of the black gun, across the greatcoat — of the best cut and fabric, and almost swashbuckling in design — to find the face beneath the lowered brim of the top hat. Somerscale.

"What the hell are you doing here, Heloise?" he snaps at me. "Bloody lucky I was here to take care of this rascal, before he blew you, me and everyone in Soho all the way to kingdom come. You nearly ruined everything. I've been after this man for days."

I'm stung momentarily out of my shock. "I'll have you know that I'm working for the War Office too, and I was doing fine taking care of this fellow. You needn't have taken a pot shot at him."

Mr Beveridge's mouth gapes open, his tongue working, an awful clucking noise rising from his throat. Clug, clug. Trying to form words against a gurgle of blood. Clug.

Somerscale eases the case from Beveridge's right hand. The bus driver blinks as blood bubbles through his slackening fingers.

"He's done for," says the constable, wiping his forehead with the back of his sleeve.

Again, Beveridge seems to want to say something, but the force of speaking pushes a fresh flood of blood into his mouth.

I kneel down and lean over him, wrenching off the damned spectacles when they slide down my nose. What is he trying to tell us? His pale eyes are fixed above, ablaze with fear, and I can see the clouds, the blue sky, reflected in them.

Finally, one last *clug* clicks from his throat, and the struggle is over. Beveridge lies still.

I climb to my feet again with the help of the constable, and I'm thankful, for my knees feel wobbly indeed. "What's in the bag, Somerscale? Should we check?" My words sound muffled to my ear; my mouth is dry, feels as though stuffed with wool. A woman slowly pokes her head out from a top window before she withdraws, shutting the window behind her.

Somerscale squats, placing the gun on the ground while pulling the square case in front of himself.

"Careful, now, sir," says the constable.

Somerscale gingerly unlocks the left clip, the constable flinching at its snap. Somerscale then unlocks the right. Slowly, he raises the lid. Nestled amongst masses of cotton wadding lies an ironclad sphere.

"It's a bomb," breathes the constable.

"You are correct," says Somerscale, his voice light. "They must teach you well at where ever they educate you people." His long finger traces a sliver of wood embedded in its side. "And this, I believe, is the fuse. Once lit, we would not have long to make ourselves scarce."

My thoughts are a jumble as I take in the bomb, lying so close to Beveridge's corpse. Blood stains the ashen skin of the dead man's face. A fly lights upon his nose, rubs its grubby little paws together. Hearing voices, I glance over my shoulder at where the dray driver looks like he might approach, but hesitates, steadying his horse. The morning light has a metallic tinge to it, and I lift my hand for a moment, to shield my eyes.

Somerscale folds down the bag's lid, clicking it shut. He gets to his feet, picking up both the case and his gun. I take in Somerscale's lovely cheekbones, his fine lips. The high collar of his greatcoat, and his cravat, a dapper number, white with thin, red pinstripes. Red. White.

My eyes drop to the gun in his right hand. I can see it clearly now, smooth long muzzle; superb gold panels of filigree etched into its barrel. A small letter *H*, also golden, engraved into the handle. It's Hatterleigh's revolver. The one I took from his room in Paris. The very same one stolen from my pocket at the Dernier Livre. For one black moment, it's as though a shutter falls across my mind, leaving me bathed in darkness.

Somerscale peers at me. "What is it, Heloise? You must stop catching flies like that."

I clap my mouth shut. Think, Heloise, think. The man — black, bushy beard — stole the revolver from my pocket. The next day he was dead in the cemetery. The revolver must've been stolen from him then, by whoever murdered him. I look sideways again at the black and gold revolver, licking my dry lips. My eyes flicker back to Somerscale's face, hitch on the cravat. Red and white.

My velvet bag — my own little pistol — lies on the ground, near Beveridge's leg. "My bag," I say, annoyed my voice is no louder than a whisper. "My bag," I repeat, bending to retrieve it. I stagger as I clasp it, and Somerscale catches my wrist in a strong grip.

"What is the matter, Heloise?" he asks again. He tilts his head at me, then lifts the revolver. "Something about this firearm has unnerved you." He studies Hatterleigh's revolver for a few moments and then chuckles. "Well, haven't I been the fool. This is the very gun stolen from you at the Demier Livre, I surmise." He shakes his head. "When I took it from that blackguard, I really only had in mind to frame this fellow," he nods towards Beveridge's body. "Not you; certainly not that useless idiot, Hatterleigh."

"You took it?"

Taking in a deep breath, he says on the exhale, "Damn you, Heloise. You have forced my hand."

He lifts the revolver's muzzle. His thumb levers the hammer into position, its slow creak a roar in my ears.

The tip of his finger whitens as it pulls against the trigger.

CHAPTER
TWENTY-NINE

Another loud report. Quick. Too quick. A smother of smoke, settling in the still air.

My hands grasp my bodice, press against my neck, squeeze my stomach. No pain. Perhaps I am numbed by the shock. My fingers feel for anything wet, gaping, any kind of tear in body or dress, but there is nothing.

The smoke clears. Something heavy thuds against my thigh, slides down my leg. The constable rolls onto the ground at my feet, clutching his chest. He groans, his shoulders shuddering.

"What have you done?" I shout at Somerscale.

The constable's hands stop fluttering. His head flops to the side.

I go to kneel by the policeman but Somerscale grabs me by the arm, mutters, "Come on, you. I might have a use for you," and marches me towards the lane from which he appeared. The revolver's muzzle is hot where it digs into my ribs; I am sure it sears a small circle into my skin like a tattoo. Somerscale's pulled the cravat up over his mouth and nose, keeps his head averted from the men who have come out from the brewery to gape. As we round the corner, I glance over my shoulder and take one last look at the poor constable, lying in the dirt. The dog stands by Beveridge's head, still yapping and baring its teeth.

Somerscale bundles me into a coach that is parked a little way down the main thoroughfare. As we trundle along, I stare out the coach's window, but I don't really see the buildings, people, trees. Even when the coach grinds to a halt, making way for other traffic, the world seems to quiver, as though dipped in aspic.

"What the hell is going on, Somerscale?" My voice sounds dull, not as strident as I'd like.

"What's going on?" he says, exasperated. He sits on the opposite bench, the revolver trained on me. Both my velvet bag and the hard case lie on the seat next to him. "You've ruined my plans, Heloise. But do not worry, I will rally. Just give me a moment to think."

"It was you all along?"

He smiles. "All along."

The gold trim of Hatterleigh's revolver glimmers in the dim interior of the coach. "You took that gun from the man with the black beard? The man who placed the note in my pocket?"

"Indeed I did."

"And you murdered him."

He looks a little surprised. "You know that?"

"Yes. I tried to make that rendezvous, but I was too late. But why kill him, if he was working with you?"

"Well, by then I knew White was onto him, damn her, so I had to make him disappear."

I wrench on the door handle, but it won't give.

262

"Locked in, I'm afraid. Only Victor — you must remember my valet — can open that door now. He sits above us, with my coachman. Very reliable men, I might add." He speaks in that light conversational tone, a pleasant smile on his face, and my skin positively crawls with horror.

"But what are you hoping to achieve, Somerscale? By bombing the police? The palace?"

"Those bombings were all a smoke screen, Heloise. A smoke screen for my real goal." It's as though he wants to impress me. "It was during my time in the Crimea War that I became fascinated with explosives, you know. I have a special cottage in Shepherd's Bush, especially for me to work away in when everyone thinks I'm at my club."

The coach rolls to a stop, caught between a wagon carrying coal and two buggies. I slam the palm of my hand against the glass of the window, but my cry for help is cut short as the warm muzzle of Hatterleigh's revolver is pressed to my neck.

I huddle back into the corner of the seat. "I don't understand. Why are you doing this?"

"Well, Heloise, imagine my surprise when White contacted me in Paris, asking me to pose as the contact in some devilish bombing scheme. Imagine my consternation. Little did she know I was the actual contact. That I was the one who had arranged the bloody meeting. I couldn't exactly turn up, could I, and have that damned stupid blackguard, Berger — the fellow I had this gun from — make clear his familiarity with me. I knew White would have other spies on hand.

Turns out that allowing myself to be imprisoned became the ultimate alibi."

He leans in towards me, leg crossed over the other in a cosy manner. The revolver lies limp in his hand, yet I have no doubt he would use it on me. I think of a flash of crimson blood, streaking through Beveridge's fingers. His blind, pale stare up at the morning sky. "So you sent me?" I say.

"Nobody knows you, do they? Well, they didn't then. There would be no tying you to me, in Paris, and certainly not in a job such as this."

The coach rolls forward a few feet, stops again.

"And, of course, I was expendable." I can't help the acerbic note. "Why send me at all?"

"Well, I still needed to know who I could contact here in London, and we had already arranged the red and white scarf thing. Luckily — or so I thought at the time — Berger must've guessed something was up, and slipped you a note instead about the new rendezvous place and time."

"And you did meet him? In the cemetery?" Just before I got there.

"Yes, Heloise. Swapped places with Victor. Those dozy guards at the debtor's jail never really checked who exactly was in residence, as long as someone was. Berger was a very efficient fellow. It was almost a pity I had to knife him."

I try to swallow, but my throat sticks. "And he told you of Beveridge?"

His smile widens. "He did, the fool. He told me that this Beveridge chap would be very keen to plant the bomb for me today. How he had grandiose ideas of dismantling the system or some such nonsense."

My mind jumps to Violette and the anger of it seems to clear my mind. "And poor Violette? Was that you too?"

A horse gallops by my window; a costermonger touts his pea soup in a drawling baritone. The coach trundles forward, at a snail's pace.

"That was very unfortunate. On many fronts. I should never have sent Victor to do my work. Look at the disorder that happens when you don't take care of a thing for yourself."

"She was murdered because your valet thought she was me?"

"Craven, he was too, when he realised his mistake. Nearly didn't tell me. Mumbled something about her being dressed as you, in a damned purple bonnet, or some such. Couldn't really blame the poor man, in the end. He tried again, outside La Maison Dorée, but said some interfering buffoon yanked you back from the road."

"You monster." Every nerve in my body leaps, stretching to their very extremes, screaming to hit him, punch him, kick. Hatred runs molten beneath my skin, but drops away suddenly, plunging me in chill water as I glimpse a familiar face duck into view outside Somerscale's window.

Ripley. On horseback.

He gives me a quick salute, his horse trotting on just as Somerscale glances out onto the street. "Don't be so dramatic, Heloise. You are not on the stage here."

Ripley! My thoughts are muddled. Is he hand in hand with Somerscale? Or is it merely a coincidence he is here? Surely not. How would he know to look into this coach in particular?

The coach wheels lurch over a stone, and I glance out the window to see two ladies step out from Gunter's Tea Shop. We are near Berkeley Square. I frown. Are we heading for Mayfair?

"Ah," says Somerscale. "We are nearly at our destination." He pulls out his pocket watch. "We still have plenty of time."

I think back on Mrs White's words earlier. "Who is this Thomas, Somerscale? In Audley Street. I suppose he is your target?"

His fine lips widen into a smile. "Clever girl. I really did underestimate you, you know. Thomas — who of course is a close chum of your Mrs White — is none other than the War Secretary."

Again, Ripley trots past, this time travelling in the opposite direction.

"But why, Somerscale? Why murder him?"

"Why? For money, of course, Heloise."

"But you're rich."

He looks surprised. "Rich? Heloise, you must know better than anyone that there is never enough. And would you have me sitting around, twiddling my thumbs? And in any case, it is not the Secretary I am after, it's the man he is meeting today. Of course, everyone will think it's the Secretary who is the intended target but actually it's a Brazilian businessman. I've had my eye on him for a while, for he is constantly cutting me out of business."

"Business?"

"Dealing arms, my dear. A very profitable venture, I've found. British arms sustained the Confederates for a certain period — some provided by our government, but a lot supplied by me. Incredibly lucrative, it turned out to be. But what with their little civil war petering out, I have been on the hunt for new buyers, and have hit upon a nice stir-up in Paraguay. Unfortunately, so has this Brazilian . . . mmm . . . nemesis of mine. But, if he were simply to be murdered — shot in the night, or stabbed in his bed — I assure you, all eyes would be turned on me. That would put me and my business in a very awkward position. Much better for people to think his death is the sad result of an assassination attempt on the Secretary."

"And he's here?"

"Yes. Having a meeting with the War Secretary at 11 a.m. I overhead Thomas speaking of it purely by chance at White's, and it gave me time to distract London with these other bomb attacks."

The coachman calls out for the horses to halt, and the coach rocks as someone — Victor, surely — climbs down from above. We've pulled in next to a red brick building. I quickly scan the street for a policeman, Ripley, anybody, but apart from a girl who runs past carrying an armful of twigs, and a bent old beggar pulling a rickety cart on a length of rope, there is no one I can call on for help.

Somerscale unclips the case, revealing the bomb. "Now, Heloise, slowly reach over here, if you would, and take up your pretty bag."

267

Victor, a tall, bulky fellow, with a moustache as thick as a tarbrush, takes up position outside the door that leads to the pavement. He tips his hat at two ladies who stroll by, swinging baskets of flowers by their sides.

I shake my head. My head whirls, dizzy, as my heart skips the odd beat.

"Don't be foolish, dear. Pick up your bag."

I don't know what his game is. I eye the door handle to my left, but even if it were to be unlocked, I would only plummet into Victor's arms, after all.

"Fetch your bag," Somerscale barks.

Reaching over, I pick up my bag. Dare I risk diving into it for my pistol? But I stare too long and Somerscale chuckles. "Don't be foolish, Heloise. There would not be time before I would shoot a hole in you. Think of Beveridge and that dreadful racket he made as he lay dying."

With the muzzle of the revolver he indicates for me to open the bag. My fingers are stiff, my joints almost ache, as I slowly undo the clasp.

"Open it wider, dear."

I rest it on the seat and pull the bag's mouth wide.

His voice is very soft when he says, "Now, lift up the bomb, here, and place it in your bag."

"I will not!"

He leans forward, presses the small, round tip of the revolver to my breast. I can feel my heartbeat drum back against it. "Heloise, Heloise. The bomb is quite stable. It won't explode unless ignited. Take it. Place it in your bag."

I bend forward, reach towards the bomb. My skin jumps as my fingertips touch the bomb's cool frame. But nothing happens. Keeping well away from the wooden fuse, I press my thumb to the sphere and grip. I'm not sure of its weight though, and I'm scared I might drop it. But the longer my fingers rest on the iron casing, the more I worry that maybe the warmth of my skin will ignite it, change its composition in some way. I lift it and, as gently as possible, nestle it into my velvet bag.

Finally, I look back up at Somerscale. Sweat stings my upper lip.

"Well done." With the revolver still trained on me, he looks out the window, towards a large Georgian house on the next corner. A short, barrel-chested man, in a dark overcoat and bowler hat, stands, stalwart, by the front steps.

"A guard," murmurs Somerscale. "Mrs White has been busy."

"What do you plan to do?"

"Well, of course, the original plan was for Beveridge to disguise himself as a delivery man, in order to leave a nice little package on the doorstep. But when I saw him cornered like that by you and that policeman, I knew he'd talk."

"So you killed him."

"Yes. However, that plan has come unstuck."

"Why don't you take it yourself?" I say, glaring across at him.

He peers at me. "But I've had a better idea, Heloise. A plan that I believe Victor could manage for me. I rather think that if he were to rush to that guard for assistance, surely the man would lend Victor assistance; perhaps even — hopefully — allow entry to the premises? The only problem would be ensuring the fuse lasts long enough for Victor to escape, or else . . ." His eyes widen, and his head tips to the side. "I might have to offer him a bonus of some sort. But he's a loyal sort of chap, he'll do my bidding I daresay."

I don't like the smile that hitches the side of his mouth. Every muscle in my body tenses. "Why would Victor need assistance?"

Somerscale taps the glass with the revolver, catching Victor's attention. "He'll have an unconscious lady and her bag clasped in his arms, of course."

He drops the revolver to the seat and lunges for me, his hands aimed at my throat.

I struggle against him, kicking as hard as possible with my boots. His thumbs dig into the base of my throat, cutting short my scream. He presses hard, his fingernails piercing my skin. The door to my left swings open, and Victor, eyes starting from his head, makes ready to climb in to assist his master.

Glass crashes about my ears. Shards fall over my shoulders, my right sleeve. Somerscale falls back, just as the muzzle of a Colt nudges its way through the broken window, fires one shot. Victor rears back, clutching his shoulder. Through the gun smoke I see the valet lift his own pistol, firing back through the middle of the carriage.

"Take care, you fool," roars Somerscale.

270

But Ripley — for it could only be Ripley — has dropped out of sight.

Somerscale picks up the revolver again, and shifts over on his seat, craning to see through the broken glass without making a target of himself. "You'd better sit still," he growls at me. He bangs the roof of the coach and screams at the driver to get a move on.

The coach starts to rock again, and we look upwards as footsteps clamber across the top of the coach. Somerscale leans out the open doorway, and fires his gun once, then a second time, into the air. Someone screeches, and tumbles to the road beside me. A fat man, balding, a dark stain blooming across the back of his red coat. The coachman.

"Blast," says Somerscale. "Get up there, man," he shouts at Victor. "Get us out of here," but Victor stares above us, to the top of the coach, and turns tail, scuttles off down the street, his hand still clapped over his wounded shoulder. "Blast," Somerscale shouts again, stamping his foot. He pants, looking swiftly from right to left. He grabs my sleeve, forces me through the doorway. I fall to the pavement, scraping the heels of my hands, but don't have time to catch my breath before he picks me up by the scruff of my gown and hauls me to my feet. Grabbing me around the waist, he tugs me close into his body. The black tip of Hatterleigh's revolver wavers close to my right eye. I hear that terrible creak again, as he cranks the hammer ready.

I stumble as he backs us both further onto the pavement, so that I'm between him and the road. I stare up at Ripley, who stands atop the coach, hat pushed to the back of his head, a Colt pistol, cocked and ready, in each hand. The man guarding the Georgian house has run forward, but stands frozen at the sight of so many guns.

Somerscale calls out, from where he crouches behind me, "If you don't drop those firearms, sir, I will surely blow a hole in this pretty head here." He taps the muzzle to my temple. He's regained his composure. His voice is calm and pleasant again.

Ripley considers us for a moment, his eyes narrowing, measuring the possibilities. My heart sinks when he shrugs, disarms his pistols, flips them into his hip holsters.

"You got a deal, there, Mister. Don't want anyone else to come to harm, do we?"

"Come now," calls Somerscale. "You mustn't take me for a fool. You think I don't know how quickly you can draw those Colts of yours again? Throw them to the ground, would you?"

Ripley's wide jaw clenches tight. He shakes his head a little. Everything seems to slow down, drowned in aspic again. Ripley takes the guns from the holsters. The two women with the baskets of flowers look back over their shoulders. Ripley keeps a sharp eye on us as he kneels, dropping one pistol to the ground, where it clatters against the coach's wheel. The beggar crosses the road towards us, dropping the rope to his cart. As Ripley stretches out his arm to drop the second gun, I sense Somerscale's attention is focused on the American, and the black and gold revolver wavers, is no

272

longer pointed directly at my head. I decide that this might be my only moment to act, and if I am quick enough, maybe Ripley will still be in possession of the second Colt.

I wriggle in Somerscale's grip, try to break free. As we sway, a bullet lodges in the bricks behind us, and Somerscale lifts his arm instinctively, fires his gun at Ripley. I lift my arm under his, twist free, and think of trying Ripley's stamp to the foot, or palm-smash to the nose, but I'll resort to my usual line of defence. I steel my frame and, with all the force I can muster, I lunge my knee into Somerscale's groin. I can't make perfect connection because of my blasted skirts, but it's enough for him to gasp and step away. The revolver shakes as he lifts it again, but another bullet tears the skin from the fleshy part of his hand and he throws his head back and howls. The revolver falls with a clunk against the toe of my shoe.

The shots still ring in my ear as I turn around. Ripley stands atop the coach, looking about himself, puzzled, his hands empty. My eyes find both his Colts, lying in the gutter where they have fallen. The two women run towards us, shedding lilies and peonies behind them. They shove me out of the way as they draw truncheons from beneath the flowers in their baskets. They wrench off their bonnets and wigs, shouting at Somerscale to get to the ground.

"Constable Jones and Merryweather, madame," the taller one explains to me, in a deep voice, sweat trickling down his forehead.

"Good work, Mrs Chancey." I turn to look at the beggar. Behind the dirt and charcoal that darkens her face, Mrs White's eyes glitter out at me. "I didn't know how we were going to get you out of such a sticky situation, but you managed very nicely indeed." Her fat cheeks lift into a smug smile as she holds up a silver pistol. "With a little help from me."

CHAPTER
THIRTY

Amah

Taff helps Amah climb the stairs to her rooms in Mayfair, Bundle following close behind with her bag.

"Thank you, Taff," she says to the coachman, as he stands, watching her from the middle of her sitting room. She sinks into the armchair, and stares at her linen handkerchief. It's positively black with soot from rubbing her hands upon it on the train.

"You sure you'm all right?" he asks again.

"Yes, Taff, yes, I am." She's terribly tired, and only wishes for bed, and she struggles to keep the snappish note from her words, for Taff has been good to her, patient. When Christopher Crewe had sent for him to fetch Amah in the middle of that dark night at Crewe Hall, Taff and the coach had arrived with the orange glow of dawn, careening up that long driveway, pebbles spitting from beneath the speeding wheels. He'd taken her back to the hotel, telling her how much he had worried; how he'd scoured the docks and tormented the local police about her disappearance. In her room, he packed her portmanteau in between bullying her into eating more chicken soup and what he called 'stirabout'.

"Them oats were'm good enough for my mother — who, I might add, lived until she were sixty-eight years old! — and they be good for you too," he said, stirring swirls and swirls of sticky treacle through the hot porridge.

Bundle returns with a tray of tea things which he places on the round table. He bends to light the fire, and she sees he's in his dressing gown. "I am so sorry to have woken you," she says to the butler. "I had no idea it was so late. Please, leave it. I can light the fire myself."

But he ignores her and carries on with his task. "It is no problem, Amah. I was still reading the newspaper, in fact. Not yet asleep."

When he's satisfied the flames have caught, he taps Taff on the shoulder, says, "Come, Taff. Share an ale with me. I'm sure Amah is in need of rest."

The door clicks behind them as they leave. On the tray is a shallow pile of post for Heloise, reminding Amah of that fateful day she opened the letter from that woman, demanding she meet them at that tavern. Amah shakes her head. That woman and her spineless husband. Christopher said that he'd take care of them, threaten to take them straight to the magistrate should they persevere with their idiotic prank. That was the word he had used. Prank. Not 'blackmail'. Not 'kidnapping'. Not 'violence'.

Amah shakes her head again at the unfairness of it all. What could she expect? He was that woman's brother, after all. She lifts the teapot and pours herself a cup.

Christopher had also promised to send her jewellery back to her, and the other earring, the twin of the gold orb she has locked away. She prays he does. It would make her so happy to own the pair of earrings again, so she could pass them to Heloise. They would be the girl's only inheritance from an ancestor who wasn't Amah herself. For Amah doubted she would receive anything from Christopher or his wicked sister, despite the fact that if there was true justice, Heloise's place in the world would supersede that woman's. Amah would be Lady Crewe. She almost smiles at the thought. But of this she would never tell Heloise. Never. If she were to tell Heloise of her half-brother, Sir Christopher Crewe, it would go to Heloise's head in some way. She would either peacock the news, or worse, rage at the unfairness of it all. Either way, it was best Heloise didn't know more of who her father truly was.

The teaspoon trembles against the china as she remembers what Christopher told her, of how her John passed away. Originally, she was too numb, too dazed by her escape to truly think on Christopher's words. And since then, her exhausted mind has shied from dwelling on it. She places the spoon down, stares at the pattern of lilac flowers on the teacup, trying to gauge how the idea of John's death sits in her heart. She thinks of how his fair hair feathered across his forehead, of the brush of his skin against her thigh, of the first night she had lain in their cold bed, quite alone. Her mind lingers over the memories like she might shift a morsel of food in her mouth, tasting it, savouring it. Her chest feels a little heavy, but perhaps the sadness is

277

not for him, Jonathan Crewe, this man she didn't really know, but for her youth, for those early, cheerful days in Liverpool.

There's a soft scratching at her door and she feels a slight peak of exasperation. Surely Taff is not still worrying at her.

When she opens the door though, her impatience falls away.

"Amah." Agneau breathes the word. His dark eyes take her in. "Amah, I heard Bundle and Taff talking of you, of the hardship you have faced . . . Please, do not stand here in the cold draught of the hallway. Go back, go back, to your fire." He touches her elbow lightly, guiding her back to her armchair.

He places a piece of cake next to her teacup. "Your favourite *gâteau*, Amah. The one with the cherry filling. Not too sweet, how you like it."

Again, his eyes search her face. Before she can stop herself, she tucks a stray strand of hair behind her ear, hopes she doesn't look too haggard. Prays the firelight is kind.

"That is very nice of you, Agneau."

"*Non*, Amah. To tell you the truth I was anxious about you when you went away so suddenly."

"Oh. That's very nice of you," Amah says again. Heat rises to her face, and her heart beats uncomfortably.

"I can see you are tired. I will not pester you. But tomorrow I will prepare your favourite dishes. Please visit me in the kitchen."

He cups her cheek in his hand, softly rubs his thumb across her brow. And then he is gone. She closes her

278

eyes, and for a few moments she can still feel the gentle sweep of his thumb.

Carrying her cup of tea into her bedroom, she places it on her dressing table. As she unbuttons her blouse, she gazes at herself in the oval mirror. Her hair tumbles to her shoulders as she unpins it. She angles her face from side to side, so that the light of the fire catches the shadows of her cheekbones, the lustre of her dark skin, and in her reflection, she can almost see that young woman who first found love.

CHAPTER
THIRTY-ONE

I plunge into the soft cushions of the sofa, so glad to be home. I take in the details of my drawing room — the blue and white porcelain, some of which is for show, some of which is of actual value; the bronze buddha who's laughing, clad in a blue cloisonne robe; the sumptuous brocade and polished mahogany; the gilt framed portrait of myself above the mantelpiece — trying to calm my mind which is still filled with bombs and bullets, and the way my skin jumped when I thought Somerscale shot me. My thoughts creep even further, to poor Violette. What a terrible waste. I close my eyes, and when I open them, I think of how lucky I am that I have my home to return to, when my travels and adventures are done. If only Amah were home too, though. On returning to South Street, the first thing I did was rush up the stairs to her rooms, but Abigail informed me that she had just left for her afternoon walk. I wait patiently, listening for Amah's return.

I think of the evening before, how I spent so many hours in Mrs White's office, a high-ceilinged room, bare of decoration apart from a lovely rosewood desk, and three matching chairs. Over a platter of cold meats and bread, Mrs White told me that most likely Somerscale would have murdered Beveridge anyway, after framing him for the Secretary's death. Beveridge was to be the one blamed for all the bombings. He was to be the disgruntled citizen, taking his revenge upon the state. I press my eyes shut against the sudden memory of Beveridge; the blossom of red at his throat, the shock in his pale eyes. I feel a bit sad for the man, even though, of course, I realise he was likely intent upon robbing many people of their lives today. What pushes a man to take such evil action? What drives a man to such rage, that he wants to kill others? I have known real bitterness in my life, real demoralisation. And when I think of my lowest days, wrapped in a stifling cloak of pain and hatred, I wonder if perhaps I was pushed one more inch, if hunger, fury, the injustice of it all became too much, if I too could have taken a life.

"It was only your talk of the red and white scarf that tipped me off to Somerscale, you know," Mrs White had said, sipping on black coffee. "For nothing in the original correspondence mentioned this form of contact. Somerscale could only have known about the red and white scarf if he were involved himself." She explained that, after that, it hadn't taken her long to make connections between his finances and a possible target. Hence her rapid manoeuvres to protect the War Secretary.

By the time White finished with me it was well past midnight, so instead of rousing my household, and facing the possibility of interminable questions, I decided to spend a peaceful night at Brown's. I have only been home again a little over an hour and am glad my house doesn't reek of fish and mould like the house in Green's Court. Much better to be surrounded by the scent of lavender and fresh roses.

Bundle opens the drawing room door, says, "Mrs Chancey, a visitor. A Mr Ripley I believe," and before my poor butler is quite finished speaking, the American strides into my drawing room.

Ripley hooks his thumbs into his coat pockets and gazes about my room, an admiring smile on his face. He whistles. "Well, this is certainly a fancy parlour for a little governess to have."

I cast my eyes to the ceiling but grin too. "Ripley, how on earth did you find me here?"

He taps his finger to the side of his nose and winks. "You wouldn't have any bourbon for me to drink, would you? I'm parched after all that excitement yesterday."

I point to the side board littered with crystal decanters of spirits and wines. "No bourbon, I'm afraid. But plenty of whisky. Bring a large one for me, too, will you."

He passes me a healthy-sized whisky and takes a seat in the armchair opposite. Lifting his own glass, he says, "Here's to catching that devil. I always enjoy a good gunfight."

"It was damned lucky for me you caught us up. Where did you come from?"

"Heard talk of the ruckus on Green's Court in the bar at the Clover, so I thought I'd have a gander. Found a bunch of constables twirling their noisy rattles, running for the next lane over. That's where we found

282

that poor policeman, shot through the chest, and lying next to him were your glasses, squashed into the dirt. Turned out the constable was clear-headed enough to tell me in which direction you'd headed."

"He was alive?"

"Sure. Said he pretended to be dead so that Somerscale didn't shoot 'im again."

The whisky sits sweet on my tongue, then burns its way across my throat. I think of what I can do for the constable, perhaps send my surgeon to him, some fruit. I must find out where he is at. Taking another sip, I savour the taste of the amber spirit, so much more pleasant than gin and milk, I think, shuddering.

"You all right? Thinking of yesterday, are you?" Ripley looks concerned.

"Not at all. I'm reliving my stay at the Modestos'."

A smile widens his mouth again. "You certainly had me bamboozled when I first caught sight of you in Soho, that's for sure. Thought perhaps you had your eye on me."

"On you? Why would I be spying on you? I was sure you were trying to murder me!"

Ripley laughed, slapping his leg. "I'm not in the murdering game. I followed you and your maid back to your hotel after we shared those absinthes. Couldn't work out what your game was. Felt mighty curious. Grateful, too. I'm not one to forget you saved my skin in the bar that night. Paid you back, in fact."

"Outside La Maison Dorée? It was you that pulled me out of the way?"

"Sure was." He throws back the rest of his whisky and stands to pour himself another.

"But why did you seem to be everywhere I turned?"

"Pure coincidence, I reckon, apart from the fact that Somerscale dipped into the same murky pool of people I found myself amongst." He contemplates me for a few seconds. "I think I can trust you to not give me away. Last year, word leaked that a new Fenian faction was purchasing large quantities of arms, heading them towards Canada. Meanwhile some of their men were being sent to Paris for training. It was organised with the General I was serving under that I'd be struck from the American army list so I could follow 'em. Keep an eye on 'em. Spy on 'em, I guess you'd call it. It was in Paris that I heard of a plan to recruit more men and money here in London. Which led me to Soho."

I remember what he told me of his upbringing, his father, the copper mine. "I thought you were sympathetic to their cause. Or was all you told me a cover, Mr Ripley?"

"Nah. That was all true what I told you. And don't get me wrong — I do understand what they are agitating for, I am totally on their side with that — but we must make a stand against them taking it with violence."

I nod, but really, I wonder if it might be the only way Connolly and his fellows will ever find justice: in suffrage, work conditions, independence. By wresting it for themselves in any way they can.

Ripley takes to his feet, placing the glass down on the side-table. "Well, that was a pleasure, Mrs Chancey. I sure hope when this is all over, we can meet up again. You might even want to visit me in America some day soon, when all the dust has settled."

Looking up into his broad, cheerful face, I realise I'd really like that. "Sounds lovely, Mr Ripley. Keep me apprised of your movements when you are done here in London." I walk with him to the drawing room door. "And thank you, Mr Ripley, for saving my life that night. I didn't realise what real danger I was in."

He winks at me, and shakes my hand. "Well, like I said, I was already in your debt at that time. And I sure hope I can be of assistance again."

Taking his wide-brimmed hat from Bundle's hands, he shoves it on his head. A single leaf blows through the door as Bundle sees him out.

"By the way, Mrs Chancey," says Bundle, "Amah arrived home from her walk while you were with your guest."

As I climb the stairs, I think of Ripley's offer. I've never been to America, but I've heard wonderful things. Rowdy masquerade balls, crocodiles, saloons, iced tea.

But all thought of the Yank leaves me when I stride into Amah's rooms. She sits by the fire, working on a silk shawl. Even from across the room I can see she is slighter, more fragile in some way.

"Mama, have you been sick? You are skin and bone." I lift her wrist. It's as slender as a bamboo shoot. "Agneau must fatten you up."

The trace of a smile lifts her lips as she lifts her head from her embroidery. I feel bad, because perhaps she is pleased that I show such care. How I do neglect her, leaving her here, in boring Mayfair, quite alone.

"I think you need a change of air, Mama," I say as I pour her a cup of tea, stirring in a brimming spoonful of honey. "I will take you to Venice, just as I promised. I'll look into the arrangements tomorrow."

"Venice?" Amah replies. "No, Jia Li. No. I think I will just stay at home, if you please."

A NECESSARY MURDER

M. J. Tjia

Stoke Newington, 1863: Little Margaret Lovejoy is found brutally murdered in the outhouse at her family's estate. A few days later, a man is cut down in a similar manner on the doorstep of courtesan and professional detective Heloise Chancey's prestigious address. Meanwhile, her maid, Amah Li Leen, must confront events from her past that appear to have erupted into the present day. Once again, Heloise is caught up in a maelstrom of murder and deceit that threatens to reach into the very heart of her existence.

SHE BE DAMNED

M. J. Tjia

London, 1863: Prostitutes in the Waterloo area are turning up dead, their sexual organs mutilated and removed. When another girl goes missing, fears grow that the killer may have claimed their latest victim. The police are at a loss, and so it falls to courtesan and professional detective, Heloise Chancey, to investigate. With the assistance of her trusty Chinese maid, Amah Li Leen, Heloise inches closer to the truth. But when Amah is implicated in the brutal plot, Heloise must reconsider who she can trust, before the killer strikes again.